From a Whisper to a Scream

As the Vampyr  the heavy end of us arc, the brass wol in the heart, doubling g dropped from the man's hand. A pistol.

The Vampyr kicked it away with a booted foot and pushed Maddersly back against the brick wall.

"You are *Damphyr*," he said, his face no more than a few inches from the other man. "I smelled it on you. . . ."

"I don't know nothing about no Damphyr or whatever you call them, mister."

"You lie," said Enoch Bale. "But not for long." The Vampyr's jaw slid and locked. He whispered against the man's throbbing temple and into his ear, the terror almost palpable, like a fluttering bird in the grip of a cat.

"Tell me what you know," he said, his lips sliding down the man's cheek to the salty, sweat-stubbled throat above his collar. . . .

The VAMPIRE *of* NEW YORK

LEE HUNT

A SIGNET BOOK

SIGNET
Published by New American Library, a division of
Penguin Group (USA) Inc., 375 Hudson Street,
New York, New York 10014, USA
Penguin Group (Canada), 90 Eglinton Avenue East, Suite 700, Toronto,
Ontario M4P 2Y3, Canada (a division of Pearson Penguin Canada Inc.)
Penguin Books Ltd., 80 Strand, London WC2R 0RL, England
Penguin Ireland, 25 St. Stephen's Green, Dublin 2,
Ireland (a division of Penguin Books Ltd.)
Penguin Group (Australia), 250 Camberwell Road, Camberwell, Victoria 3124,
Australia (a division of Pearson Australia Group Pty. Ltd.)
Penguin Books India Pvt. Ltd., 11 Community Centre, Panchsheel Park,
New Delhi - 110 017, India
Penguin Group (NZ), 67 Apollo Drive, Rosedale, North Shore 0632,
New Zealand (a division of Pearson New Zealand Ltd.)
Penguin Books (South Africa) (Pty.) Ltd., 24 Sturdee Avenue,
Rosebank, Johannesburg 2196, South Africa

Penguin Books Ltd., Registered Offices:
80 Strand, London WC2R 0RL, England

First published by Signet, an imprint of New American Library,
a division of Penguin Group (USA) Inc.

First Printing, January 2008
10 9 8 7 6 5 4 3 2 1

To the real Sheila Maxwell:
Good true friends are hard to find.

"I am Dracula and I bid you welcome."
—Bram Stoker

"I am the last of my kind."
—Gary Oldman as Draculiya

"If there is in this world a well-attested account, it is that of the vampires. Nothing is lacking: official reports, affidavits of well-known people, of surgeons, of priests, of magistrates; the judicial proof is most complete. And with all that, who is there who believes in vampires?"
—Jean-Jacques Rousseau

PROLOGUE

The black man in the worn canvas trousers and blue jacket that made up the rough uniform of a seaman in the Union navy walked down the narrow street, surveying the damage done by the riots. Half the ramshackle tenements he saw had been scorched or showed fire damage of some kind, and all had been ransacked. For the moment they were all abandoned, left to the rats until folks came back and tried to take up their lives again.

The sailor now wondered whether that would ever happen. Lincoln had emancipated the slaves, but that seemed to have angered the white folk even more than usual. Sometimes the sailor thought being a field slave in Alabama or Mississippi had more joy than being a freeman in a city like New York. If a black man had a job, it meant he'd taken it from a white. If he had no job, then he was just a lazy nigger who thought the world owed him a living. Being in the navy wasn't much better, but at least the food was regular and the pay was better than cleaning up horse crap on the streets or humping cotton bales onto the ships bound across the sea.

At least the lynchings and the burnings and the beatings had ended. With the arrival of troops from Pennsylvania and Maryland, an uneasy quiet had fallen over the city streets. Nobody was doing much business yet, but the sailor knew that in time everything would go back to looking normal. The glass would be swept up, the burned buildings repaired, and the newspapers would find some other cause to promote or decry. A city trying to eat itself alive wasn't something the average resident of New York City wanted to remember— much better to forget it ever happened and go back to the business of making money.

The sailor reached the end of the street. The building where he was supposed to rendezvous with Miss Kate had been burned to the ground. The tenement was now nothing but blackened beams and a skeletal stairway that had somehow managed to survive. He stepped up onto the remains of the front stoop and looked into the twisted wreckage of the building. The air was ripe with the sour smell of wet ash, made worse now by the light rain that had begun to fall even before he left the Jersey shore. The rain had calmed the rioters almost as much as the soldiers he had fetched.

He struggled through the half-blocked remains of the doorway. The hallway in front of him was a charred passage, but at its end he could see the sagging, half-destroyed entrance to what was probably a cellar laundry, or maybe even a gin mill. He saw something silver in the debris at the head of the cellar steps. Easing himself carefully along the passage and skirting sagging areas in the floor, he reached the basement doorway and pushed the cinders and ash away to reveal a long knife, its blade made of some dark stone, the handle worked silver. Holding the knife, he peered down the dark stairway. It looked reasonably intact.

"Miss Kate?" he called out.

There was only cold silence. He stood there uncertain, frowning, every fiber of his being whispering faint warnings, almost willing him to turn and leave. But his feet felt like lead, and warnings or no, he felt a terrible, consuming curiosity.

"Miss Kate?"

This time there was an answer.

"Barnabus?" A strange, soft voice.

Clutching the knife, the black man started down the stairs.

"It's me, Miss Kate. What in the name of all that's holy are you doing down there?"

"Barnabus?" the soft voice queried a second time.

He reached the bottom of the steps. Ahead there was nothing but pitch-darkness and the smell of wet earth. Something else, he thought suddenly. Something very old and as dry as time itself: the scent of an autumn leaf, crumbled in your hand. The smell of a dead thing.

Barnabus stood in the darkness, waiting. There

was a scratching sound and the flare of a phos-
phor match. The match was applied to the wick
of a lamp, and suddenly everything was revealed.

"Dear God," said Barnabus. The room was a
horror. He saw in the flickering lamplight that a
massive pair of planks had been nailed together
to form an X. There were leather thongs fixed to
every corner of the monstrous instrument as well
as rusty-looking spikes of iron. The plank was
stained with splashes of deep russet brown.

Beside the wooden X a man stood wearing a
sergeant's uniform with a pair of big Colt Navy
pistols pushed through his belt. The man's hair
and the uniform were slick with mud, as though
he'd crawled up from a sewer or a grave. His
right hand was gone, the stump blood crusted, the
neatly cut end of a yellowish white bone poking
out through the putrefying flesh. The sergeant was
smiling, tossing a coin into the air and catching it
with his good hand. A gold coin. Barnabus watched
the spinning gold piece, mesmerized.

"Barnabus the ferryman," said the sergeant.

"Yes," whispered Barnabus. Fear was clutching
at him, but he could not move. He stared at the
flickering coin.

"Throw me the knife," said the sergeant, and
Barnabus did. It dropped into the mud at the sergeant's feet. He crouched and picked up the blade,
then stood and pushed it into his belt beside one
of the pistols.

"Come closer," said the sergeant, and unwillingly Barnabus did. The sergeant's voice was barely

a whisper. His eyes were like black hailstones. Something moved in his jaw, and Barnabus saw that the shape of the soldier's face had changed, elongating like a snake or a wolf about to leap upon its prey.

"Do you know who Charon was?" the creature hissed.

"No," whispered Barnabus. Dear God, his eyes, his eyes!

"He was a ferryman, just like you, the boatman of the dead. In ancient times they placed a coin on a dead man's tongue to send him on his way. The price of passage for your soul."

"Please," whispered Barnabus, the single word a prayer.

"I'll pay for your soul, Barnabus; you've nothing to fear." The sergeant stepped forward, bringing the black-bladed knife up in his hand and sweeping it across the sailor's throat. The obsidian blade was sharper than any sword, and there was almost no pain at all. Blood began to fountain from the ghastly wound, and the sergeant leaned forward, enclosing the slashed throat with his lips, sucking noisily. He drank, supporting the entire weight of the other man's sagging body with one hand beneath his arm. Finally the blood stopped pulsing and the sergeant dropped the carcass onto the dirt floor. His face and chin were dripping, staining the already filthy front of his uniform.

"I always pay for what I take," the ghastly creature slurred. "Always."

CHAPTER 1

Shortly after eleven o'clock in the morning on Monday, April 27, 1863, the steam packet RMS *Anglo-Saxon*, an iron-hulled mail ship of the Montreal Ocean Steamship Company out of Liverpool, was beating around the distant rocky point of Cape Race, Newfoundland, in a heavy, concealing fog of a type all too common for that bleak and lonely part of the world. The sun, almost directly overhead, was nothing more than a dull copper disk casting little light and no shadow. The world was a flat gray expanse, the sea a dark undulating mirror, reflecting nothing.

The man in the dark frock coat and heavy wool walking cape stood at the port deck rail smoking an Egyptian cigarette and staring out into the fog. He was tall and pale, long black hair framing a narrow face with high Slavic cheekbones. The nose was aquiline, the nostrils slightly flared above full lips. His teeth were naturally very white. His eyes were a startling shade of jade green. His name was Count Vladislaw Draculiya, once a Prince of Walachia, now a fugitive from British justice, wanted for a crime he did not commit: the brutal murder of the noted Dutch philosopher and naturalist Abraham Van Helsing.

He knew of Van Helsing, of course, and the strange little scientist's obsession with him. It was Van Helsing who had followed him to England, and it was Van Helsing who had convinced Thornton Hunt at the *Daily Telegraph* that he was a terrible threat to the population of London. Some sort of archvillain, tantamount to a demon in human disguise. He had left his home in Bohemia in the midst of just such a panic, and it had happened again in England, with Thornton Hunt snapping at his heels like the snarling dog that he was. Rumor, always rumor, and then the fear followed by the never-ending hunt. Like the *Judensjagen*, the Jew hunts of not so long ago.

The Count continued to smoke his aromatic cigarette and thought idly of his future. He'd moved so often, lived in so many worlds and times, that it often seemed nothing but a blur or half-remembered dream. All he knew of Montreal was that they spoke an old sort of French there, and having himself lived in Paris for a time many years ago, he knew he'd have no trouble acclimating himself to the city.

It certainly seemed an unlikely place for Van Helsing's people or the police to come looking for him. He sighed and pinched out the remains of his cigarette before tossing it over the rail. All he really wanted was peace and quiet. And to be left alone.

He lifted his head, suddenly alert, his sensitive hearing picking up a distant warning. His nostrils, equally sensitive, twitched to the familiar waft of earth and land when he knew they should still be well out to sea. He peered ahead into the fog, but there was nothing to be seen. There was only the urgent, deeply felt sense of imminent danger.

"Breakers!" a terrified voice screamed from high above him in the crow's nest atop the mainmast. "Breakers dead ahead!" There was barely time to make sense of the words. Seconds later the ship lurched into a sudden turn to port as the helmsman on the bridge threw the wheel around. It was too late.

The Count was suddenly thrown against the rail with stunning force, and he only just barely managed to keep himself from being thrown overboard. An instant later there was a terrible crashing sound as the stern slammed into hidden rocks and a sheer black wall of stone appeared out of the fog directly in front of them.

The stern of the ship pounded even harder into the rocks. The *Anglo-Saxon* was hard aground, the terrible grinding waves of the North Atlantic pushing broadside against her hull, forcing her inexorably toward the massive granite cliffs of Cape Race, a frail ship of wood and iron trapped between an unstoppable force and an immovable object.

Panic and unholy terror gripped the entire ship

within seconds as the rudder, sternpost and propeller were torn away with a ghastly screeching sound like Hell's fury. Water began rushing into the forward stokehold, putting out the fires and filling the engine room. There was no way the ship would ever move under its own power again. The bow and stern anchors were dropped in a vain attempt to hold the dying, sinking ship in place, but water steadily began to pour into the ship.

Several observant and nimble members of the crew, seeing that the jib boom actually jutted above the cliff face, ran along it with ropes and made it to the shore before the whole sail tore away and fell into the foaming sea. First-class passengers were beginning to swarm up from below, and lifeboats were prepared for lowering on the port side of the ship, away from the rocks that hemmed in the boats on the starboard side. There were only six lifeboats available, and all of those were used by first-class passengers and crew since the steerage passengers, more than three hundred of them, had not yet been allowed on deck.

As the boats were lowered, they were almost immediately hammered against the side of the ship, some overturning, some breaking up and some simply swept away to smash to pieces on the rocks. The fog still hung thick, the air full of the noise of the dying ship, the sobbing and screaming of desperate passengers and the shouted orders of the crew, all set to the horrible rolling drumbeat of the unceasing waves.

Suddenly the decks were even more crowded as the first steerage passengers forced their way onto the upper deck, adding to the melee. There was another great lurch as the remains of the ship settled in the sea and the mainmast fell, killing a dozen people and tangling twice that many in fallen rigging.

The main deck was now fully underwater, and people were being carried off in all directions, some clinging to debris, others flailing, almost all eventually being thrown against the stark black rocks of the cliff only a few dozen yards away. Some people clung desperately to the rigging, but even they were eventually swept away or drowned when the *Anglo-Saxon* suddenly rolled away from the rocks as her waterlogged weight shifted, almost turning turtle as she was totally dismasted, sinking fast. Parts of the deckhouses and the bridge were ripped away, their remains used as rafts by people clinging to them.

Fights broke out between survivors, passengers and crew alike, as they fought for space on the makeshift life buoys. More fell from the rigging to be dashed on the rocks; still others were crushed or simply drowned. To make things even worse, a slanting rain began to fall. All this happened within fifteen minutes of the first shouted warning.

It was hours later when the Count awoke from a dark, dreamless sleep to find himself on the upper edge of an angled piece of the main deckhouse roof, now a life raft tossing easily on a heavy swell. Above him the fog had partially lifted in the cold night air and he could see a sliver of the risen moon.

Far ahead of him he could just make out a distant phosphorescent line where the swell broke on the face of a sloping pebble beach. Above the beach, like a dark pillar, was a lighthouse, its beam sweeping in a regular pulse across the wide black sea. He heard a beating heart close by and then a groan. He turned his head and saw that he was not alone.

A young man, fair-haired and perhaps twenty, was curled up on the lower edge of the raft. His leg was broken, awkwardly bent, and he was pale and shivering. The Count edged down until he reached a point just beside him. The Count's wool cape was sodden with rain, but it would offer some warmth to the shivering boy. He gasped when he breathed, and the Count could see a huge wound in his side where a splinter from a falling piece of one of the masts had pierced his flesh. The young man was clearly dying, slowly and in great pain. The Count drew the cloak over him, tucking it below his shoulders.

"Thank you, Father," the boy whispered, seeing the black-dressed figure above him.

"I'm no priest," answered the Count gently, smiling at the irony of the young man's mistake.

"I was on my way to make my fortunes in the gold fields," said the young man. "Now, isn't that a laugh! I didn't even make it ashore!" His accent was Irish, probably one of the steerage passengers they'd picked up at their brief stop in London-derry the day after leaving Liverpool.

"Ma told me to stay, but I wouldn't listen. Stub-born like my da—that's what she said I was." The boy gave a great shudder and his eyes stared. "Jeez, Father, but ain't it cold?" he managed. He blinked. "Christ! I could use a smoke!" He real-ized what he'd said. "Sorry, Father."

The Count felt around in his pockets and mirac-ulously found his cigarette tin and box of wax vestas. He lit a cigarette and placed it between the young man's lips, holding it for him. The boy drew deeply, coughed and then exhaled.

"Jeez, but that's good, Father!" He shuddered again and winced. "Christ, it hurts!"

"What's your name?" the Count asked quietly. They were much closer to shore now.

"Enoch, Father. Enoch Bale, from Ballynew, near Castlebar in County Mayo."

"Enoch. A good name," said the Count. "Lots of brothers and sisters and cousins to greet you when you arrive?"

"None, Father. I'm alone. All the family, what there is of it, is back in Ballynew. I was one mouth less to feed, so Ma didn't complain too much in the end." The boy shuddered horribly and his teeth grated with the pain of the spasm. He gripped the Count's wrist hard and moaned, rain sheeting off his upraised face like shining tears.

"Would you like the pain to go away, Enoch?" the Count asked quietly. "Would you like me to take away your pain?"

"Oh, jeez, Father, yes. It hurts so bloody much!"

He gave the boy another draw on the cigarette, watching as his chest heaved. The Count looked toward the shore. It would be only a few minutes more until the floating deckhouse broached and they were thrown into the sea, but for the boy it would be an infinity of agony and a drowning death. There was a better way. A gentler way.

The Count bent low over the dying boy, his voice pitched peacefully and very softly. "Think of your mother, Enoch, and think of home."

"Yes, Father, oh, yes! Pray for me, Father, dear Jesus God!" The young man's back arched and he screamed in pain.

"Home, Enoch, you're going home now." The Count bent over the boy's shattered body, and with his long pale fingers he turned the young man's head aside, exposing the frantic pulsing of the great artery in his neck. The Count leaned down, his mouth parts shifting in their familiar way, the shining eyeteeth descending in twin saber arcs like great snake fangs, the hollow razor points shining with the silvery emission that would dull the boy's pain and ease his inevitable death. "Home now, Enoch. Home to Ballynew." And the long fangs slipped deeply into the soft, waiting flesh, and the young boy sighed in sweet relief.

An hour later, the Count, alone, made it to the beach and staggered up the long, winding path to the lighthouse. He hammered on the lighthouse keeper's door, and his knock was answered by a thin-faced man dressed in boots, sweater and oilskins.

"What place is this?" the Count asked.

"Cape Race Light. I'm John Halley. Who are you?"

Count Vladislaw Draculiya—son of no mother, raised by no man, once a Prince of Walachia in Bohemia and now a shipwrecked fugitive—barely hesitated before answering.

"My name is Enoch," he said firmly. "Enoch Bale."

CHAPTER 2

At thirty-six years of age, Dr. Carrie Elizabeth Andrea Norton, BA, MA, PhD, was convinced that she would have been far better off if she'd kept her summer job flipping burgers at her local Mickey D's twenty years ago and never gone to university at all. By now she would probably own her own franchise, drive a hot car and be married with a couple of kids, or at the very least have a boyfriend. It wasn't as if anyone really needed an anthropologically based native herbology of North America. Did anyone really care if the Kalispel Indians of Montana, sometimes called the Bitter Root, used the herb of the same name as a laxative? Just to make herself really depressed, she'd once checked the computer files in the Columbia University library to see how many times her doctoral thesis had been consulted in the past seven years. The answer was the one she'd expected: never.

As a child she'd preferred to read books by

Mary Renault and Rosemary Sutcliff rather than Nancy Drew mysteries or *Little House on the Prairie.* As a teenager she'd dreamed of finding another Tutankhamen or Rosetta stone rather than being a movie star or a model. Her parents, one a teacher in a prep school, the other the principal of a nearby high school, had stressed education and paid for her tuition along with her braces, and the die was cast: she was doomed to a life of academic poverty and overqualification and a social life where a guy still didn't go out with a girl who was smarter than him, even if she was relatively good-looking, had a nice body and was perfectly willing to sleep with him on the first date if she really liked him.

Instead she'd become an itinerant "shovel bum" or "dirt digro"—a contract field archaeologist who wound up going to all sorts of exotic locations around the world to dig holes, type up somebody else's notes, be sexually harassed by an endless series of beardie-weirdies who thought all graduate students with breasts were fair game and get nowhere with her career. There just weren't that many top jobs in the archaeology profession, and much to her disgust she discovered that it really wasn't *what* you knew but *who* you knew, and that was being polite about it.

In the end, as the years rolled by and her passport filled up with stamps and scrawls from just about anywhere you could name and others you couldn't pronounce, she was surprised, like people are who do one thing very well for a very long time, that she'd become something of an expert. Instead of being a run-of-the-mill field-worker, of which there were an endless supply, some even willing to pay for the privilege, she was now considered to be a "China Hand," someone who generally had more field experience than the academics often hired to oversee a project by the consulting firm, and someone who was often the real intelligence behind a dig and able to bring it home on time and on budget.

Contract archaeology—research, surveying and excavation contracted by government agencies or private companies to protect or identify sites in danger of destruction due to development—was big business, and the ability to do things quickly and economically at a dig site was a valuable commodity. The only problem was that the work was intermittent and rarely had much in the way of benefits, and the pay was smiliar to that of a supermarket bag boy. On the other hand, you didn't have to buy an expensive work wardrobe: construction boots, jeans and a flannel shirt were the de rigueur uniform for a shovel bum. In winter long johns, a cable knit and something padded from Galaxy Army and Navy on Sixth Avenue at Thirtieth filled out the ensemble.

All of this wandered through her thought processes between the time she got up and the time she stepped into the shower in her tiny fifth-floor apartment on Second Street and Avenue A in the East Village's Alphabet City. Some people, usually landlords, referred to the area as "trendy," but to

Carrie it was still the slum she'd used as a base of operations for the better part of ten years now.

After the shower she went across her hallway office to her closet bedroom and dressed for a summer day, which meant a T-shirt instead of a flannel one. Today's shirt was a classic SHOVEL BABES DO IT IN THE DIRT design. She did up the laces of her dependable old Wesco Jobmasters, completely ignored the dishes in the mini-sink in her mini-kitchen and went out the door.

She rode the creaky, coffin-sized elevator down to the street, then went across to Nicky's and picked up a six-inch *bánh mì*, the Vietnamese version of a submarine sandwich. She thought about the fried egg breakfast version but knew it would drip, so she went for the basic: pâté, ham, roasted ground pork, pickled carrots, cucumber, cilantro, jalapeño, easy on the mayo, all on a mini, crusty baguette. She got an iced Vietnamese coffee to go with it, then walked over to Second Avenue and two blocks down to Houston Street, alternately munching at her sandwich and sucking up her iced coffee through a straw.

She finished her breakfast, then rode the uptown F train to Fourth Street and Sixth Avenue. She came up out of the subway on West Third, watched a group of kids shooting hoops in the public court for a minute or two, then walked back down Sixth Avenue past the drugstore, the sex shop, the Taco Bell and the abandoned Wendy's, finally turning left onto Minetta Lane. Mamoun's was only a block away on MacDougal

Street, and the *makdoos*—the $3.50 stuffed egg-
plants with garlic and walnuts marinated in olive
oil—were without a doubt the best thing about
the job she was working on: a parking lot excavation and preliminary site analysis for an eighteen-
story, ten-million-a-pop condo building being
developed by the Lincoln Corporation on the corner of Minetta Lane and Minetta Street, once the
center of the neighborhood known as Little Africa
during the Civil War period.

The Lincoln Corporation had purchased the old
tenement property years before and put it into
typical New York City development turnaround
by tearing down the building, paving over the remains and turning it into a parking lot. Property
prices had risen to a point where somewhere deep
within the Lincoln Corporation's pulsing, heartless
infrastructure a little bell had tinkled and the
plans for the Avalon Tower on Minetta Lane, a
LinCorp Lifestyle Development Project came to
life.

But to get the official go-ahead required a pass
from the New York City Landmarks Preservation
Commission, and that's where Cornwell-Maibaum
Urban Archaeology Consultants ("We Won't Let
Your Project Become a Thing of the Past") and Dr.
Carrie Elizabeth Andrea Norton, BA, MA, PhD,
came into the picture. William Augustus Cornwell
and David Maibaum, two new-age archaeologists
with more degrees in business and computing
than in archaeology, sat in their Tribeca loft offices

making all the money while as project manager Carrie did all the work under the supposed "direction" of the senior archaeologist on the project, Vaughn Erickson, a dull-witted twenty-seven-year-old boob with a minty-fresh doctorate from a nothing university in Ohio or Iowa or Arkansas or someplace like that and no field experience whatsoever, who just happened to be David Maibaum's son-in-law. He also had bad breath, Maibaum's equally dull-witted, flat-chested, spotty-faced daughter for a wife and no sense of humor whatsoever.

All part of the ongoing life of an American shovel bum. Maybe someday she'd write a book about it. If she ever got the time, which was unlikely. For Carrie there were two states of existence: working and looking for work. It didn't leave much time for anything else, including vacations. The last one of those had been four years ago, half of the time spent trout fishing on the Willoughby River in Vermont with her dad, the other half spent looking for antique spinning wheels with her mom, and all the time fielding questions from both of them about why she wasn't married and making them grandparents.

She went through the doorway in the plywood utility fence surrounding the site and headed for the grimy, graffiti-covered ten-by-twenty-foot trailer they used as a field office. She was surprised to see everyone clustered at the far end of the site around the last test trench they'd started on the day before. Nobody was working. They were just standing around, jawing and looking into the trench. There was no sign of Vaughn Erikson.

She went up the three plank steps and into the office. Erickson was at the phone behind his paper-covered desk. As Carrie stepped into the office, he covered the mouthpiece of the phone and stared at her. His eyes were wide and he looked nervous.

"We've got trouble," he said.

"What kind of trouble?" Carrie asked.

"We found a body."

"Oh, crap," said Carrie with a sigh. "That's all I need."

Detective Max Slattery of the NYPD Cold Case Squad looked like Winston Churchill in a butch-cut toupee. He had the kind of face that belonged on a bald head, but his snow-white hair was a perfect bristled flattop exactly half an inch long over a vast expanse of glowing pink scalp. His hangdog jowls were clean shaven and the thought of growing a mustache had never occurred to him. Everything about him was square: face, shoulders, barrel chest and short, powerful legs. Years ago someone had taken a Spuds Mackenzie Budweiser poster and taped Slattery's picture over the dog's face. The caption read: AREN'T YOU GLAD HE'S ON OUR SIDE? A lot of people thought he'd been the inspiration for the Andy Sipowicz character on *NYPD Blue*, and the average reaction on meeting him for the first time was that he was nothing but a dumb Mick cop. He wasn't. He was an extremely smart Mick cop who'd solved more homicides than anyone else in the history of the New York Police Department.

He was also getting old, with twenty-eight years on the force, having worked everything from Warrants and Central Robbery to Missing Persons and Manhattan North Homicide. He'd now been with the Cold Case Squad since it was formed in 1996— more than a decade. In two more years he'd reach mandatory retirement, and he knew the boredom would probably kill him. He'd been a cop for almost thirty years and with very few exceptions he'd enjoyed every minute of it. He'd chewed up a few marriages and countless other relationships, lost partners to violence, disease and promotion, and never been on the pad for more than a cup of coffee.

The offices of the NYPD Cold Case Squad are located in a squalid little building in Brooklyn. It looks like every other police squad office only more so. Everything is out-of-date, from the telephones to the computers. Everything is either green or brown or beige. Everything is worn out, one way or another. There are filing cases lined up against the walls, battered lockers and rows of battered desks. There is a police administrative assistant—PAA—named Doris Dubukian, who is a bottle blonde, as old as Max Slattery, and who has a memory that is unbeatable when it comes to the mundane. Ask her the names of the first five batters struck out by Sandy Koufax in the first game in the 1963 World Series and she'll answer immediately: Tony Kubek, Bobby Richardson, Tom Tresh, Mickey Mantle and Roger Maris, just like that. Behind Doris and Max's back there were whispered rumors of a long-standing affair between the two of them. Rumors that were utterly unfounded.

At ten thirty in the morning Max was at his desk, working his way steadily through a pile of DD5s, his reading glasses barely hanging on to the end of his Bob Hope nose. Out in reception he heard Doris's phone buzz. A few seconds later his light started to blink. He picked up. The voice belonged to Max's boss, Charlie Groman, an inspector who was in his office one floor up.

"What do you know about Minetta Street?" Groman said.

Max sat back in his chair and closed his eyes. He thought for a moment. The rest of the squad called the look on his face "doing a doris." Finally he spoke. "Stephen Crane wrote an essay about it. A crook named No Toe Charley lived there. It used to be a high-crime spot, worse than Five Points. Before that it was a black ghetto. Al Pacino lived on Minetta Lane in 1973 in *Serpico* and he spied on his girlfriend there in 1993 in *Carlito's Way*. The Minetta Tavern on the corner was used in another mob movie called *The Legend of Jimmy Blue Eyes*. The Minetta Tavern was also the place where *Reader's Digest* was founded. In the basement."

"You've got a sick mind, Max—you know that, don't you?"

"Sick minds solve crimes," answered Max. "What's new on Minetta Street that would interest us?"

"An archaeological site. They found a body."

"Isn't that what they're supposed to find?"

"This one took a bullet to the back of the skull, had his throat ripped out as well, his lips sewn together with binder twine and apparently is wearing a uniform. Civil War. A naval uniform by the looks of it."

"Which side?"

"Ours."

"Which presumably means the uniform is not Confederate."

"Correct. Which is odd."

"Why would that be?"

"Because the corpse is black."

"I see."

"No, you don't. The property belongs to the Lincoln Corporation. You're going to have to tread very softly here."

"Why do we have to tread at all?"

"You know the rules. Article seven, item six of the New York Landmark Preservation Act says that in the event of unanticipated human remains being discovered, the NYPD and the Office of the Chief Medical Examiner shall be informed."

"So, consider yourself informed."

"Quit being a pain in the ass, Max."

"Okay."

"Get yourself down there. Your contact is a woman named Dr. Carrie Norton. She'll give you the dirt, so to speak."

"Don't try to be funny, Charlie. It doesn't suit you."

"Go." Groman hung up.

"On my way," said Slattery to the dial tone.

CHAPTER 3

Ten days after the wreck of the *Anglo-Saxon* on the ragged rocky shore of Cape Race, Newfoundland, the schooner *Sheila Maxwell* docked at Pier 18 on South Street at the foot of Maiden Lane carrying sealskins and salt cod. The *Sheila Maxwell* had been one of the first rescue ships to arrive at Cape Race to pick up survivors and the very first to leave St. John's en route to New York. The Count assumed by then that the British authorities would know he'd fled England aboard the *Anglo-Saxon*, and getting away from Newfoundland as quickly as possible had become an immediate priority. Even with the adoption of his new identity it had seemed prudent to travel to a city outside the formal jurisdiction of the British Empire.

The Count, now calling himself Enoch Bale and carrying the ticket receipt from the dead boy's pocket to prove his identity, went down the *Sheila Maxwell*'s gangplank to the pier in the early morning. It was midweek and South Street was throbbing with vibrant life. A forest of masts blocked the view of the East River, and the bowsprits of the hundreds of ships docked along the long row of piers almost poked through the windows of the ship chandlers, warehouses and taverns on the far side of the broad cobbled street that ran along beside the docks.

The air was heavy with a rich combination of smells made up mostly of a hundred thousand tons of horse manure, coal smoke from ten thousand stoves and the animal odors and rich, thick blood of the Hell's Kitchen slaughterhouses. Over all of this was the simple stink of almost eight hundred thousand people living in close proximity to one another.

The noise of it all was equally incredible: squeaking cartwheels rumbling on cobblestone streets, the creak of ships' masts down by the piers, the neighing of horses, the rattle of cranes, the yelling calls of thousands of tradesmen, the clatter of hooves, the ringing of bells, laughter, screams, shouts, roars and singing all mixed together in a raucous music you could sink into like a man drowning in a sea of incessant babbling, carousing and madness.

Enoch Bale was entranced. The narrow alleys were capillaries, the streets were veins, the avenues arteries, the rush of horses, carriages, carts and people the lifeblood of a huge living organism that was the city. Here was a place to settle, vanish, live and satisfy any possible appetite. He had found a home at last, perhaps the first he could call that for the better part of nine hundred years.

He saw a Hasid come out of one of the South Street warehouses and followed him to a cramped and crowded street called Maiden Lane, where he immediately discovered what he wanted. Continuing for a little way up the street and into the city, he found a rooming house with an eatery nearby called the Fraunces Tavern, and he took a room. Over the next several days he followed a familiar routine: removing the hidden pouches sewn around the cuffs and side panels of his frock coat and extracting the secret cache of gems he carried there, mostly diamonds, pearls, emeralds and rubies, all of the finest quality and of moderate but not excessive size.

Maiden Lane, as he'd discovered on his first day in New York, was the center of the city's gem trade. He had no difficulty in converting a portion of his collection into gold, making sure not to attract too much attention, but selling enough to give him a substantial sum, which he put on deposit at the Irving Bank and Trust, which was also traded on the stock exchange. Consulting with an officer of the bank, he opened a trading account with George Peabody's office, a counting house and brokerage he was already familiar with, having dealt with its London branch as the Count Draculiya, a name now rapidly becoming infamous in England.

The people at Peabody's, seeing the size of his

deposit at the Irving Bank, quickly arranged a mortgage for him on a recently vacated and fully furnished property decorated by the well-known firm of Pottier & Stymus at 15 Gramercy Park in the more socially acceptable area of Kips Bay, close to Irving Place and Madison Square.

The house was four stories, made of brick, and elegant in a plain and unobtrusive way, which was precisely what Enoch Bale was looking for. A good, but not overly ostentatious, bespoke wardrobe from the people at Brooks in Catharine Market completed his transformation. So thus it was that in the space of two weeks, Enoch Bale, fugitive and shipwrecked castaway, was transformed into Mr. Enoch Bale, resident of New York and respected man of means. During those two weeks he managed to liquidate the rest of his store of gems without arousing suspicion, spreading his resulting gains through several banks. Enoch Bale was a wealthy man. All he needed to make his new life in New York complete was the services of his friend. If he was to survive here, he needed Chang Fu Sheng.

Echo Van Helsing and her younger brother, Matthew, arrived at Norddeutscher Lloyd's Pier 3 in Hoboken, New Jersey, on the steamship *America* almost two weeks to the day after Enoch Bale's arrival in New York City. Well-seasoned travelers after many years with their late father, Dr. Abraham Van Helsing, Echo and her brother had very little luggage and it was with a minimum of fuss and bother that they made their way to the Hoboken Ferry Terminal a few blocks down from the pier. They had only to wait for the quarter hour before traveling across the North River to the foot of Christopher Street.

From there they took one of the hansom cabs that were apparently fresh to the streets of New York but which they were quite familiar with themselves from their time in London. An American acquaintance of their father's had suggested the Sturtevant House on Broadway and Twenty-ninth Street as both a dignified and relatively inexpensive hotel in the city, and by early afternoon they had secured a set of adjoining rooms on the American plan for a reasonable fifty dollars per week.

Echo Van Helsing looked out the window of her sitting room. On the other side of the avenue called Broadway, two teams were playing at English cricket, one dressed in plain white uniforms, the other wearing jackets of striped brown and gold with matching caps. The game seemed very sedate, which made the players look all the more ridiculous since Broadway itself was bustling chaos: carts, barouches, hansom cabs, expensive-looking phaetons, farm wagons and pedestrians crisscrossing in all directions, no one paying the slightest attention to the others.

Like in London, the atmosphere was a slightly foggy yellow even though the sun was trying its best to shine down through the smoky gloom. Unlike in London, the buildings seemed much less cramped, the sidewalks and the streets themselves much wider and the buildings taller. Even the people in their masses seemed rather different: the men wore the same sort of dark suits and the women the same sort of fan-front bodices and full, flouncing, silly skirts, but somehow the men's strides seemed longer and the women's movements much less proscribed than what she was used to.

It was a grimy, enormous city certainly, with an all-too-apparent rubbish problem piled by the curb in heaps and manure in staggering volume in the streets, but there wasn't the soot of centuries on the brick or the rounded, worn-out look of ages on the cobbles. Big, brash and bustling, it was a young city, and a city fully enjoying its youth.

And somewhere out there, she thought, staring moodily across the smoky, fuming chimneypots toward the distant river, somewhere out there is the beast that killed my father.

She refused to think of the Count Draculiya as a man, for that he decidedly was not. But neither could she think of him as the supernatural creature her father had supposed. Rumors abounded about his powers to transform himself, to fly, to make himself invisible, but those were only rumors, not proven fact. The only thing she knew for sure about Draculiya was his sinister and seductive ability to bring people under his power, and once they were under that power to destroy them utterly, and in the end, kill them with savage ease and a terrible indifference.

She knew that because she'd felt the first powerful taste of it during their single brief meeting with him at Carfax Abbey on the eastern outskirts of London along with his odd friend and companion, Robert Renfield. It was a fateful meeting that had eventually led to her father's murder at Draculiya's hand and her own voyage halfway round the world to bring him to justice. Certainly no man and no demon either, but a beast, an animal, some ghastly primal creature out of history, but a creature that could be caught, and once caught, caged.

"Don't worry, sister. We'll find him."

She turned away from the window and smiled at her brother, who had just entered the room.

"Do you really think so, Matthew? It seems an awfully big city."

"Not as large as London."

"Nor as familiar," said Echo with a sigh. "We have no friends here."

"We'll make friends," said Matthew, trying to look stern. Echo smiled at him. He was handsome, a young version of his father, slight and sandy haired, with freckles, unlike Echo, who had dark features and dark hair. He looked very dapper in his proper frock coat and collar, neck cloth neatly tied, but clothes unfortunately could not hide the fact that Matthew was more boy than man. He was only seventeen and not even shaving yet. Had it not been for the infuriating impossibility of being a woman and traveling without a male escort, she would have sent him back to Breda Castle and to his place at the royal military academy, where he belonged.

"You're right, of course," she said trying to put on a smile. "But first we must unpack."

"Then eat!" Matthew replied enthusiastically. "They have a restaurant here that serves something called 'ruddy duck' and 'tutti-frutti.' Doesn't that sound interesting?"

"That depends on how much it costs," said Echo cautiously. Their father had left them comfortably endowed, but the money would not last forever; they had to be careful. A few weeks in the hotel would be enough; after that they would have to look for cheaper lodgings. The only asset Echo Van Helsing truly possessed was her intelligence, and for a woman in these times intelligence was worth absolutely nothing.

"Don't be so glum, sister," chided her brother. "You always look for the worst, never the best in things."

"That is because the worst inevitably seeks you out and the best is always simply a pleasant surprise." It had been her father's credo and now it was hers. She felt a tug in the pit of her stomach and could feel tears welling in her eyes. She turned away and looked out the window so Matthew wouldn't see her crying. If her father had followed his own best advice perhaps he'd still be alive.

She regained her composure and shooed her brother out of the room. She took one last look out the window before unpacking and preparing for a much-needed bath. The cricket game was over and the players were all shaking hands. In one corner of the field by the gate, a table was laid out with cakes and sandwiches and glass jugs of lemonade. Young black men and women in simple uniforms served the men and women clustering around the table now that the match was done. The women were laughing and chatting with one another beneath their colorful parasols. Down there on the cricket field was the innocent best that Matthew spoke about, but in her heart Echo knew that the worst was coming, and soon.

CHAPTER 4

Carrie Norton stared at the body on the autopsy table, scanning it with a practiced eye. This wasn't the first time she'd dealt with human remains, but these were by far the best preserved. The body had been laid out under the bright lights of the Special Projects room at the Office of the Chief Medical Examiner at NYU Medical Center.

The corpse was that of a man with definite African-American features, approximately five feet seven inches in height, wearing the remains of what appeared to be a Civil War–era naval uniform, complete with white duck pants stained to a shade of oversteeped tea, a waist-length "monkey jacket," a shirt and even an old-fashioned flat-cap sailor's hat. His feet were bare. The remains looked as though they'd been dropped into a vat of sheep dip and then left to cure. Horribly, the best comparison that jumped to Carrie's mind was a piece of human-shaped beef jerky. As she'd already noticed, the man's lips had been sewn together with what looked like heavy string or a leather thong.

"He looks black but he's got red hair like an Irishman," said Max Slattery, standing beside Carrie. "How's that possible?" He looked across the table at Dr. Harold Potter, the assistant medical examiner, with the inevitable nickname of "Hogwarts."

"Not my field," said Potter, tactfully deferring to Carrie.

"It's the acid content in the soil. Most bog bodies have red hair," she explained.

"That was no bog," said Slattery. "You said that was a basement you found him in."

"The basement had an earth floor. There was no real foundation," replied Carrie. "The whole area was bogland, almost a swamp. There used to be a creek that ran right through the middle of it named Minetta Brook, from the Dutch for 'little stream'—Mintje Kill. It went through Washington Square Park, through the Minetta Street area, and exited in the Hudson. That's why the land was so cheap."

"Not these days," snorted Slattery.

"Can we get on with it?" Potter asked a little testily. "Dr. Norton tells me we're on quite a deadline. Our friend here's been dead for a hundred and fifty years or so, but she's in a hurry."

"Because he's drying out," said Carrie. "Your examination is just a formality; we've still got CAT scans, PET scans and electron microscopy, not to mention simple X-rays. The longer he's out of that

acidic environment that kept him so well preserved, the more he's going to deteriorate, even
decompose. We're going to have to freeze-dry him
if we want to hang on to him."

"So now he's instant coffee?" Slattery said.

Carrie nodded. "Something like that. The Museum of Natural History is lending me their
freeze-drying chamber if they can have a bit of
tissue for their DNA database."

"Instant coffee and chopping him up into little
pieces. The *Post* is going to eat this up," said
Slattery.

"Try this," said Potter, easing the bog man's
head to one side. "He was murdered at least
twice, maybe three times."

"I beg your pardon?" Carrie said. She leaned
over the wizened, leathery object on the table.
Hogwarts exposed the neck. It looked as though
the man had virtually been beheaded.

Potter used his scalpel as a pointer. "There's a
definite ligature mark here. A wire. He was gar-
roted. He also had a section of his throat literally
torn out. And there's a hole in the back of his
head that looks like a bullet wound. Very. large
caliber, no exit wound. If I dug around I'd probably find it in there."

"That's consistent," said Carrie thoughtfully.
Slattery turned and stared at her. He still hadn't
made up his mind, but he was well on his way
to disliking the woman.

"Consistent with what?"

"Most bog bodies found have been the victims of

some kind of ritual sacrifice. Bludgeoned, hanged, throat slit, sometimes all three." She pointed at the sewn lips. "The mouth is consistent too—it was done to keep the spirit from escaping."

"Murdered."

"Sacrificed," said Carrie. "It's not quite the same thing."

"It is in New York," he answered. He stared down at the body. "Why is this so familiar?" he muttered to himself.

They spent another twenty minutes with the John Doe from the Minetta Lane site but didn't learn much more beyond the fact of the man's general physical characteristics and the three potential causes of death. Potter promised to send the remains on to the museum when all the requisite tests had been completed, and Slattery and Carrie rode the elevator back up to the main-floor reception area together.

"So now what?" Slattery asked.

Carrie shrugged. "I go back to the dig; you go back to wherever you came from. Like I told Hogwarts, this isn't a homicide; it's a formality."

"You don't care that this guy was murdered?"

"Look, I'm an archaeologist, not a detective. Dead bodies are part of the deal. I'll admit this one's better preserved than most, but it has nothing to do with what I'm doing at the Minetta site. It's a sidebar. Interesting, but not necessarily very important in the bigger scheme of things."

"What scheme would that be?" Slattery asked as the elevator thumped to a stop.

"A big corporation wants to put up a big building and I have to ascertain if there's any real historical reason why they shouldn't bring in the pile drivers and start putting up steel."

"It's a crime scene!"

"Like Hogwarts said, a hundred-and-fifty-year-old crime scene. It's a dead issue, so to speak."

The elevator doors opened. Three people were waiting in the reception room. One of them was a man in a police uniform with more gold braid than Carrie had ever seen, the second was the slightly lumpy figure of David Maibaum, one of her two employers, and the third was a woman in a power suit carrying a notebook computer like a purse.

"I don't like the looks of this," said Slattery. He knew who the man in the gold braid was: Chief Richard "The Dick" McNichols, head of Community Affairs. The PR commander of the entire NYPD. If you needed something covered up, the Dick was your go-to guy.

"I don't like the looks of this at all, at all," Slattery repeated.

"Me neither," said Carrie. David Maibaum had a disgustingly obsequious expression on his face, which probably meant the woman in the power suit was a client, in this case the Lincoln Corporation. The suit was black, the shoes were Dolce & Gabbana, and the hair was blond, pulled back so tightly it was stretching her perfect eyebrows back up her Botoxed forehead. She was forty going on thirty and her lips were puffy. Carrie hated her on sight.

"Chief," said Slattery with a nod. The chief nodded back.

"Dr. Maibaum," said Carrie.

"I'm Karen White from LinCorp," said the woman in the black suit, holding out a manicured hand to either Slattery or Carrie Norton. Neither one shook it.

"You've been examining the artifact, presumably," said Maibaum, addressing Carrie.

"It's a body," said Max Slattery. "Not an artifact."

"In fact it's the body of a black Civil War sailor who was murdered," said Carrie. Maibaum winced at the words "black" and "murdered." Slattery glanced appreciatively at Carrie with a new respect. He altered his opinion of her a notch or two. The resulting pregnant pause went into overtime.

"We have a situation I think everyone would like to see resolved," said the woman from LinCorp, finally. Maibaum nodded. So did McNichols.

"Resolved how?" Carrie asked.

"No one wants to see the Avalon Project slowed down," said Maibaum slowly. "We want to keep things on track here." He glanced at Karen White.

"On the other hand," put in the LinCorp flack, "we recognize the importance of the find at the site."

"Crime scene," put in Slattery.

Carrie spoke up. "I wouldn't quite put it in the

category of a 'find' either. Whoever it was, it was a human being."

"No matter how we slice it," said McNichols bluntly, "this is going to be big news. As big as the African Burial Ground." The African Burial Ground had been an accidental discovery by construction workers in lower Manhattan who had unearthed a "Negro Burying Ground" at the corner of Duane and Elk streets. The building that was supposed to be put up had never been built. A few hundred million in construction had gone up in smoke. The city fathers put on a bold face, but no one was pleased.

"We are obviously in the midst of a very sensitive situation here," murmured Karen White. "Especially considering the political overtones, which I am sure we are all aware of."

No kidding, thought Carrie. Henry Todd Lincoln, the CEO of the Lincoln Corporation, and a direct descendant of President Abraham Lincoln, was in the middle of a mayoralty race with James Washington Stone, the charismatic black activist and filmmaker. Both men were playing the race card, with Lincoln advocating more cops, more rules, fewer foreigners and less welfare, as well as a "border guard" and identity cards to keep "undesirables" out of the city. Stone was responding by calling his opponent an economic racist and an isolationist bigot. In the final analysis Lincoln was the rich New Yorker's choice and Stone was the poor man's candidate.

"In light of that," said Maibaum, "we have decided to take steps."

"Really," said Carrie.

"Really," said Maibaum coldly.

"LinCorp is providing you with office and laboratory space at one of our buildings. A corporate loft on Lispenard Street, to be precise."

Slattery smiled at that. He knew what a corporate loft was: a nice, discreet place to tear off a private piece of ass without Mrs. Corporate seeing it on Mr. Corporate's MasterCard bill.

"Name what the two of you will need and it will be provided," said McNichols.

"What 'two of us' are you talking about?" Slattery said.

"What he said," said Carrie to Maibaum.

"Detective Slattery is being put on detached duty under my orders," said McNichols. "It's already been approved by One PP and the chief of department. This is a Special Task Force investigation."

Slattery smirked. In the business it was known as a "stiffy"—an exercise in public relations to get the chief off the hook and sound as though something serious was being done, when you were really just spinning your wheels.

"And who else is on the task force?" the heavy-set cop asked.

"She is," said Maibaum, pointing his chins at Carrie. "She'll provide you with any archaeological help you need and liaise with my office. I'll liaise with Ms. White."

"Whole lot of liaising going on," murmured Slattery.

"Sounds like an R and B title," muttered Carrie.

Within two minutes, cards and telephone numbers had been exchanged, promises made about being kept in the loop, a few direct orders given; then the suits vanished, leaving Carrie and Max alone in the reception room. A few seconds later a stone-faced man in his seventies was led into the reception area by a much younger man in a white jacket. Slattery watched the man as he was led through a set of swinging doors, then turned to Carrie.

"You get the feeling we've just been handled?"

"With bells on," said Carrie. "I guess I'm a detective after all."

"And I'm an archaeologist."

"Trade you."

"There's an Italian place down the way," said Slattery. "They do great paccheri in Sicilian eggplant sauce; you interested? We could make some kind of battle plan maybe. Figure out how to handle them back. I'll get the food; you get the wine. A nice Barolo maybe. Put it on separate expense accounts."

"You're on," said Carrie. "A good autopsy always makes me hungry."

CHAPTER 5

Echo Van Helsing sat at the writing desk in her room at the Sturtevant and scribbled in her diary. The silver mechanical pencil she used had been her father's, and the diary itself, a beautiful thing with a picture of the Taj Mahal on the cover, inset with small chips of mother-of-pearl, had been a Christmas gift from him. The writing of a journal had also been his suggestion, not so much for what was written but as an aid to focusing one's thoughts and giving direction to considered action. To make a plan was to write it down, and to write it down was the best way to observe its strengths and weaknesses.

She put down her pencil for a moment and stared at the vase of wildflowers Matthew had collected for her from a nearby vacant lot. They were nothing spectacular, just trout lily, wild daffodil, sweet white violet, greater celandine and periwinkle, but together they were an impressive bouquet, all the more so for coming from the heart of an enormous city where one really didn't expect to find growing things at all.

But what of Draculiya? Like the wildflowers, his physical aspects were nothing to single him out in a population as large as New York's. He had enormous presence certainly, but you couldn't go about the city in your hired carriage saying "Have you seen a man of great presence anywhere?" He could be described, yes; in fact she even had a sketch of him she'd made from memory, but what was that except a rough portrait of a man with high cheekbones, a pale complexion and the deepest, darkest, most sinister and seductive eyes she'd ever seen?

It was at once the face of Saint Augustine, of Hamlet and Lothario, all combined, and she knew what anyone would say if she showed it: this is a portrait of her phantom lover, the man she seeks but has never had. She veered away from that thought quickly and picked up the silver pencil again. Her father had found Draculiya once by following what he referred to as "the Logician's Path": observe, hypothesize, predict, and finally, prove.

What then had she observed about Draculiya? He was a secretive man and not particularly sociable. In London he had attended only affairs where it would have been more suspicious if he did not attend. He lived well, if discreetly. Carfax Abbey had been a grange house in Purfleet, a suburb, not a house in Cheyne Walk or Mayfair. He had few friends, if any, other than Renfield, who had gone mad and was now in an asylum. The only other person regularly in his company was that quiet little Oriental who was his batman and butler in one. Chin? Chung? No, it had been Chang. Chang Fu Sheng.

What had Draculiya been beyond a prince? What did a prince do? She tapped the silver pencil against her upper lip and pondered. She had no idea what a prince did, or a count. Did royalty actually work at all in any proper sense, or did they just sit about looking at the family jewels and running their fingers through great cauldrons filled with gold coins?

The family jewels. That sparked a thought. She made a little lozenge-shaped drawing on her diary page, then filled it with triangular facets. The first place her father had gone in London had been the pawnbroker's in Drury Lane, looking for anyone who'd recently sold a store of gemstones, both set and loose.

In the notes he'd left behind it was clear that this was how Draculiya financed himself, transporting his wealth in the form of gems, then liquidating them for cash. When leaving a place he would do the reverse, spending cash to buy gems. She knew little about gems, and diamonds in particular, but two things she did know: the people who traded in diamonds were generally Jews, and furthermore they were Dutch or Belgian, coming from Amsterdam or Antwerp.

Born in Leiden, Echo obviously spoke Dutch, learned Flemish and simply enjoyed French. Traveling for so many years had added English, German and a smattering of Russian. She would have no difficulty communicating with the Jews of New York. Find the Jewish ghetto in any city and inevitably you would find the jewelry traders. She turned back to the diary briefly and jotted down that fact below the little drawing of the diamond.

So, following her father's scientific method, what could she hypothesize from what she knew? Draculiya, undoubtedly traveling under another name by now, would be living quietly, but in good fashion, somewhere not in the social whirl, but perhaps not far from it. He would have recently traded jewels for cash, and he might well still employ a Chinese manservant named Chang.

She wrote all this down, then added a few notations somewhat outside her father's method: she'd noted herself that Draculiya had dressed extremely well, his bespoke suits from Saville Row or Bond Street, as were his shirts and boots; none of this would have been noticed by her father, who preferred tweeds and wooly German vests and whom she had once seen give a lecture at the university in his carpet slippers.

He was also perfectly shaved, which meant a good barber, and he smoked Turkish cigarettes, which meant a tobacconist. All of these were small hints but depended more or less on having Draculiya's new name. To get it would require a visit to the Jewish ghetto, and to find that she'd need some sort of guide. According to the hotel manager, Mr. Boone, Appleton's published a more than adequate handbook, which he'd promised to purchase for her.

She laid down her pen as Matthew came into the room, biting on an apple. He'd been down watching the cricketers and there were grass stains on his trousers from sitting on the ground. Such a boy, she thought, half fondly and half with worry at what was going to become of him without a father.

"There's someone here to see you," said Matthew, without much interest. "A Mr. Warne, from the Pinkerman Agency."

"Pinkerton," corrected Echo.

"Yes, that's it," said Matthew.

Echo frowned. She knew that the Pinkertons, with their unsleeping-eye signature, were detectives, but she hadn't sent them a note or telegram and she didn't know any Mr. Warne. On the other hand, if it wasn't too much of a financial strain, perhaps hiring a detective wasn't such a bad idea at that.

"Send him in," she said to her brother. Matthew withdrew and didn't return. A moment later a slim, narrow-faced man in slightly tinted spectacles, boots, a rumpled brown sack suit and a shapeless felt hat of the same color entered the room. His collar was a little grimy and his necktie was poorly adjusted. He held the stub of a narrow cigarillo in his gray-gloved hand. A tradesman without the manners to remove his hat indoors or the good taste to match his gloves to the rest of his dress. Not to mention the foul-smelling cigarillo. It smelled precisely like the nasty things her father had smoked incessantly in his study at home.

"Mr. Warne? I asked for no agent from your company. Why are you here?"

"Mrs. Warne, actually," the figure said, taking off the ugly brown hat. Removing one glove, the person in the suit reached up and unpinned a long cascade of brown curly hair.

"*Krijg het apelazerus!*" Echo whispered, using one of her late father's favorite exclamations. "You're a woman!"

"Since birth," said Warne. Her voice was a little rough, the timbre more like a young man's than a woman's. She took off the tinted glasses and smiled. She held up the cigar. "Gives me a bit of a rasp, helps with the disguise."

Echo dropped into her chair and stared at the woman. With the hair under her hat, the effect had been perfect. "How wonderful!" she said at last as the implications sank in. The smile on Kate Warne's face widened.

"Walking around, playing at being of the masculine gender?" she said. "It has its benefits." The woman shrugged. "It also has its drawbacks. You have to pay for everything yourself for one, and not to be indiscreet, but there are problems of hygiene to consider."

Echo blushed. She hadn't thought about that.

"Still," she said.

"Still." Warne grinned. "It does cap the climax! Smoke on the street, spit on the sidewalk and go where you want and as you please without a man on your elbow! Grand fun, Miss Van Helsing!"

"But I'm afraid I still don't understand," said Echo. "We have never met and I have made no request to your agency."

"Allan is friends with Sir Richard Mayne."

"The Scotland Yard commissioner?"

"That's him."

"I see," said Echo, who didn't see at all.

"There's more to it than that, but suffice it to say that I'm supposed to render you any and all assistance in the pursuit of this Count Draculiya fellow. So here I am."

"And you're a detective?"

"According to Allan, Mr. Pinkerton, that is, I'm one of the best, in a dress or out, if you know what I mean." She smiled.

Echo didn't quite know what she meant, but she had certain ideas. "What do you know of Draculiya?" she said at last.

Kate Warne shrugged. "Just what they told me. A foreigner, Hungarian or Romanian or some such; I can never keep all those countries straight. Came to London about a year ago. Suspicions of him being involved in the death of some girl named Lucy Westenra, but nothing was ever proved. He's also been implicated in the murder of your father, Abraham Van Helsing." At this point the female detective gave Echo a curious look. "The weapon used in that murder having been a wooden stake which was plunged through his heart."

"That's right," said Echo, blanching at the description of her father's death. "Initially Dr. Seward thought it had been Draculiya's companion Renfield who had escaped from the asylum, but it was later discovered that Renfield was already dead himself, a suicide in his cell."

"Dr. Seward?"

"An alienist."

"Who worked at an asylum?"

"In Purfleet. He was the chief administrator."

"Where's this Purfleet place?"

"East London. It's where Draculiya lived. Carfax Abbey."

"Your count lived in an abbey?"

"The Abbey Grange. The manor house occupied by the lord who gave the land to the monastic order occupying the abbey," explained Echo.

"So he had a great deal of money, this count of yours?"

"He wasn't my count." Echo bristled. "He's a fiend."

"So I hear tell," said Kate Warne dryly. "A rich foreigner count comes to England, buys a big house next to an old church and starts killing people by sticking wooden stakes through their hearts. Is that about right?"

"Put crudely, yes," Echo said. "Although Lucy wasn't killed that way."

"No?"

"No," said Echo. "She had her throat torn out."

"Some kind of animal maybe?" Kate Warne suggested.

"She was found in her bedroom. The sheets

were covered in blood; in fact she was bled dry, if you must know."

"Yes, I must, actually, if we're going to find this character," the detective said. "Why does everyone think it's this Draculiya doing the murders? How is he connected?"

"He made advances to her at a dinner party. She complained of a headache and he cured it through some kind of Bohemian magic. Animal magnetism, he called it."

"Mesmerism? Hypnosis?" Kate Warne said.

"I suppose you could call it that, although my father always thought Mesmer and Baird were both charlatans."

"You know much about that kind of thing?"

"I was my father's assistant. He was a scientist."

"So Draculiya cures a headache and he's the killer?"

"There was more. She met him in secret several times after that. She was engaged to Arthur; it was quite scandalous."

"Arthur?"

"Lord Godalming."

"Rich?"

"Very."

"Was Lucy's family rich?"

"Not especially."

"So she was going to marry money and Draculiya interfered."

"It wasn't like that." Echo frowned. "The Count seduced her. He seduced everyone. His manners, his wit, his elegance, his aristocracy . . ."

"Handsome?"

"Some thought so." Echo shrugged, trying to make her tone cool.

"Handsome foreign royalty sweeps Lord Godalming's fiancée off her feet and has his way with her. Lord Godalming objects, kills her and blames it on the Count. Your father finds out what Godalming's been up to, and he kills him. Could it have been that way?"

"No," Echo said firmly, "it could not." She heaved a great sigh. "Mrs. Warne, you'd have to have known Arthur. He was devoted to Lucy. He loved her with all his heart."

"In my experience those are often the most dangerous ones," said the detective. "Love and jealousy go together likes roses and thorns."

"Like Draculiya and death," responded Echo. "There was no problem before he arrived. My father and I were investigating the possibility of blood disease as a cause of madness at Dr. Seward's asylum, Lucy was engaged to Arthur; even little Mina, Lucy's companion, was engaged to Arthur's solicitor, Mr. Harker. And then the Count arrived at that drafty old hall of his and everything was ruined." She turned and went to her valise, perched on a chest of drawers beside her bed. She withdrew a long dagger, the haft ornately carved silver, the blade made of a black, shining substance, more like polished wood or stone than metal. "When I find him I will kill him with this. I will pierce his heart and then remove his head in the old way. My father thought it the only way."

Kate stared at the wicked-looking weapon and frowned. "But there's no real evidence that Count Draculiya was involved, no living witness to any crime?"

"No," said Echo after a long moment. "No evidence. No witness."

"Then," said Kate Warne brightly, "we'll just have to find some, won't we?"

"You sound very sure," said Echo.

"I'm not a great believer in coincidence, Miss Van Helsing. Let me be forthright about my position, which to be completely honest goes well beyond your own concerns. Over the past several weeks in New York there have been reports of a number of murders such as the one you describe . . . young women, all with their throats savagely torn out, as though by some sort of terrible, savage animal where no such animal could possibly be. Mr. Pinkerton, at the request of President Lincoln himself, has asked me to investigate the matter in as discreet a manner as possible. There's trouble enough with the war and the draft coming up; we certainly don't need a panic about some monster roaming the streets of New York murdering young women."

"You think it's Count Draculiya?" Echo said.

"Let's find out," said the lady Pinkerton agent.

CHAPTER 6

Lispenard Street in New York runs confusingly between West Broadway on the west to Broadway just south of Canal Street on the east. Pearl's Paints is at the Canal Street end, and Nancy Whiskey's is at the West Broadway end. In between there are dozens of old warehouses going back to the days when Lispenard Street was the center of the garment industry. Later it was the crackhead and paint-spattered center of the Tribeca art scene, but now it is all upscale galleries for the bridge-and-tunnel crowd, with most of the Bogardus wrought-iron buildings turned into million-dollar granite-kitchen condos.

The loft at 45 Lispenard was in the first block off West Broadway. It was on the second floor above a coffee and juice bar and a place that sold old architectural bits and pieces such as ornamental lions and the concrete pediments from old building columns. In the two days since the promise of office and lab space, it was obvious that the Lincoln Corporation and Carrie's bosses at Cornwell-Maibaum had been hard at work.

The condo had been cleared of furniture except for a couch and a few chairs around the entrance foyer, and then loaded up with desks, worktables, computers and every piece of electronic gear that an archaeologist had ever dreamed of, from infra-red digital cameras to fluid detectors and very-high-end discriminating metal detectors and even a big, bright yellow Seeker ground-penetrating radar unit that looked like a robotic version of an outsized kiddie stroller. Two spaces in the loft had been turned into offices, one for Carrie Norton, the other for Max Slattery. The walls were white, the floors were hardwood and big windows looked out onto Lispenard Street on one side and an alley on the other. The view onto Lispenard was the back end of a postal station with delivery trucks parked up and down the street.

The day before, a huge shelf unit had been installed in the living room area and loaded with every reference book imaginable, from Jordan Kerber's *Lambert Farm: Public Archaeology and Canine Burials Along Narragansett Bay* to Barbara Meil Hobson's *Uneasy Virtue: The Politics of Prostitution and the American Reform Tradition*. There was even the Seymour Greggs famous inventory of two hundred cesspits and privies excavated in downtown New York, including his seminal essay on the variety and uses of female urinals in the early

treatment of venereal disease and the differences
in basic diet between Polish and Irish immigrants
based on the coprological evidence at hand.

"What's coprology?" Slattery asked, biting into
his dripping cheeseburger at the bar in Nancy
Whiskey's pub at the end of the block.

Carrie picked up one of the fat, beer-battered
onion rings from the basket they were sharing and
took a crunchy bite. "The study of shit," she said.
"Not to put too fine a point on it."

"You've got to be kidding," said Max. He shook
some hot sauce between the bun halves of his
burger and took another bite. "People actually
study shit?"

Carrie nodded. "Coprologists do. You've never
heard of the Lloyd's Bank turd?"

Slattery put down his burger. "No."

Carrie smiled. "Eight and a half inches long,
sharp at both ends. Dropped by a Viking in a
hurry at the Lloyd's Bank site in London. The big-
gest fossilized human fecal deposit on record. It's
insured for fifty thousand dollars."

"No." The cop sounded impressed, either at the
size of the artifact or its value.

"True," said Carrie. She took another onion ring
and sprinkled some salt on it. She took a bite.
"They had it on display in a glass case in the
lobby of the bank for years."

"So maybe what we're doing isn't such a wild-
goose chase after all," said Slattery. He sipped at
his pint of Kilkenny.

"It's a bit of overkill, if you ask me." Carrie

shrugged. "But it's smart marketing by the Lincoln people."

"You mean it'll keep James Washington Stone and his Rollnecks off guard," grunted Slattery. He picked up his burger again and chewed. Stone, in an updated homage to Malcolm X, had all his volunteer workers, male and female alike, dress in black roll-neck sweaters and black trousers or skirts. There had been a few ugly comparisons to Mussolini's fascist Blackshirts from the thirties, but the quasi uniforms were certainly impressive in a sinister way. One way or another it made the point: black isn't just beautiful; it's powerful as well.

Carrie nodded. "Something like that. We'll take whatever heat comes along, and that loft is going to look great for press conferences and photo ops."

"Dear Lord," murmured Slattery. "The media." He chomped through the rest of his burger in silence, wiped off his hangdog jowls with a napkin and took a slug of beer. "So where do we start? I've never done a hundred-and-fifty-year-old murder. An old lady clubbed to death in Flatbush in 1958 is my personal best."

"You told me your computer's hooked up to every cop database they could think of, and mine's hooked into just about everything New York and every major university and museum the country has to offer. I figure I'll track down the victim and you see what you can do with any of the stuff the other guys at the site have for us."

"You really think you can find out who he was?" Slattery asked.

"That should be the easy part," said Carrie. "It's definitely a Civil War naval uniform he's wearing, and they kept pretty meticulous records back then. The fact that he was an African-American should make it even simpler."

Slattery picked up his Kilkenny and stared at the condensation on the side of his glass. "Why couldn't the poor bugger have come from County Cork and saved us all a lot of trouble?"

"Think positively, Detective; the guy was killed during the Civil War. That means between 1861 and 1865. During the Civil War there were less than a million people here, against eight million now. That's seven million suspects you don't have to worry about, right there."

"You are going to be a joy to work with, aren't you, Dr. Norton?"

"Finish up the onion rings, Detective Slattery. We have to get back to the über-office to greet our new assistant." An assistant had been assigned from the Administrative Division at One Police Plaza to take care of any filing and paperwork. He or she was due to arrive later that afternoon.

The assistant turned out to be a young black officer in patrolman's uniform wearing horn-rimmed glasses. He was as lean as Slattery was fat, and his name was Archie Kling. Somehow he'd been given the nickname Diddy Kong by his companions at the Police Academy and it had stuck. He didn't seem to mind. He'd been at Central Registry for two years and knew enough about police pension plans to put everyone to sleep in five minutes.

He was twenty-three years old and willing to do anything to get out of his assignment in the bowels of One Police Plaza. As far as Diddy was concerned, Max Slattery was his knight in shining armor. By the time they'd finished their lunch at Nancy Whiskey's, Diddy was seated behind his desk in the foyer making up telephone call sheets for both Carrie and Slattery on his computer. He'd also made a fresh pot of coffee from beans ground in the shop downstairs.

"It's Sulawesi," he said after he introduced himself. "It's my favorite, but I can get something else if you like." He stood up when he talked to them.

"I like my coffee brown, with lots of Sweet'N Low," said Slattery. "Beyond that, I don't much care." He stared at the young man. "Sit down," he said.

"Yes, sir," said Diddy. He sat. Carrie smiled.

"Don't call me sir. My name is Max. Or Slattery, or if I start drinking with you I might even let you call me Slats. Get it?"

"Yes, sir."

"Don't be a smart-ass."

"Yes. Max."

"Do you know what a coprologist does, Diddy?"

The young man barely hesitated. "Yes, Max. He studies shit."

"Crosswords?" Carrie asked.

"*New York Times*, every day," the young man said proudly. "Top ten at Stamford every year."

"Stamford?" Slattery asked.

"Connecticut," explained Carrie. "The American Crossword Puzzle Tournament. It means he's one of the ten best crossword puzzle solvers in the United States."

"Yeah, you'll fit right in," said Slattery.

"Some people from Cornwell and Maibaum brought in some big plastic containers about an hour ago," said Diddy. "They're on the first examination table in the living room area. And this." He held up a Sony Memory Stick.

"They tell you what it was?" Carrie asked. She took the mini–storage device from Diddy. The young patrolman consulted a notebook on the desk in front of him.

"They said to tell you it was the stratigraphic analysis of the interment site."

"Which means?" Slattery asked.

"A three-D diagram of where the body was found and what else they discovered there. Come and take a look if you want," said Carrie. "You too, Officer Kling."

"Diddy, please."

They went into the living room. The boxes were big, translucent Rubbermaid containers neatly labeled S-1 through S-9. There was a separate box off to one side simply labeled RD. Carrie switched on the computer at the end of the table and waited for it to boot up. "S stands for strata. Each of these boxes represents what was discovered in a one-foot deep, six-by-nine area around the body."

"What about RD?" Slattery asked.

"Remains detritus," explained Carrie.

"Come again?"

"Pocket litter," said Diddy. "Right?" he asked Carrie.

"Right," she answered.

"Maybe I should go and sit in a rocking chair somewhere," muttered Slattery.

"Your time will come, Max, believe me."

The computer went through its cycle and Carrie plugged in the memory stick. A few seconds later there was a wire-frame image on the screen that looked like a pale yellow elongated three-dimensional rectangle dotted with red, black and bright blue squares. Each of the squares had a tiny number beside it. In the middle of the rectangle, like an alien corpse in a sci-fi coffin, was a solid representation of the bog man in the naval uniform.

"What are we looking at?" Slattery asked, looking over Carrie's shoulder.

"Red is organic material, black is bone or ceramic and blue is metal."

"What's all that metal stuff around where his feet are?" Diddy asked, pointing to a little cloud of blue squares.

"Max?"

"This some kind of test, Doc?" the cop said with a sour note in his voice.

"No test. Just wanted to see if you could figure it out."

"Hobnails," said Slattery easily. "From his boots. The smaller pieces are the tips from the laces."

"Not bad," said Carrie. "I'm impressed."

"Good," said the grizzled old detective. "Show some respect for your elders."

"There's something big and metallic on the edge of the S-3 layer," said Diddy, pointing at the screen. "What's that?"

"We'll get to it," said Carrie. "But let's go through the man's pockets first."

She left the computer terminal and crossed to the pile of Rubbermaid boxes. She pulled a pair of disposable surgical gloves from the container on the table, snapped them on and peeled back the lid of the box marked RD. She began examining the scattering of objects with Slattery and Diddy looking on.

"Coins," said Diddy, peering into the box. Carrie lifted one out and held it under the extension-lamp magnifier attached to the end of the table.

"Knickerbocker token," she said. The one she held between her fingers had the figure of a stooped old man on one side and 1 CENT—PURE COPPER-I.O.U. on the obverse. She went back to the remains detritus box and picked up another token. This one had a bearded old man, a circle of stars and a date, 1863, on one side and a beer mug inside a laurel wreath with the name GUSTAVUS LINDENMUELLER and NEW YORK on the other side.

"Not like any money I ever saw," commented Diddy.

Carrie peered closely at the coin under the magnifier. "They were store tokens, made of cheap copper alloy, sometimes bronze or cardboard or rubber. Lindenmueller ran a saloon; he gave them out in change after people started hoarding government coins. Every big store used them. They were used in general circulation, but they pretty much date the body because they were only used in New York for about a year: 1863, just like it says on the coin."

"Oh, great," said Slattery. "Time of death: sometime during the year 1863."

"You're such a pessimist." Carrie grinned. She went back to the RD box and quickly looked through the rest of the objects: two more tokens, a broken piece of a clay pipe, a pair of wire-rimmed spectacles with one lens cracked and the other missing altogether, a wooden button, a penknife corroded shut and what appeared to be a piece of cardboard folded down the middle. Somebody at the dig site had wisely placed the soggy piece of cardboard into a separate plastic bag to keep it from drying out unevenly.

Carrie set out a large blotter under one of the infrared heat lamps clamped to the table and used a small instrument called a bone folder to gently open the cardboard, laying it flat on the blotter. There was a picture of a black man on it in a dark blue naval uniform. He was smoking a clay pipe and wearing wire-rimmed circular spectacles.

"There's our man," murmured Carrie. She pulled the big extension magnifier over to look at the little photograph more clearly. "They used to use photographs like these as calling cards back in the Civil War. It was fashionable." She paused, reading the ribbon on the old-fashioned flat hat the man wore on his head. "My God," she whispered, "he was one of the crew on the USS *Monitor*."

"As in the *Monitor* and the *Merrimac*?" Diddy asked. "The first ironclads?"

"That's the one." Carrie nodded. "Our bog body was famous, once upon a time."

"Wonderful," said Slattery. "Just what I need, a hundred-and-fifty-year-old celebrity killing."

CHAPTER 7

They left the hotel with Echo feeling almost naked wearing one of Matthew's rather outrageous checked suits and a brown, medium-crown bowler that was too big for her head but which was perfect for accommodating her excess hair. The brushing together of her trousered thighs and her complete lack of stays felt utterly scandalous and dizzyingly rude, but Miss Warne assured her that the disguise was perfect and that she'd do quite well as her younger, and handsomer, brother. For her part Echo was simply relieved that Matthew had left the hotel to go and watch the cricket game on the other side of the avenue. At Kate's instruction she hid the wicked-looking dagger in her boot.

Crossing the hotel lobby, she was sure that every eye was upon her, but somehow she and the Pinkerton agent made it to the doors without seeming to attract any undue attention and went outside onto the crowded street. Warne had a hackney coach with a Negro driver waiting. Unaided for the first time in her life, Echo climbed up into her seat, sweeping away nonexistent skirts before she sat, feeling the trousers stretch against her bottom, flushing with the sensation as she settled into the padded leather.

"You'll get used to it," whispered Kate Warne, dropping down beside her with a smile. "But stop brushing your skirts; it makes you look a bit of a Mary."

"Mary who?" Echo asked. The driver twitched the reins and they moved out into the flow of traffic on the roadway.

"A Mary, a Nance, you know," said the lady Pinkerton agent. "A sodomite."

"Oh. Yes, I see," nodded Echo, though once again she wasn't quite sure she saw at all. "Where are we going, by the way?"

"According to Allan's man at the Yard, your Count Draculiya carries his wealth in gemstones, so we're going to see a man about some diamonds," answered Warne. She leaned forward and spoke to the driver. "Tiffany's, Billy, down Broadway to Warren Street," she instructed. "Across from City Hall Park."

"Yes'm," replied the driver.

"You know better than that, Billy."

"Yes, boss," said the driver, correcting himself. "Sometimes I forgets you wearing such comfortable footwear."

Deciding for her own sake that the Negro driver and the Pinkerton detective were having some private joke together, Echo concentrated on the drive down Broadway instead. At first there were a few vacant plots of earth, like the cricket pitch across from the Sturtevant, but as they drove along the broad avenue the buildings became more concentrated, with fewer lanes and alleys and no vacant lots at all between them, and very little to be seen in the way of greenery.

Unlike London, where old soot-covered stone was the rule, most of the buildings along Broadway were plain, square and brick, four and five stories high, their facades glaringly covered with gigantic painted signs, the street-level entrances and windows shaded by broad canvas awnings. In a single block she saw signs advertising Meads Hats and Clothing, Bailey's Signs, Brawley's Hardware, Shoonmaker Paper Hanging, three different hotels, eleven saloons and restaurants and the appropriately solemn Underhill Casket Company. She remembered gawking down the length of Regent Street in London, but Broadway seemed to go on forever, block after block, as Billy maneuvered his two plodding steeds through the morning's smoky haze along a never-ending parade of buildings that bought, sold, made, traded, imported, exported and warehoused every object, product, service or commodity one could think of, guiding the carriage and his two passengers through a steady elaborate design of traffic going in every direction possible with no discernible rule or right-of-way.

And such traffic it was! Carts and wagons heading south loaded with produce, some drawn by mules, some drawn by oxen and even pushcarts drawn by human brawn. Heavy wagons loaded with barrels and boxed goods, lumber or bales of yard goods trundled north, offloading when necessary, blocking lanes and turning without any sort of signal beyond a shrill whistle or a yell lost in the general tumult.

In among the turning, swaying, rumbling and roaring of all this was the squeak and shriek of the omnibuses being pulled along their embedded iron rails like so many angry yellow bumblebees. The muck carts roamed like kitchen flies. The mucking boys, usually barefoot ragged children, busily scooped up the horse dung almost as it dropped. The cart was generally pushed by an adult foreman while the muckers did the dangerous work of dodging wheels, whips and horses' hooves as they gathered up the stinking waste that would eventually be sold as fertilizer.

Even the darting boys and overflowing carts couldn't seem to keep up, because there was manure and all sorts of garbage piled at the curb. According to Kate there were entire blocks above Fifty-seventh Street and in the borough of Queens devoted to horse dung called manure blocks. Here and there on the hour-long drive down from Twenty-ninth Street, Echo saw dead horses rotting by the side of the avenue, covered in maggots and clusters of flies. Once again Kate explained that there was no organized system for dealing with such occurrences—frequent in a city where almost

two hundred thousand dray animals were kept—
and except for itinerant butchers willing to sell
cuts of meat from the freshly dead creatures, local
merchants had no alternative but to pay for the
removal of the dead animals out of their own
pockets, and few in the midtown area were willing to do so.

The result of this, combined with the night soil
of close to a million people, was that as well as
being a giant stinkpot, the city of New York,
grand as it was and a center of wonder and fabulous commerce, was also a cesspool of disease and
incipient disaster. Cholera, plague, malaria and
even yellow jack were fairly common, and there
were almost as many fires as there were firemen.

"And there's thousands of them," said Kate
with a laugh. "More every day with the boss in
charge."

"The boss?"

"Boss Tweed," explained Kate as the carriage
bounced and rattled over the cobbles.

"The mayor?" Echo asked.

Kate laughed even louder and puffed happily
on her cigar. Echo was beginning to wish she had
one of her own; the stench of the street was almost
overpowering, mixed now with a faint breeze
tinged with an odor that was sickeningly sweet.

"Better than that," said the Pinkerton detective.
"He's the new Tammany boss, the big fixer, a pol.
He owns the Seventh Ward, lock, stock and barrel,
has every Irishman in the city in his hip pocket

and the Germans and all the rest on his watch
chain. Some people say that Bill Tweed has more
money than God and the Devil as his best friend."

"I'm not sure what that has to do with firemen,"
said Echo. It seemed the farther she went down
Broadway the more confusing New York was
becoming.

"It has everything to do with firemen," explained Kate. "The city is divided into wards,
each ward has an alderman, and each alderman
controls the fire station in that ward. Some wards
have two or three. The firemen are appointed by
the aldermen, but their salaries are paid for by
the city. The aldermen are all Tammany, and
Tweed's the Tammany boss. Understand things
better now?"

"No," answered Echo honestly.

"Say you'd like your son or your friend or your
brother to have a good job as a fireman. Slip your
local ward pol—your alderman—a bribe and the
job is yours. A little piece of that bribe will find
its way into Bill Tweed's big, deep pockets, and
so will a piece of every other city dollar spent on
just about anything you'd care to name."

"This Tweed is corrupt?" Echo said. "Is that it?"

"Corruption is his mother and his father, my
dear Van Helsing. This city runs on corruption
like a steamship runs on coal." Kate glanced up.
"Ah," she said, "here we are."

Echo looked out of the open coach. The park
was triangular, with City Hall itself, an impressive
building of granite with a narrow clock tower at

the widest end of the park, and a pleasant stand of trees at the narrowest, marred now by a wooden platform draped with bunting and hung with signs looking for new recruits and offering county, state and U.S. government bounties for the willing. An ancient-looking cannon stood on the grass in front of the platform, and several older-looking soldiers in uniform were clustered around the rickety gun trunnion, smoking clay pipes and laughing together.

"Another good reason to be a fireman," commented Kate, climbing down from the carriage. "Being one of Tweed's appointees automatically exempts you from military service."

Echo followed the Pinkerton agent down to the street. Tiffany's was a slope-roofed wooden building on the corner of Warren Street with a figure-headlike sculpture of Atlas over the door, painted bronze and supporting a large clock on its shoulders.

The interior of the store was cool, with all the counters' glass set into wooden display cases. The walls were paneled in dark wood and the floors were marble. The clerks all wore dark morning suits and to a man they were all clean shaven. There were more soldiers in the store than outside at the recruiting platform. They were all officers and most were examining the large displays of ornamental swords the store had on offer as well as cases showing an array of gold braid for uniforms and various models of Colt revolvers with chased barrels and cylinders and fancy ivory- or

silver-etched grips. Well-dressed women in volu-
minous skirts hung on the officers' arms, their
eyes wandering from the swords to the brooches,
rings and necklaces laid out on plump blue velvet
pillows behind the curving glass of the cases.

"Something I can do for you . . . Mr. Warne?"

Echo turned and found herself staring up at a
very tall, quite handsome man in his forties, slim
and dark-haired except for a sprinkling of gray at
the temples and at the edges of his full, perfectly
trimmed beard. It was clear from the twinkle in
his eye that he knew Mr. Warne was no mister
at all.

"Mr. Tiffany," said Kate, smiling. "This is my
friend Mr. Van Helsing." She turned to Echo. "Mr.
Van Helsing, Mr. Charles Tiffany, the proprietor."

Echo shook the man's hand but said nothing,
following Kate's instruction to remain silent.

"We need your help," said Kate.

"Certainly," said Tiffany with a short, bowing
nod. "Anything to be of service to Mr. Pinkerton,"
he added in a murmur.

"Your office, perhaps?" asked Kate.

"Certainly," said Tiffany, nodding again. "This
way."

The two women followed Tiffany down the
long, narrow store, Echo silently delighted that
not a single one of the customers paid her disguise
the slightest attention—not a single deferential
"ma'am," not a bow or even a finger to a hat
brim. By putting on a pair of trousers and a man's
tie she had become invisible.

They reached a narrow stairway at the rear of the store and followed Tiffany up to an expansive office on the second floor that had a large, balcony-like gallery that looked out over the store below. The office, like the store, was dark paneled. There were several leather chairs, a large desk and a scattering of mantel lamps on small occasional tables in various corners of the room. A small painting was displayed on an easel. Echo thought it looked like a landscape by the popular French painter Camille Corot. Tiffany gestured to the leather armchairs and seated himself behind the desk.

"Well, then," he said, sitting back in his chair. "What can I do for Pinkerton's today?" The eyes twinkled again. "Somebody going to rob our next shipment of pearls?"

"Not that we're aware of," said Kate. "We're looking for someone associated with Mr. Van Helsing, here."

"Oh?" Tiffany said, arching an eyebrow. "Associated how?"

"We're almost sure it's in a criminal fashion," answered Kate. "Murder, in fact."

"Dear me," said Tiffany.

"Dear me, indeed," agreed Kate. "He deals in gems."

"Deals in them?"

"Travels with them from place to place," responded Kate. "He was recently in London. We think he's come here."

"Do you have a name?"

"Draculiya," murmured Kate. "A foreign count."

"Strange name," answered Tiffany with a thoughtful frown. "I've never heard it before."

"He almost certainly changed it when he came here," said Kate.

"What kind of stones would he have traded in?" Tiffany asked. "Was there any gem he seemed to prefer especially?"

Echo thought for a long moment, trying to remember whether there'd been any indication of a preference that she'd noticed when she'd visited Draculiya at Carfax Abbey. Suddenly she had a brief vision of a pendant she'd seen around Lucy Westenra's neck that night, and the carved stone of the vile monster's signet ring. "Rubies," she whispered harshly, speaking aloud for the first time. "Rubies the perfect color of blood."

CHAPTER 8

The USS *Monitor* was the first of three ironclad
warships in its class ordered by the U.S. Navy
early in the Civil War. Unlike the ironclads used
by the Confederacy, which were merely wooden
ships clad with iron armor, the *Monitor* was a
brand-new class of ship, the hull almost completely underwater and built with a rotating turret
with two cannons that could fire in any direction.
In terms of armed warfare, it was as great an inno-
vation as the tank was to mounted cavalry, or the
machine gun was to the musket. The *Monitor*
wasn't particularly successful as a warship, but it
became famous as the first ironclad to engage another ironclad in battle, at Hampton Roads, Virginia, engaging the CSS *Merrimac*, by then renamed
the CSS *Virginia*, on March 8, 1862. Neither ship
did much damage to the other, but in the end
the *Virginia* was forced to withdraw, so it was
considered to be a victory for the Union navy.
Unfortunately, the USS *Monitor* sank during a

storm off Cape Hatteras on December 31 of the same year, but the so-called "cheese box on a raft" had earned its place in history, and the forty-six surviving crewmen were treated much like the crew of the B-17 *Memphis Belle* eighty-two years later during World War II. Being a member of the *Monitor* crew was to be automatically conferred with the status of hero.

"It looks like our bog body was the real deal," said Carrie, looking up from her computer in the Tribeca loft. "His name was Barnabus Andrew Coffin, originally from St. Lawrence, New York. He signed up in New Bedford, Massachusetts, as a seaman, which probably means he was a whaler before that. He was twenty-three when he enlisted. He was sunk not once, but twice. He was part of the original crew at Hampton Roads, but then he was transferred to the USS *Cairo*, another ironclad, this one on the Mississippi, probably because they were looking for experienced crewmen. The USS *Cairo* was sunk clearing river mines at a place called Haines Bluff, Mississippi, on December twelfth, 1862, and our guy asked for a transfer back to the *Monitor* and his old crew, which he got. He rejoined the crew in Hampton Roads just in time for her to be sunk by a storm on December thirty-first. He survived that too and came to New York on leave sometime in July 1863. He was supposed to report for duty at the Jeronemus S. Underhill Dry Dock and Iron Works in Brooklyn for an assignment to the USS *Keokuk*, another ironclad that had just been commissioned. He never showed up."

"How can we be sure it was him?" Slattery asked, sitting behind his own desk, which had already become a mess of papers, coffee cups and stacks of file folders.

"There were only two black crewmen on the *Monitor*," said Carrie, glancing at her computer screen. "Coffin and a guy named Siah Carter. Both men survived Hampton Roads and the Cape Hatteras sinking. Carter was honorably discharged in 1865, married a former slave named Eliza Tarrow and had thirteen kids in a place called Bermuda Hundred, Virginia. It's not Siah Carter, so it has to be Barnabus Coffin. The age is right, and so is the height. Five eight and three-quarters."

"Or maybe it's somebody who borrowed his uniform," suggested Diddy, sitting at his reception desk close to the door.

"Just in time to have his throat ripped out. That's a stretch," said Carrie.

"It's all a stretch," responded Slattery in a moody voice. "And the kid's right. Just because he's got a hat on that says USS *Monitor* doesn't mean he's this Barnaby Coffin or whoever. It's not like we can call up the guy's dentist."

Diddy beamed at Slattery's agreement. Carrie tapped her teeth with the eraser end of a pencil and stared at the screen. "Let's assume it's Barnabus Coffin," she said quietly. "What was he doing in the basement of a tenement on Minetta Lane?"

"It was a ghetto back then," offered Slattery, "Worse than Five Points. He was black. Maybe he was visiting friends. Maybe he had family there."

"Do you know much about Minetta Street and that area in the 1860s?" Carrie asked.

"Like I said, it was a ghetto." He paused and looked across at Diddy. "No offense, kid, but it was called Niggertown."

"None taken," said the crossword champion. "Just a six-letter word to me. Like 'whitey.' "

"Or 'cracker.' " Carrie grinned.

" 'Cracker's' got seven letters," said Diddy. "Good if you're playing Scrabble."

"What's the point you're trying to make, Dr. Norton?" Slattery sighed.

"The point is I can tell you more than any sane person would want to know about that address on Minetta, and the first thing I can tell you is that it was built in 1861 after a house owned by a man named Louderback had been torn down. The builder was a German named Strudder. Strudder built a standard five-story brick tenement with small windows and off-the-rack doors and fittings. It was an early form of prefab. It had a raised first story and a storefront supported on cast-iron piers. The storefront sold dry goods for a while, but it went out of business and turned into a laundry. The building was forty feet wide and sixty-eight feet deep on an eighty-eight foot, six-inch lot. The remaining twenty feet was used for a cesspool and privy for the whole building, which consisted of twenty apartments, four to a floor, two in the front and two in the back. Each apartment was somewhat less than five hundred square feet and generally housed at least eight people."

"I still don't see your point," said Slattery.

"No basement?" Diddy suggested.

"That's right," nodded Carrie. "No basement. The ground was too soft, so they hammered iron piers into the mud and built on that. There was a subfloor with the laundry, and then five floors of apartments over that. The bog body was buried below the subfloor level."

"Under the laundry?" Slattery asked.

"We've got pretty extensive plans of the building. He was under everything."

"How could that be?" Slattery asked. "Somebody in the laundry dug through their own floor?"

"No. He was in the sewers," said Carrie. "It's the only answer."

"I didn't know New York had sewers back then," said Diddy.

"They didn't," the archaeologist responded. "Not ones that carried actual sewage, but they did have a system of storm drains and aqueducts to control water flow. Minetta Creek flowed down the street to the Hudson; the city just covered it over with planks and bricks. That's why the street still has a curve in it; the street follows the path of the old creek bed."

"Then it's even more of a mystery," said Diddy. "Strange enough to be in the basement, but what was he doing in the sewer?"

"That's an easy one," said Slattery. "And now

it's actually beginning to make some sense." He got up and went to the giant map of Manhattan pinned to the wall and found Minetta Street with his thick, blunt-nailed finger. "In my day they used to hide bodies in the Jersey Pine Barrens. Back then it looked like they just stuck them down the sewer." He peered closely at the map. "I wonder where they put him into the system."

"There's eleven thousand miles of sewer, about a hundred and fifty thousand catch basins and almost five hundred legal outflows for sewage and wastewater in New York. Six thousand miles of pipe in Manhattan alone."

"Why don't I ask my dad?" said Diddy brightly.

"Your dad?" Slaterry asked.

"He's a professor of history at Columbia," explained the young man. "If he doesn't know himself, he'll know somebody who will."

Slattery grinned. "I knew I was right about you," he said.

"What was that, Detective?" Carrie said.

"I knew he'd fit right in, just like I said."

Diddy picked up the phone and dialed.

Carrie got up and crossed over to where Slattery was standing. She stared at the map. After a minute she traced a pathway with her finger. "Water flows downhill," she said. "Most people think Manhattan is flat, but it's not. It's always been highest in the center, like a spine that runs the length of the island on a midline that Fifth Avenue follows roughly." She tapped her finger on Washington Square. "The square used to be a swamp, then a potter's field, and then the original quad for NYU. This is where Minetta Creek originates, so the dumping point will be somewhere between here and the tenement site."

"You'd make a pretty good detective," observed Slattery. "Or have I told you that before?"

"Just an old smoothie, aren't you?"

"While Diddy's calling his dad, why don't we see what else is in those little treasure chests of yours?"

They crossed the room to the big examination table and pulled the top off the box marked S-3. On the three-dimensional grid it had been Diddy who'd first noticed the presence of a relatively large metal object. In the box they discovered more coins, all of the same 1863 vintage, what might have once been a child's toy whistle, and a large rust- and dirt-encrusted object approximately five inches long, with a large circular disk at one end and an oblong of oxidized metal at the other.

"This shouldn't be too difficult," said Carrie. She picked up the object in a pair of rubber-guarded tongs and carried it across to the far end of the main room, where a large glass-sided electrolyte tank had been set up. She attached an alligator clip to the central portion of the object, wrapped it in a piece of stainless steel mesh for an anode and attached a second alligator clip. Using the tongs again, she lowered the object, now wrapped in steel mesh, and then turned on the current. By that time Diddy had left his post at the reception desk and joined them.

"My dad said he's got a friend who did his PhD on the New York sewer system. He'll have all the possible access points by tomorrow at the latest." He peered into the glass tank. Bubbles were beginning to form on the rusty object, and flakes of scaly red were magically beginning to drop off, falling through the steel mesh to the bottom of the vat. "What's the electrolyte solution?" Diddy asked.

"Weak H_2SO_4," said Carrie.

"Huh?" Slattery said.

"Bobby was a chemist's son, but Bobby is no more. What Bobby thought was H_2O was H_2SO_4," rhymed Carrie. "It's a fairly strong solution of sulfuric acid. Run an electric current through it and you've got the world's greatest rust remover." She stared into the tank. "It's working."

"A key," said Diddy, excited, as more flakes of rust peeled away. "There's some kind of design at the top." They kept staring into the tank.

"Archaeology TV," grunted Slattery. "Like watching clocks tick or paint dry."

"Archaeology is patience. Just like being a cop," said Carrie.

"Being a cop is donuts and free coffee at the 7-Eleven," answered Slattery.

"It's two letters, intertwined, " said Diddy. "A design. Old fashioned."

"A *G* and a *P*," said Carrie, squinting. She straightened, remembering an illustration in a book on the architectural history of New York she'd once seen. "Good Lord," she said. "It's one of the original keys to Gramercy Park." Carrie frowned. "Now, how did our friend Mr. Barnabus Coffin get his hands on *that*?"

CHAPTER 9

In terms of actual distance, Gramercy Park was only two blocks from the tumult, noise and concentrated filth that Echo Van Helsing had encountered on her drive down Broadway from the Sturtevant Hotel, but two blocks might just as well have been two hundred blocks given the separate worlds they occupied.

The small park had been donated to the city by its original owner, Samuel Ruggles, with the single condition that no commercial enterprise be permitted on the facing streets or in the park itself. The park, a simple square of trees and shrubs and carefully groomed gravel pathways, was enclosed by a wrought-iron fence, and only those people who owned one of the sixty-one lots on the square had the keys that allowed them access.

A number of illustrious people lived on the privileged square, including James Harper, one-time mayor of the city and well-known publisher, at Number 4; Edwin Booth, world-famous actor

and present manager of the Winter Garden Theater at Number 16; Roosevelt, the glass manufac-
turer, at Number 18; and a number of other city
notables, including the Henrietta Haines School
for Young Ladies at Number 10, thought to be the
finest place in New York for the education of the
gentry's daughters.

The park was a quiet place except for a brief
period every morning and afternoon when the
girls from Miss Haines's school played there with
their hoops and jacks and balls. Carriages came
and went, but there were no carriage houses or
stables within the square itself, and any manure
or other objectionable material was quickly removed by a small army of gardeners and caretak-
ers employed for that purpose.

Local tradesmen delivered foodstuffs, coal,
firewood and any other commodity, and the negro
tubmen and other night-soil workers employed by
the owners of the houses on all four sides of the
small, prestigious neighborhood came and went
in the back gardens of the residences with the
dawn and with the greatest discretion.

In the winter, snow was removed almost as
soon as it fell, in the autumn leaves were raked
up as rapidly and in the summer the gardeners
ensured that the grass and shrubbery within the
park itself were always kept well watered. A pair
of constables from the Eighteenth District Patrol
House on East Twenty-second Street were fully
employed with a beat encompassing the park and
its environs, and there were rarely disturbances

beyond an occasional drunkard meandering off his course in the small hours of the morning.

For the most part, the illusion of perfect propriety and dignity was kept, and it was here, on the south side of the square, that Enoch Bale had purchased his new residence for the price of a ruby that had once graced the now-severed neck of Her Grace, Claire of Saint Mauris, Marchioness of Laubespin, and a diamond brooch rumored to have been worn by his distant relative, the equally unfortunate Countess Erzebet Báthory, the so-called Vampyr Princess of Čachtice—absurd, of course, since the woman was barely a countess let alone a Princess of the Blood.

There was a certain irony in the history of the stones, since Number 14 Gramercy Park was undoubtedly a house of the dead. Designed twenty years before by a forgotten architect, it was one of four essentially identical four-story townhouses built of locally quarried brownstone. All four had a lower half story for kitchens and servants and four floors above. Each house had a simple stone porch and a granite-lined entranceway. Number 14, by a peculiar reason having to do with Ruggles's original survey, was possessed of a lot that went all the way back to East Nineteenth Street, while the other properties on the south side of the park were not so deep.

The first owner of Number 14 was a portly, unhappy man named Norburn who invested heavily in Mexican gold mines and lost everything to Santa Anna and his hordes when the Mexican-American

War was declared. Norburn committed suicide by hanging himself from the front-parlor chandelier. The chandelier separated from the ceiling under Mr. Norburn's ponderous bulk, but his effort was not wasted, as the central spike at the chandelier's center struck the dazed, half-strangled man in the center of his forehead, crushing his skull completely and skewering what was left of his head to the polished cherrywood floorboards.

The second owner, Dr. Charles Allnutt, fared a little better and lived in the house for almost ten years. Allnutt, a successful society physician, was a friend and medical consultant to the Astor family and, like them, was one of the first to enjoy healthful summer holidays away from the city on Mackinac Island, a tiny speck of land where Lake Huron and Lake Michigan meet.

It later turned out that the holidays spent there by New York's highest society were more than simply good for the general constitution. Allnutt, as an enterprising *New York Herald* reporter discovered, was also performing illegal operations on young ladies of elevated social position and somewhat lower morals, including his own seventeen-year-old daughter. The daughter died, the story appeared in the New York press and Dr. Allnutt and the remainder of his family vanished into the far west without ever returning to the house.

The final owner before Bale of the plain-faced narrow house on Gramercy Park was a shipmaster named Andrew Barclay. His tragic story was the simplest and most unhappy of all. Barclay had been a mail-ship captain with the Inman line for a number of years, and in that time he had amassed both a fortune from bonuses and cargo shares as well as a family.

After living at Number 14 for a little more than a year, and with two of his young daughters, Emily and Rose, enrolled at the Miss Haines School, Barclay had been offered a position as master of the brand-new liner, SS *Phantom* of the Anchor Line, an Inman rival. The benefits were too generous to ignore, so he accepted the position and to celebrate decided to take his wife, Elizabeth, son, Andrew Jr., and the two girls on the vessel's maiden voyage from New York to Glasgow. On September 18, 1862, the ship left New York Harbor and was last seen off Bird Rock in the Gulf of St. Lawrence three days later. Then, in imitation of her ill-omened name, the ship and all its passengers, including Andrew Barclay and his entire family, simply disappeared, swallowed by the fog and sea, never to be heard from again.

Number 14, now in the hands of Captain Barclay's friend and lawyer, Mr. Tobias Strong, mourned vacantly, shutters bolted, curtains drawn, furniture shrouded in ghostly drop cloths waiting for the next visitor to its dark interior. It was here, in this deeply shadowed and unfortunate place, that Enoch Bale now slept and dreamed, transforming the passing daylight hours into more welcome night.

In his dreams he traveled as he once had in

his distant past, from his first remembered home beyond the Balyanos Pass, where the wide Tatros River flowed, to later days in the stolen midnight armor of the Knight of the Seven Castles, Nicholas Callisto, carrying the Great Sword Fragarach, the Sword of Air, the Whirlwind, reaping like Death's own scythe.

What days those were, and what nights and lessons learned! The first true lesson for his kind and the last: that the world was made up of only sense and memory—the taste of blood, first on the sword's edge, then on the tongue, the stink of fear, the sight of death and the hot breath of descending angels, their wings as black as shadow, their streaming hair blotting out the sky. And above all the memory of it to feed you through the unrolling years, decades, centuries, filling you with the same desperate desire and eternal ambition: to feel and taste and see it all again.

In his dreams he rode Abderus, one of the flesh-eating Mares of Diomedes, and together they roamed from the Karpitans, where they fought against their dread enemies the Cumons, all the way to the ford of the Harbachtal and beyond to the mountains of the Tromelei. These were the days between the Old Gods and the New, when his kind were like an army in the world, but those times faded at last when the Old Gods finally were swept away and reason began to rule the land. Draculiya and his kind, once lords and masters of the earth, were hunted down and destroyed, all in the holy name of this white and savage god who showed no mercy, especially in death.

Then came the final battle on the slopes of Slieve Gullion, where the hag-witch Calliag appeared and cursed the last of his family, and forever more the tears shed that terrible day were known as *Calliag Szikes To*, Calliag's Lake of Sorrows. On that day the Ten Vampyr remaining dispersed across the world, leaving nothing of themselves behind, vowing never to meet again until the Old Gods returned and time came to an end. Six hundred years or six thousand since that evil day on the dark, volcanic mountainside, but in his dreams it was always only yesterday, and the dreaming, as it was for all of the Ten, was his only salvation. Without those dreams his only memory would be the loneliness of a shadow life everlasting.

In his dreams he was a warrior, not a wraith; a hunter, not a wanderer searching for a soul that was no longer his to own. In his dreams he was the dream of everything, but with the passing time the dreams passed too. Some of the Ten faltered and chose to live in the other world, and the bastard, ill-gotten breed of Damphyr was born, half true to the blood, half human, relentless but not eternal, and cursing the true Vampyr for their other, more secret powers. Of these the Outcast, the Other, was the most fiendish, the one who had made the Ten into the Nine and who knew no rule but his own and followed no law except slaughter.

In his dreams the half-caste Damphyr began to

triumph, breeding and breeding again in a perversion of the ancient ways, nine by nine by ninety-nine until they seemed to be almost anywhere, disguised and sinister, waiting for a time when pretence would be unnecessary and they could rule the world. Along the centuries more than one had tried and a few had almost succeeded, and their ascension sometimes seemed almost inevitable, for there was very little left to stop them. The sleeping Vampyr Draculiya knew in his dreams that only six of the Nine were left, two consumed in their own balefires by intent, and the last, his old companion, Saint Germain, Prinz Ragoczy, by the brutal hand of a man much like his own nemesis. The *Vampyr-vadász*, the late and unlamented Abraham Van Helsing, inexorable vampire hunter. All in his memory, all in his dreams.

"Lord." The voice came out of the shadows in the room, familiar. "Lord," said the voice a second time.

"Fu Sheng?" Enoch Bale opened his eyes, the dreams shredding away like old cobwebs and tattered shrouds. A hundred pasts became the present.

"Yes, lord."

He remembered then. Chang Fu Sheng had fled London well before him to prepare for his arrival in the New World. Only the night before he'd found his servant waiting, alone in a gaming house on Baxter Street between the Bowery and the docks. A basement opium den full of lonely sailors far from home.

Enoch Bale searched the darkened room with his eyes, the furniture anonymous beneath the sad muslin veils that covered every piece. It was dusk, and the bars of light seeping through the shuttered windows were pale and dying with the sunset. Almost night again. Dusk filled the master chamber on the second floor like the inside of an old tomb.

"I have news, lord," said his servant, standing close to the bed. He was dressed in his usual dark tailcoat with shirt and tall collar so bone white and starched they seemed to glow. The face above the collar was the texture and color of ancient parchment. The hair, sleek and oiled and tied back in a long queue, was black, shot with streaks of wolfish gray. The servant was old, older even than his lord and master knew. Men of his race and name had served him since the Mongol hordes swept across the steppes back in the time of the Great Khan himself. This Chang could be the fifth generation of his clan or the fiftieth; there was no way to know.

"Tell me," said the Vampyr.

"They are here, lord," said the Chinese man in his soft, faint voice. "The trail is almost invisible, but there have been mistakes, a definite spoor."

"Killings?"

"Yes, lord." Chang Fu Sheng nodded. "Savage ones."

"Women?"

"Yes, lord, so far only women."

The Vampyr nodded. It was always the same.

The Damphyr would settle somewhere and begin to prey on the surrounding populace, usually beginning with prostitutes and other forgotten castaways of society. The longer they remained, the bolder they would get. Enoch Bale sensed something in the servant's demeanor.

"Is there something else, old friend?"

"Yes, lord," said the old man, hesitating.

"What is it?" The Vampyr slid his legs off the bed and sat up. It was almost fully dark now; the night smelled of fading bergamot and wormwood. Faint scents from the fenced-in park, perhaps, or a distant memory of another time and place.

"There is Another, lord. Nearby."

"One of the Nine?" The Vampyr asked. It was impossible. It was part of the vow and sacrosanct. No one of his brethren would dare to break the covenant. "I don't believe it."

"It is not one of the Nine, lord. It is the Outcast, the Other."

"The Tenth of Nine," said the Vampyr. "The Forgotten One."

The Vampyr stood. A memory stirred. Something in the scent of the flowers outside.

"What does he call himself now?"

"Adam, lord. He has taken the name Adam Worth."

"Adamo!" the Vampyr whispered into the darkness. "Adamo!"

CHAPTER 10

"It's Adam Worth, of course," said the tiny man, staring at the autopsy photographs of the Minetta Lane bog man's wounds. He tossed the sheaf of pictures down onto his already cluttered desk and leaned back in his old wooden office chair.

He took a bent old pipe out of the pocket of his ratty green cardigan, clamped it between his teeth and lit it with an enormous table lighter in the shape of Daffy Duck. When he thumbed down the tail, flame spurted out of Daffy's beak. Carrie stared, fascinated. She tried to imagine what an archaeologist of the future would make of such an artifact a thousand years from now. After a few seconds she gave up; it was just too bizarre. The little man put down the lighter and puffed up huge clouds of smoke that wandered up toward the clusters of pipes and electrical conduits in the ceiling above his shiny bald head.

His name was Dr. Ennio Morricone, and according to him he was absolutely no relation to the music composer of the same name, although he could whistle the entire *The Good, the Bad and the Ugly* theme without missing a note—which he ably demonstrated to Carrie and Slattery within two minutes of their first entering his basement office in Schermerhorn Hall on the Columbia University campus in Morningside Heights.

Schermerhorn was one of four buildings making up a pleasantly treed quadrangle just east of the Low Memorial Library. The other three buildings were Saint Paul's Chapel to the south, Avery Hall to the west and Fayerweather Hall to the east, directly on Amsterdam Avenue. All the buildings were brick and dated from the late nineteenth century. Morricone looked as though he came from roughly the same period. "*The Good, the Bad and the Ugly* theme. The world's best-known music associated with the American Wild West with the possible exception of the William Tell Overture." He whistled a few bars of the *Lone Ranger* theme and snorted. "Imagine that, the American West musically defined by two Italians, Morricone and Rossini." He smiled.

"Then there's 'The Star Spangled Banner,' of course; Francis Scott Key wrote the lyrics, but the tune was stolen from a drinking song composed by a Brit named John Stafford Smith." He shook his head. "How very proud we all are about our Americanness." He gave another snort. "Even the word 'America' is Italian." Morricone put a finger in one ear as though he was afraid facts were going to come leaking out all over the floor.

His face was cracked and seamed like a road map folded once too often. What little hair he had was nicotine white and stuck up on his temples and made him look like some sort of infuriated rodent. He was dressed in a pair of corduroy pants from another dimension, a swamp green cardigan, a checked shirt and a pair of bedroom slippers in Macintosh plaid.

Ennio Morricone, vaguely rumored by Diddy's father to have some connection to the Mafia, looked about a hundred years old and was professor emeritus of urban history at Columbia University, having received his first degree while Hitler was still alive and his last, an honorary doctorate from Harvard, just after the death of James Brown, who, according to Morricone, was far more important than Hitler when it came to historical significance since they'd be playing James Brown albums long after *der Führer's* rather dull and fatuous speeches were forgotten. Morricone was the world's leading expert on the history of New York City and he'd written three dozen books to prove it. The professor, however, emeritus or otherwise, had a certain difficulty in getting to the point.

"This whole place used to be an insane asylum—did you know that?" said Morricone, puffing more smoke. "Some people would say it still was." He gave a little hooting laugh around the stem of his pipe. "The Bloomingdale Asylum. No relation to the department store." He glanced up at the pipes above his head.

"It's all radioactive, too, of course." He smiled. "They didn't call it the Manhattan Project for nothing. The original bits for the first cyclotron are still down here in the tunnels somewhere." He grinned again. "History never really goes away, you know. It just gets mislaid. I can think of presidents who would have done well to remember that." He let out his hooting laugh again, and Carrie began to see the connection to Daffy Duck.

"Who was Adam Worth?" Slattery asked.

"Good Lord, you don't know who Adam Worth was?"

"If we did, we wouldn't be here, would we?" Slattery said patiently. He'd interviewed thousands of witnesses and suspects in his time, and the professor was just another in a very long line of eccentrics and weirdos who had crossed the big policeman's path.

"No, I suppose not," said Morricone. He rubbed the bowl of his pipe against his old, leathery cheek. "The Napoleon of Crime? The man Conan Doyle based his Moriarty on?"

"I thought he was English," said Carrie. "The Napoleon of Crime."

"German, actually. 'Werth' with an *E*. Changed it when he landed in Boston. 1849. Then to Cambridge. His father was a tailor, if I remember correctly. Left Cambridge at thirteen, came to New York and went to work for Brooks Brothers down by Schermerhorn Row. Named for Paul Schermerhorn. Same as the building we're in, as a matter of fact. . . . New York's very much like Miss

Marple's St. Mary Mead, when you get right down to it . . . just a village. Everything interconnected and intertwined. You know Miss Marple, surely, Agatha Christie. Mystery writer?"

"Adam Worth," said Slattery. Carrie marveled at the even tone in his voice. He was handling the little professor far better than she could have.

"Ah, yes. Mr. Worth."

"Brooks Brothers," the cold case detective reminded him.

"Quite." Morricone nodded. He picked up Daffy, clicked his tail and relit his pipe. More clouds wafted to the ceiling. The crowded basement office was beginning to smell like a cherry orchard on fire.

"Something happened while he was working there. A clerk, I believe. Something to do with the wife of one of their customers. Came a cropper in some mysterious way. Worth was blamed. Fired. Vanished briefly. Turned up again in the army." Morricone lurched forward in his chair and began to rummage through the pile of books and papers piled on his desk. He finally found what he was looking for, read it and tossed it back into the general pile.

"Interesting subject," he murmured. He closed his eyes and seemed to be falling asleep. He blew smoke up at the overhead pipes.

"What is?" Carrie asked.

"Military crime. Fascinating, really. Wonderful environment for a serial killer, don't you think?"

"You're saying Adam Worth was a serial killer?" Slattery asked.

"I'm a historian, not a policeman, but if pressed I would say it's a definite possibility."

"Why?" Carrie asked.

"Worth joined the Second New York Heavy Artillery. Battery L, to be specific. They were a detached battery and served in and around Washington, D.C. During the time Worth was with the battery, there were six identical murders of Washington prostitutes. They all had their throats ripped out, just like your friend in the pictures."

The professor tapped the photographs on his desk with the stem of his pipe. "And they all had their lips sewn shut, just like your man."

"When was this?" Slattery asked.

"June and July 1862," said Morricone. "On August thirtieth he fought in the Second Battle of Bull Run. The night before the battle, a black steward named Pinckney was murdered in camp. His throat was torn out. People were suspicious of Worth by then, but an investigation was put off until after the battle. During the fight, Pinckney's friend and the only witness to the murder, another steward, named Jedediah Hoseason, went missing and was presumed dead. Worth was wounded in the arm and was sent to Georgetown Hospital.

"There was a bureaucratic mix-up and he was listed as killed in action. He left the hospital and reenlisted in five separate regiments in three days, picking up the fifty-dollar signing bonus every time. Then he vanished. He turned up in New York in January 1863 and started working as a high-end pickpocket and burglar. Not surprisingly, that's when the murders began again. Eleven of them in five months that fit his profile. Nobody made the connection to Worth. There was no real reason why they should, not to mention the fact that army records had him listed as killed in action. He had the perfect alibi. He was dead."

"What happened after that?"

"He put together his own gang. Some people say he went to work for the Assassin's Club; others say he was on his own. Anyway, by 1869 things got too hot for him in New York and he fled to London. The rest is history and Sherlock Holmes. You'll even find a few obsessive types who think Adam Worth was Jack the Ripper. The timing fits. He was living in London by then. Pinkerton's followed him around for years. They caught him for a mail robbery, and after he served his sentence he retired. Died in London, supposedly. No one knows for sure."

"There was no record of him knowing this Barnabus Coffin?" asked Carrie.

"Your victim?" Dr. Morricone said. "No. I checked the big Civil War databases. As you mentioned, Dr. Norton, Coffin simply never showed up for his assignment to the USS *Keokuk*. He was listed as a deserter. There was no reason to connect him to the New York murders in the spring and summer of 1863, and no reason to connect him to Adam Worth."

"You mentioned something called the Assassin's Club," said Carrie. "What was that?"

"They were a group of rich men, mostly young, mostly involved with stock trading. They made 'killings' on the stock market—hence the name. I think Jay Gould and some of his nastier cronies were members. They were also rumored to get their information in rather dubious and even illegal ways. A man like Adam Worth could very well have been useful to them." The gnomish history professor puffed on his pipe and squinted up at the ceiling. "Did I mention that the murders here in New York were called the Double Eagle Killings? One presumes it has something to do with the lips being sewn shut. *Harper's Weekly* ran quite a lurid illustration at the time by that scallywag Thomas Nast."

"Why were they called that?" Carrie asked.

The old professor smiled. "Because after the victim had his throat torn out, the killer forced a twenty-dollar gold piece down his esophagus. A double eagle."

Slattery frowned. He leaned forward, about to ask a question. Carrie's cell phone warbled. She excused herself and took the call. She snapped the phone shut a few moments later.

"That was my friend at the Museum of Natural History. They've got Barnabus Coffin over there so they can keep the body in a climate-controlled environment. They ran a CAT scan because they weren't satisfied with the X-rays from the medical examiner's office.''

"And?" Slattery asked.

"They found something in the gut. It looks like a coin.''

CHAPTER 11

Echo Van Helsing and Kate Warne spent the rest of the day fruitlessly going down the list supplied by Charles Tiffany, ticking off the possible dealers in gem-quality rubies one by one. They reached the last name, Mr. Solomon Morowitz, just as the sun was setting and the lamplighters with their long poles were beginning to move up both sides of Maiden Lane.

Solomon Morowitz's address was listed as being 14 Maiden Lane, putting it in a five-story building with stores on the main floor and arched window offices above, directly on the bustling corner of Broadway. Even with dusk on the way, the corner was still filled with vendors and their carts selling everything from wedding rings to ladies' hat pins and "gold" chains that would turn a neck green within a day.

Bright yellow omnibuses loaded with the inky-fingered clerks and writers from the exchange were making their plodding, squeaky way up the broad avenue, its lamps, each one a prescribed one hundred feet away from the one before, already lit, a twin row of glowing fireflies showing the way north to hearth and home and away from the whirlwind of daily commerce.

With the lighting of the lamps, the first ladies of the evening had appeared in their bright costumes, and so had the first flocks of dapper dandies who would eventually employ their services in the squalid rooms a few blocks away, above the taverns on Coenties Slip and the maze of narrow streets along the waterfront.

Echo Van Helsing could still feel the pulsing excitement of the strange city, but she was also exhausted as well as frustrated. Keeping up the pretense of being a man required a great deal more effort than she'd first imagined, and so far it didn't seem to have done any good at all; there was no sign of her father's murderer anywhere. It was as though he'd simply vanished into the enormous, frightening maw of the city without a trace.

Back in London, in the full fury and grief of her enormous loss, all she could think of was revenge, but now she was beginning to regret her decision. She was a woman in the world, alone and frightened, and even with the help of the remarkable Kate she doubted that she could ever manage to bring Draculiya to justice. With a sinking heart she followed Kate Warne through the narrow entrance to 14 Maiden Lane.

The building was a gloomy maze, larger suites

of offices and small manufactories having long ago been subdivided into small rooms along dark corridors barely lit by narrow, grime-sealed, nailed and soot-covered windows that looked down into some sort of interior air shaft. The climb was a hot one as well, since there didn't seem to be any proper ventilation, and Echo was becoming uncomfortably aware of her bladder, although she was much too embarrassed to mention her predicament.

They found Solomon Morowitz's office on the fourth floor at the air-shaft end of a dismal passageway. The only sign was a small square of card attached to a plain wooden door with a black-headed mourning pin, the man's name inscribed in a spidery hand and two words beneath as the sole indicator of his profession:

FINISHED GOODS

Above the sign, at eye level, was a peephole covered over with a piece of tin. Kate knocked firmly on the door. There was a faint sound as though a drawer had been opened, then shut again, and then a thin, almost reedy voice spoke out.

"Who is it?"

"Warne," said Kate in her best smoke-rasped voice. "Pinkerton's."

"I don't employ Pinkerton's. Go away."

"I'd like a moment of your time, Mr. Morowitz. It's important."

"How do I know you are who you say you are?"

Kate reached into the inside pocket of her suit jacket and took out a small leather folder. In it were several four-inch by two-inch "visiting cards" with a photograph on one side and PINKERTON'S IDENTIFICATION on the other. The card showed Kate in her man's costume and the identification referred to her as Karl Warne. The cards, standard for all Pinkerton agents, were made by Alexander Gardner, a personal friend of Allan Pinkerton.

"I'm going to slip my card under the door," said Kate.

"Go away. I don't need Pinkerton's. Leave me alone."

Kate bent down and slipped the card under the door, then stood and waited. For a moment there was silence, and then they heard the shuffling sound of footsteps. She could almost see the old man, white haired, with a long gray beard and dark clothing, a wide-brimmed black hat on his head like the Sephardic Jews she used to see traveling to and from the Bourse in Amsterdam. She'd already seen a dozen or more just like that in the hours she'd spent in the diamond and jewelry markets of Maiden Lane. The sound of the footsteps stopped and a few seconds later the piece of tin over the peephole slid aside. Echo saw a dark, suspicious eye staring out. The man was obviously wearing spectacles.

"You don't look like you're a Pinkerton," said

Morowitz. The eye swiveled to take in Echo. "Who's your friend?"

"A client. We'd like to speak to you about a stolen ruby."

"*Geh cocken offen yom*; I don't deal in stolen goods—understand me?"

"You'd have no way of knowing it was stolen," said Kate, trying to soothe the old man's irritation.

"Go away."

Kate sighed. "Mr. Morowitz, the Second District Station House is just a few blocks away on Beekman Street. I can go and get a constable and tell him my story, and I can make him walk back here in all this heat, and then I can get him to climb all those stairs to your office here, but I assure you, Mr. Morowitz, if I make him do that, he's not going to pay much heed to you telling him to go away. He's more likely to put his shoulder to the door and his billy club to the back of your skull, and believe me, Mr. Morowitz, I wouldn't want that to happen. No, sir, indeed I would not."

The eye continued to peer out at them, flickering back and forth between Kate and Echo. Finally the man spoke again.

"I'm going to unbar the door. Wait for a count of ten, and then come in when I call upon you. When you enter you will bar the door behind you. Is that understood?"

"Yes," said Kate.

"You will do as I ask?"

"Yes."

"All right."

They heard the scraping sound of a heavy metal bar being lifted away from the door and then the shuffling sound of footsteps. They waited for the full count of ten and almost to the second they heard the man call out again.

"Enter."

Kate opened the door and stepped inside, Echo directly behind her. Kate shut the door and busied herself with barring it again while Echo stared into the room. The office was small, twelve feet by twelve at the very most, the floors wood, painted black and very scuffed.

There was a large carved pedestal desk under a narrow window. The window had been white-washed and barred heavily, even though they were four floors up. A small wooden shelf under the window held a delicate-looking set of jeweler's scales. In front of the desk sat two plain wooden chairs without arms. Behind the desk was a wooden office chair. Sitting in the office chair was a perfectly ordinary-looking man in his late thirties or early forties with a thick black mustache and black hair parted in the middle.

He was wearing a perfectly ordinary dark frock coat with a white shirt, high collar and black ribbon tie. In his right hand, which lay on the desk, was a very large Colt Navy revolver. Directly in front of him was Kate's *carte de visite*. The man looked at them from behind gold, wire-framed, circular spectacles. He looked nothing at all as Echo had expected.

"I'm busy," said Morowitz. "What do you want?"

"May we sit?" Kate asked, indicating the chairs in front of the desk.

"If you must."

Kate Warne and Echo sat down.

"A ruby," began Kate.

"What size, what cut, what clarity? How do you know it is a ruby and not so much cut glass? How do you know anything? Did you know that a ruby is nothing more than a variety of the mineral corundum? Perhaps this ruby you speak of is nothing more than a cheap spinel."

"Which would have no value," said Kate.

"Which would have no value at all," repeated Morowitz.

"In which case you would not buy it," said Kate.

"Just so."

"We're looking for the ruby you would buy," said Kate. "A large one."

"How large?"

"Very," said Echo.

"Very large tells me nothing," said Morowitz. He opened a drawer on the left pedestal of the desk and took out a sheet of paper and a graphite pencil. "Draw it," he said.

Echo leaned forward and picked up the pencil. She quickly sketched the stone she remembered in Draculiya's signet ring. Morowitz leaned forward and looked at her drawing upside down.

"Triple cut," he murmured. "Perhaps ten carats. In a ring, as you have drawn it?"

"Gold," said Echo. "A signet ring."

"And you say it is stolen?"

"We don't care about the ring, Mr. Morowitz; we just want to know who sold it to you."

"If I went about disclosing who my clients were, I would be out of business by tomorrow," scoffed the gem dealer.

"So you did buy the ring."

"I didn't say that." The man shrugged. "But if I had purchased such an object, it would be gone by now. Such items move quickly through people's hands."

"You can't tell us anything at all?" Echo pleaded.

Morowitz frowned. "I can tell you that a man who owned the Laubespin Ruby set into a signet ring would not think twice about taking the life of a simple gem dealer on Maiden Lane." He paused. "Do you know what a *dybbuk* is?"

"No," said Echo.

"A *dybbuk* is a thing out of Gehenna, out of Tartarus, what you would call Hell. A *dybbuk* is a dead soul occupying a living body. To divulge the secrets of such a creature would risk becoming such a creature yourself." The man shivered as though a sudden cold wind had run through him.

"You *do* know him, then," whispered Echo.

"I can say nothing," answered Morowitz. He paused again. "But if such a creature had asked me where I banked the proceeds of my trade, I might well tell him."

"And where would that be?" Kate Warne asked quickly.

"The Irving Bank in Washington Market," said Morowitz hastily. "I will say nothing more." He slid Kate's Pinkerton card across the desk. She picked it up and slid it back into its leather folder.

"This creature has done something to you?" Morowitz asked as Kate and Echo stood to leave.

"He murdered my father," said Echo, her voice breaking and tears coming to her eyes. She turned away so the gem dealer would not see.

"*Zol er krenken un gedenken*," murmured Morowitz. "Let him suffer and remember."

They left the office silently.

"I'm terribly sorry," whispered Echo, the tears still hot on her cheeks. "I'm also afraid I must make water, very badly."

"Don't worry," said Kate with a smile, "and don't be sorry. I know just the place."

They made their way quickly down the stairs and stepped out onto Maiden Lane once more. Kate whistled shrilly, hailing a hackney carriage.

"Taylor's," she ordered as they climbed up into their seats. "Quick as you can!"

The hackney rapidly took them up Broadway to Franklin Street and dropped them off in front of a large Italianate building with ornate curved windows. Taylor's Saloon occupied the entire main floor. Echo had never seen anything like it, even in cosmopolitan London.

It combined an exotic Eastern magnificence with the taste of a Parisian pleasure garden of the most opulent sort. The single room was at least a hundred feet long, the ceilings more than twenty feet high, with gilt pillars and cornices and walls made up of large mirrors separated by white marble panels.

The floor was also marble, with a row of fluted and polished marble columns running down each side. A large alcove at the far end of the room was divided by a low marble wall and filled with blossoming orange trees and a fountain of sparkling crystal water that kept the air refreshingly sweet and cool. More than a hundred marble-topped tables were arranged across the floor, each covered in a bright white linen tablecloth set with fresh flowers and brilliantly lit from above by a long series of candelabras that made the interior as bright as day. It also had water closets available free of charge to the patrons of the lavish restaurant and attended by crisply uniformed Negro servants.

After using the facilities, Echo, with Kate's guidance, they returned to their table in the restaurant and were quickly handed enormous printed bills of fare in large leather folders. Around them most of the other tables were filled with ladies in beautiful formal gowns and men in less ornate formal attire of their own. There were a number of men dining alone in small groups wearing business attire like Kate and Echo, and Echo was astonished to see women at tables dining without male escorts of any kind. She expressed her surprise to Kate.

"Taylor's and Delmonico's are just about the only places you're likely to see it," said the Pinkerton detective. "Emily Astor started the trend a while back, and where the Astors go, the rest of society is likely to follow." She looked around the enormous room. "We were lucky to find a table; the place is filling up."

"It's all so . . . genteel," said an awestruck Echo, trying to find the right word.

"You wouldn't think so if you knew who had their meeting hall on the third floor above the buffalo-skin warehouse."

"Who?" Echo asked.

"The New York Free Love League. Two bits' admission, dancing about, fairy lights and all the rest." Echo looked up at the ceiling and found herself blushing. Kate laughed. "Don't trouble yourself, then, Mr. Van Helsing. Let's eat, shall we?"

Echo was astonished by the variety on the menu. There were nine different soups on offer, from consommé Adelinna to shrimp bisque and cream of artichoke. There were side dishes from chutney to caviar, entrées from pigeon with peas to lamb cutlets and a seemingly endless number of on-hand dishes, roasts, cold cuts and salads.

There were entremets to clean the palate between all these dishes, including Charlotte Russe, Madeira Jelly and Cabinet Pudding Maraschino. There were at least forty desserts, from Bar-le-Duc, a sort of white currant jam usually eaten with squares of toasted bread, to ordinary stewed prunes. All of this could be followed by a cheese plate if you had any room, and several different types of tea or coffee.

"Good Lord," was all Echo could say.

"Keep it simple," said Kate, laughing, "or we'll be here all night."

"Do you have any suggestions?"

"It's been a long day. You must be famished. What would you say to a dozen oysters, the sirloin of beef with potatoes, some string beans and we'll think about dessert later?"

They both ordered exactly that, and an hour later, after thinking about the dessert and having enjoyed a fine, icy Nesselrode chestnut pudding and a frighteningly sweet, honey-dipped Persian Lala Rokh, they finished with a pot of French coffee shared between them while Kate savored one of her cheroots. The restaurant was completely full now, and the air was filled with laughter, the clink and ring of cutlery and crystal and a pleasant buzzing roar of conversation.

"Well, at least we made some progress," said Kate. She drew out a billfold and stared at the paper slip their waiter had brought them. She laid a crisp five-dollar bill on the little wooden tray.

"How so?" Echo said.

"We know where the enemy keeps his money," answered Kate. "It's not far from that to knowing where he lives."

"We can't simply loiter outside his bank all day," said Echo plaintively.

"We won't have to. We'll just ask the right questions to the right people."

"I don't understand."

Kate explained. "Pinkerton's is employed by every bank in the state of New York as well as almost every bank in Boston. If I can't discover the Count's roosting place in the city, I'll be very surprised." Kate pushed back her chair. "Come on," she said, rising from the table. "We've still got work to do. There's someone I want you to meet." She paused. "You're not the squeamish type, are you?"

"No," said Echo. "My father was a scientist, remember?"

"Good," said Kate grimly.

They left the restaurant, stepping out on the sidewalk, the noise and filth of Broadway assailing their eyes and ears once again. Dusk had gone. It was fully dark, and night had fallen.

"Where are we going?" Echo asked as Kate hailed a hackney, one of half dozen waiting at the curb.

"The morgue," replied the Pinkerton detective.

CHAPTER 12

Carrie Norton and Max Slattery drove up Amsterdam Avenue in the detective's grumbling old Crown Victoria, slipped over to Columbus, then turned onto West Eighty-first Street and parked in a metered spot halfway up the block once known as Manhattan Square, which contained the sprawling American Museum of Natural History. The exterior of the main building was a paean of praise to gothic, neo-Romanesque and beaux arts overstatement, most of it in a rusticated New York brownstone with a dash of pale, imposing granite making up the triumphal-columned Central Park entrance, named in honor of Teddy Roosevelt, whose father had been one of the founders.

Slattery flipped down his visor to show off the NYPD sticker, then lumbered out of the car, ignoring the meter.

"You're not going to feed the meter?"

"Are you kidding me?" Slattery snorted. "Does a fire truck pay for parking? I'm here on police business. I could have been really nasty and parked in a handicap zone." He grinned at Carrie. "Face it, kiddo. I'm not the most politically correct of people. I like red meat, I shoot astrologers on sight and I like reading baseball statistics, either on the toilet or at the dinner table." They headed up the sidewalk toward the main entrance on Central Park West.

"Too much information for me, Max." Carrie laughed.

"What's the name of this friend of yours?"

"Will Croaker, otherwise known as Igor, or Dr. Death."

"Why do all these people have nicknames?"

"Because we're all geeks. It helps our self-esteem."

"We?" Slattery said. "You had a nickname?"

"With a last name like Norton? I was Trixie for years."

They went up the broad, crowded steps and through the main entrance into the basilica-like lobby. There was an enormous snaking line of people buying tickets in front of the gigantic barosaurus exhibit, even though it was late in the afternoon by now.

"We can't wait to get a ticket," muttered Carrie.

"No sweat," said Max. The big cop dug into the inside pocket of his jacket and pulled out his badge wallet. "Save us twenty-six bucks." He headed for the nearest guard.

"Thirteen bucks. I'm a member," said Carrie. They flagged the guard, who waved them on, and

Carrie led Max out of the entrance hall, through the North American Mammals exhibit, then left through Northwest Coast Indians and right to a staircase leading down beside a baffle wall of an area by the side entrance toilets that was closed for renovation.

"You know your way around pretty well," said the detective.

"I interned here three summers in a row when I was at Columbia," explained Carrie. "I was in love with the place." She didn't bother to explain that there was also a young blond curator in the herpetology section that she was in love with that first summer. Both the curator and the love affair were long gone.

"You know this guy Croaker very well?"

"Drinking buddies," said Carrie. "We've got a few mutual friends."

"Can he keep his mouth shut?"

"If he needs to," said Carrie. "Why?"

"Tell you later," said the cop.

They reached the bottom of the stairs and Carrie turned into the food court. "There he is," she said, pointing to a tousle-haired man in his thirties wearing a white lab coat and piling cooked onions on an already overloaded museum version of a street-meat-cart foot-long hot dog. He waved the onion-covered plastic fork in Carrie's direction, and she and Slattery threaded their way through the lines of chattering kids and teenagers to where he was standing. By then he'd finished with the onions and was squeezing on another line of mustard.

"Bertman's Ball Park," he said, gesturing with the squeeze bottle. "Only place you can find it east of Jacobs Field."

"You must be from Cleveland." Slattery grinned.

"Born and raised. You must be Trixie's cop buddy."

"See?" Carrie said. "Still Trixie."

Max and Croaker shook hands after the assistant curator put down the squeeze bottle; then he led the way out of the food court, munching on the hot dog, spilling onions and sauerkraut and dripping mustard all the way to a door set into a plain gray wall at the end of a completely anonymous corridor. The scientist swiped the ID card dangling from his wrist through the electronic lock, and the door clicked open.

"From here on we just follow the breadcrumbs into the forest," said Croaker. "Thirty-two million individual items in storage from a T-rex skull to a frozen brain slice and liver sample from the Lee Harvey Oswald autopsy. Fourteen separate departments all wanting space from the attic to the basement. They used to say Einstein's brain was down here, but it's not. It's at some obscure university in Canada for some reason I could never quite figure out." He took another enormous bite from his hot dog and chewed heartily. "Don't tell the kiddies in the lunchroom, but the last thing anybody cares about in this place is exhibits."

The walls of the corridors had gone from neutral gray to a dull bureaucratic green. Ten minutes into the maze of narrow halls and passageways and they came to another flight of stairs. They went down to an even lower level and immediately the temperature dropped and the lighting dimmed. The walls were no longer plasterboard but quarried brownstone, the floor some kind of smooth linoleum.

Croaker hunched his shoulder and dragged his foot in a bad imitation of Lon Chaney in *The Hunchback of Notre Dame*. He waved them forward with the stubby remains of his hot dog. "This way, masters, this way!" he lisped.

"I'll bet his mother loved him, though," whispered Max.

"I didn't have a mother, master," said Croaker, turning and cocking an eyebrow. "I was a self-made man. I have the bolt through my neck to prove it." He gave a macabre little laugh and stopped in front of another door with an electronic lock, swiping his card a second time. He stood aside. "Come into my parlor," the scientist crooned.

The room beyond was remarkably modern. The walls appeared to be lined with stainless steel, and a wide bench running the entire length of the roomy chamber was crammed with an amazing collection of electronic instruments from centrifuges to gas spectrometers. In the middle of the room was a six-by-ten-foot light table, and in the center of the light table, glowing like some alien being, lit from beneath, were the reasonably well-preserved remains of Barnabus Coffin, naked now, the uniform removed, which, to Carrie at least, seemed to diminish him. The room looked like something out of an episode of *CSI*. Croaker rested the last four inches of his hot dog on the edge of the light table. He picked up one of Coffin's desiccated hands and gave it a little wave.

"It's alive! It's alive!"

"Some weird friends you got, Doc," muttered Max.

"Just trying to lighten the mood." Croaker pouted. He chewed his way through the last of his hot dog, then smacked his lips.

"He didn't look that shiny before," said Slattery, peering down at the leathery object on the table.

"Gave him a hot lanolin bath, limbered him up," said Croaker, bending down and rummaging around in a half-size lab fridge under the counter. He resurfaced with a Diet Dr Pepper in his hand and snapped the top. "Had to or I wouldn't have been able to get him into the barrel of the CAT scanner."

"What exactly did you find?" Carrie asked.

"Come on over here," Croaker instructed, motioning them to the other side of the room. He flipped on a bank of wall-mounted X-ray light boxes. There were four views under the clips.

"Check out the throat and esophagus or what's left of it. It's a simple endolateral image."

"From the ME?" Slattery asked.

"Yup." Croaker nodded.

"I can't see anything," said Carrie finally, after looking at all four views. "Just the wound, some shadows and a lot of vertebrae and stuff."

"Look again," said Croaker.

Slattery saw it first. "That thin little line."

"Good for you," said Croaker. He pulled down the first X-ray and replaced it with a color lateral scan of the bog body's esophagus. There was a definite round object caught about three quarters of the way down. "Most foreign bodies are found at the level of the cricopharyngeus muscle, but this is much lower."

"Crico what?" Slattery asked.

"Creek-o-far-in-gee-us," explained Croaker. "Otherwise known as the upper esophageal sphincter. It's the muscle that stops you choking and swallowing things down the wrong pipe."

"Gotcha." Slattery nodded.

"Hard to swallow something that big and get it past that point. Your throat automatically locks up the way your lower sphincter does when you're fleeing to the crapper with the runs."

"Very scientific of you, Willy," laughed Carrie.

"Abundantly clear, though." Slattery shrugged. "What you're saying is, our man here didn't swallow it by accident like a kid swallowing a penny he found on the floor."

"Exactly," said Croaker. They all turned back to the body of Barnabus Coffin.

"Can you get it out?" Carrie asked.

"If I can have your permission."

"You've got the NYPD's permission," said Slattery.

"Miss White from LinCorp might not like that," warned Carrie.

"To hell with her."

"We talking Henry Todd . . . that Lincoln?" Croaker asked, his tone suddenly wary. "The one with the ten-thousand-square-foot apartment at 740 Park?"

"The very same," said Carrie.

"He's a *huge* contributor to the museum," said the curator. "Am I doing something really stupid like risking my job and the possibility of any future employment in the museum business for the rest of my life?"

Carrie nodded. "That would be a possibility. But hey, it's an extreme world out there." She patted Croaker on the shoulder. "Think of it as anthropological bungee jumping. An adventure." Croaker was going pale.

"I'll take the heat," said Max. "This is a homicide investigation. Open him up."

The curator went to yet another bench and brought a tray of medical instruments to the light table. He reached into the pocket of his lab coat, snapped on a pair of surgical gloves, then used his left index finger to gently palpate the area they'd seen on the CAT scan. He found the spot and picked up a number 20 blade in a number 4 handle. He held the oversized surgical blade in a palmar, or dinner-knife, grip and pulled the blade along for about three inches. He put down the scalpel, picked up a pair of something that looked like rubber-nosed pliers, spread the newly created opening in the dead man's neck and reached into the hole. His tongue came out between his teeth as he concentrated.

"Got it," he said. He pulled up with the pliers. There was a faint, damp sucking sound and then the object that had been hidden in the dead man's throat for more than a hundred and fifty years was brought out into the light again. "Twenty-dollar gold piece," said Croaker, lifting the pliers up to examine the coin. "Dated 1863. Neat."

Twenty minutes later Max Slattery and Carrie Norton were sitting in a Famous Ray's on Columbus Avenue, a few blocks north of the museum. Max was having a Ray's Famous Special—pepperoni, sausage, meatballs, mushrooms, bacon, eggplant, green pepper, onions and extra mozzarella, with maybe an anchovy or two waved over the pie for that salty aftertaste. Carrie had a Greek salad.

"We have a situation," said Slattery, wiping tomato sauce off his chin and sipping his Snapple. Carrie poked at a suspiciously wrinkled black olive with her fork.

"Cardiac arrest?" Carrie said, staring at the enormous thing on Max's plate.

"I'm serious," the detective growled. He scooped up a slice, folded it expertly, then stuck it point first as far as it would go into his mouth. He bit down and chewed, then swallowed.

"What kind of situation?" Carrie asked.

"Murder," said Slattery.

"We know that already."

"Not Mr. Leatherhead back there," said the cop, nodding in the direction of the museum. "There." He nodded his head in the other direction.

"Where's 'there'?"

"Manhattan South."

"Manhattan South what?" Carrie said, exasperated. She felt as though she was living inside a Marx Brothers routine.

"Manhattan South Detective Squad. Homicide in particular. They've had eight murders in the last three months, all below Central Park. All homeless or crazies, or both. One down on Fulton by the river, a couple in Greenwich Village, a couple more on Seventh between Twenty-ninth and Fortieth. One just off Canal. All over the place. No kind of pattern I can figure, or anyone else."

"And?" said Carrie. She finally decided to pass on the wrinkled olive and had a chunk of feta-sprinkled tomato instead.

"They were all black."

"Yes?"

"They were all black, and they all had been killed the same way: somebody squirted Krazy Glue up their nostrils and into their mouths. They suffocated."

"Grisly. But what does it have to do with us?"

"Any criminal homicide rates an autopsy. Guess what they found inside each and every one of the Krazy Glue corpses."

"You're dying to tell me."

"Chocolate."

"Pardon?"

"Chocolate."

"Slattery, you're a very weird man. You're eating the ugliest pizza ever made and you're telling me stories about dead people eating chocolate as they suffocate. You're way beyond fetish here; you're deep into kinky."

"Chocolate and gold foil."

"Gold foil?"

"Like the kind they use to cover chocolate coins."

"Gold coins."

"That's right. Gold chocolate coins with the foil stamped to look exactly like an 1863 twenty-dollar Liberty gold piece."

"Oh, crap," whispered Carrie.

"You got that right," said Slattery. He took another bite of pizza and stared across the table at her. "The question is, *now* what do we do?"

CHAPTER 13

Enoch Bale the Vampyr walked the nighttime streets and alleys of the Fourth Ward from the park at City Hall to the Bowery and further to the East River and South Street. He wore a plain black frock coat, a white silk shirt and boots. He wore no hat, his pitch-black hair hanging freely down to his shoulders. He carried a walking stick that could be better described as a cudgel, its handle made in the brass image of a snarling wolf, like Napoleon's bees or the Dragon of Saint George, a favorite motif.

It was very dark, and here there were no gas lamps to light the streets, the only illumination coming from behind the shuttered windows of the tenement buildings, the grog shops and the occasional lantern at a doorway. Even so, the streets were as full of people as they were at midday. Prostitutes in all shapes, sizes, colors and states of inebriation abounded. On corners, lounging in alleys, strutting up and down displaying their wares. There were runners and ropers-in on every street corner, whispering in strangers' ears the delights available behind this shaded doorway or that. Open coaches rattled past with their passengers, likely travelers out for what they thought would be an adventure, hooked by the commission men in fancy clothes who spent their time in hotel lobbies scouting for prospects. Dogs, rats, women or the gaming table—it didn't matter which. The Fabulous Fourth had every diversion known and in every variety.

There were hard men about as well, with eyes like hot coals searching for likely victims, usually those who'd already been fleeced and savaged by the saloons and sporting rooms and who'd drunk far too much blindingly cheap gin or bucket grog. If they were lucky they might escape with nothing but their shoes and shirts stolen, but most would take a beating before the constables found them tossed on the rubbish tips or down a cesspit the following morning.

No one paid much attention to the tall, dark man with the unfashionably long hair. It was almost as though he were invisible, or more likely that once they'd seen him, passersby would quickly look away and pretend their eyes had never met his. As he walked, the loiterers and streetwalkers seemed to shrink back into the shadows from whence they came, and everywhere there was the faint tremor that can be felt between a predator and its prey.

The air was full of tastes and smells. Rotting

vegetables and fruit from the Fulton Market less than a block away, the stink of fish rising in a pall from the fish market on the wharves just below it. The thick odor of hops was in the air from the Empire Brewery around the corner on Cherry Street, running twenty-four hours a day and only one of hundreds brewing endless barrels to slake the city's never-ending, never-slowing thirst. There were the fetid smells of tanneries and coal tips, the waste, liquid and solid, of the slaughterhouses, the nostril-clogging too-sweet burnt caramel snout of the sugar refineries, both here and across the East River in Brooklyn. There was the hiss and faint aftersmell of the gas lamps, the wet smell of building piles as they settled into the swampy ground where the old collect pond had been. The smell of the river, the smell of fresh-laid bricks and new-cut stone, the smell of paint and turpentine, and threaded through it all like the reaching subterranean filaments of a suppurating toadstool were the smells of mankind. Man sweat, man waste, man fear, man lust, man horror and here and there, usually hidden, man blood and death, a copper taste on the tongue, the special green-guts odor of death-vented bowels and gassy decay.

To someone unused to it, the stink was suffocating, and even those who lived nearby often walked with scented rags or handkerchiefs over their noses. To Enoch Bale the Vampyr, the horrifying odors of New York were but a nosegay to some of the battlefields he'd once walked and killed on. He let the stench break over him like a wave splitting on the bow of a ship pushed on by the wind, his senses looking for something that none around him even knew existed.

A bright light caught his eye—a doorway and the fading sign it lit: 273 WATER ST. KIT BURNS'S SPORTSMAN'S HALL. The sign was in gilt and bilious green, much the worse for wear. Remarkably, the apostrophes were in their proper places. The building itself was a little out of the ordinary and at one time had obviously stood on its own, the residence of a wealthy merchant. It was good red-brick, neatly pointed, four full stories tall, the windows invisible behind heavy shutters painted a fading green. The roof was sheathed in copper. All of it was in sharp contrast to the run-down tenements and tumbledown sailors' lodgings all around it, their ground floors or basements almost inevitably turned into rough saloons, low brothels and grog shops serving bucket liquor.

The wide doors were open, two enormous men in bowler hats and checked suits standing on either side. From the large room beyond there was the sound of laughter, male and female, voices singing and even the occasional scream. From below, Bale could hear the hollow mutterings of a crowd, groans and cheers. Rats, or dogs or both. He looked up into the night sky. The stars and any moon were lost in the smoky, greasy haze.

He went up the ramplike steps to the front door. One of the bowler-hatted men took that moment to tap out the bowl of his pipe on an upturned shoe, and the second man, after one brief look, turned away, putting his broad back to Bale, making sure that both his hands were visible, offering no excuse for anger. The Vampyr went through the open doorway without hindrance or question.

The main floor was a saloon divided into three rooms. In the first room was a solid bar with mirrors, bottles of earthenware and glass on shelves behind, taps in rows beneath the counter. It was filled to overflowing with a laughing, jostling crowd and was wreathed in the smoke from cheap cigars.

The second room had banquettes against the walls and aproned waiters bringing drinks.

A black man sat playing a piano. It was a tune the Vampyr had heard aboard the *Anglo-Saxon*, and obviously a favorite here. The man was singing in a clear, strong baritone that worked its way easily above the other noise. It was called, simply, "Lorena."

> *The story of the past, Lorena,*
> *Alas! I care not to repeat,*
> *The hopes that could not last, Lorena,*
> *They lived, but only lived to cheat.*
> *I would not cause e'en one regret*
> *To wrankle in your bosom now;*
> *For "if we try, we may forget,"*
> *Were words of thine long years ago.*
> *For "if we try, we may forget,"*
> *Were words of thine long years ago.*

The third room was the salon, with stairs going up and stairs going down. There were half a dozen women in the room, all of them clearly sober and smiling, dressed or undressed in varying degrees. In age they ranged from perhaps twelve to twenty-five. Each one had a paper fan and on the fan a painted number.

There was one man in the room, a huge, utterly unpleasant figure with bulging eyes in a pale porcine face, fat lips sucking wetly on a corncob pipe, his hands as big as sledgehammers, the fingers like sausages. His eyes were pale blue and watery. Red veins spread across his cheeks and glistening forehead like the tracery of a bloodshot eye. His thighs bulged the houndstooth check of his trousers, and his belly flowed over his broad leather belt like lava. He wore high boots, a green shirt and suspenders. The fringe of hair around his knotted skull might once have been red, but now it was the color of tobacco. In the wide belt were two Remington Pocket Police revolvers, the cylinders and the triggers done in brass, and Enoch Bale could see the ivory handle of a knife in the man's right boot. An iron-banded cudgel used for stunning cows in the slaughterhouse leaned against the wooden armchair he sprawled in.

"My name's Leese," said the man, speaking around the pipe in his mouth. Both hands flexed slightly against his thighs, tensing. "They call me Snatchem, because that's what I do." He peered up at the tall man with the long black hair. "You got anything for Snatchem today, sport?"

"Not today, I'm afraid, Mr. Leese."

"You're a foreigner."

"You might say that."

"Might say?! I do say!" He laughed and turned to check the girls' expressions for approval. They were all trying not to look at the man in front of them and not succeeding. "What brings you to Kit Burns's place?"

"Curiosity," murmured Enoch Bale.

"Kit doesn't abide lookers," said Leese. "This isn't a fancy show at Barnum's, understand? Here you pay, one wise or the other."

A coin appeared in the Vampyr's hand as if by magic. He flicked his long fingers and the coin spun through the air in Snatchem Leese's direction, the glint of gold catching the glow from the gaslights on the walls around the room.

Almost as an afterthought the big man with the bulging eyes reached up and deftly twitched the coin out of the air. He examined it, then took the corncob pipe from his mouth and tried the coin between a few dark, stained teeth. "Twenty dollars," observed the man. "Very nice indeed." Twenty dollars: four times the daily wages of a skilled craftsman, forty times those of a laborer digging ditches or laying pavers. Snatchem Leese slipped the coin away into the pocket of his shirt. "Women and cards upstairs; rats, dogs and prize-fights in the pits under. Got it?" He waved his hand. "Girls you order by their numbers." He slipped the corncob pipe back between his lips. "Sheehan and Maddersly in the ring tonight, if you didn't already know."

The Vampyr went down the heavy oak steps into the low-ceilinged basement. The long room was dirt floored, the air choked with smoke. If anything, it was more crowded than the rooms upstairs, and everyone was either drinking or placing bets with the bookies standing on their wooden crates, betting slips tucked into hatbands, fists full of dollars and pockets bulging with coin.

In the middle of the room was the rat pit. "Pit" was a misnomer because it was nothing more than a ten-foot square made with a three-foot-high fence around it, the inner side sheathed in thin metal. On two sides of the ring, rough tiers of seats had been constructed using barrels and planks. The floor of the pit was sand, blood caked from the earlier round of dog fights and rat terriers at work. The corpses of headless rats gnawed by the terriers lay around the perimeter of the fence, and in a far corner the gutted body of a bulldog lay, its white and purple entrails coiled around its savaged belly.

In the center of the pit two men were fighting bare knuckled, stripped to the waist. One was shorter than the other, black bearded, with short, dark hair. He had the hard, lean look of an Irishman from one of the lower counties, Cork or Kerry, with as much Spaniard or French in him as Celt. The other was slimmer, dressed in kid-leather riding trousers, and had the look of a gentlemen. He wore a broad leather belt fixed with a huge silver buckle. The short one had a chest like a barrel and arms like hams, but the taller, slighter man had muscle too, and speed. The short man tried to pummel his taller rival with combinations to the belly and kidneys, but the taller man chose his battles, reaching out with his longer arms to jab at his opponent's jaw, dancing out of the way of most of the other man's ferocious swings. The fists of both men were slick with blood, and the short one's left eye was swollen shut and black with crusted blood.

"What round?" asked Enoch Bale to the well-dressed man beside him.

"Thirtieth."

"Of how many?"

"Until one of them drops, boyo," chortled the man. Bale looked beyond the far end of the ring and saw a group of very young, dashing-looking men cheering on the taller man boxing in the ring.

"They're friends of the man in the belt?" Bale asked, raising his voice over the steady noise in the basement.

"That's Maddersly in the ring. He belongs to Gould."

"Gould?"

"Jay Gould," said the man beside the Vampyr, pointing across the pit. "The one over there with the top hat and the cane. Looks like an undertaker." Bale stared through the smoke. The man was handsome, sallow and dark-haired, wearing an expensive-looking navy blue silk jacket and striped trousers. He looked to be in his early thirties, and the men around him seemed cut from the same cloth. His companions were all laughing and cheering, but the one called Gould wore no expression at all. His face was as impassive as a bookkeeper's.

"Who is he?" asked Enoch Bale.

"Jay Gould?" the man answered, looking surprised. "He's just about the hardest scalper on the exchange. He bulls the market, then milks the street. He's been accused of kiting and ballooning, but no one has ever come up with any proof. He arranges fights for Maddersly. Makes book on him for a hobby. He's an Assassin."

"An Assassin?"

"A member of the Assassin's Club. Posh gentlemen traders and such. Costs a pretty penny to join them, not that they take just anyone."

Maddersly landed a right hook that lifted his shorter opponent off his feet, then took a short step, raised his left to fend off a haymaker, then used his own left to pound Sheehan in his ruined eye. The short man let out a yelp and tried to cover that side of his face, but it was too late. The right fist lashed out again and caught Sheehan in the throat, and the left struck him hard high in the chest. He dropped like a stone into the bloody center of the pit. There was sudden silence in the room. Maddersly stood above his prostrate opponent, waiting. The other man lay motionless in the dark-stained sand. From somewhere a deep voice boomed out heartily.

"Pay up, gents!" And then the crowd began to cheer. Enoch Bale kept his eyes on Gould. Even with his champion triumphant, he showed no pleasure or any other emotion at all. Suddenly Gould looked up, and for a fraction of a second the young man's hooded eyes locked with Bale's, and Jay Gould smiled, almost in recognition.

As Echo Van Helsing quickly saw, Bellevue Hospital, though well away from the center of the city, had done little or nothing to deserve its name, especially in the dead of night. It was a gloomy brownstone pile in the classical tradition, and from the odors rising up around it she could tell it had been located in very close proximity to a cesspool or swamp. As the carriage pulled up at the hospital's main gate, the only view that Echo glimpsed was the moonlit wharf where the ferry to Blackwell's Island and the lunatic asylum stood.

After paying the driver and promising him a fare back into town if he waited, Kate Warne led her young friend across an open courtyard and around to the side of the main building. Hidden by the high walls surrounding the grounds were two low structures, shed roofed and windowless.

"The smaller one at the back is the dead house. The big one in front is the morgue." They went to the main door of the morgue, which was lit with a single gas lamp behind a cage of blue glass.

The door itself was heavy and sheathed in painted metal. The Pinkerton agent knocked loudly, then lifted the latch and went inside without waiting for an answer.

The interior of the morgue was simple and straightforward: a single chamber, low ceilinged and lit by a series of open cruciform gas jets in the ceiling every six or seven feet. The walls were cut stone with workbenches up against them, and the floor was made from heavy paving stone and set at intervals with drains. On the far wall there were a number of taps and large sinks, and running down the center of the room were eight stone pedestals, each one supporting an eight-foot-long marble-topped table, its edges raised all around. There was one cross-shaped gas lamp for every two tables.

There was only one other living person in the chamber. He was tall, fair-haired and clean shaven, wearing a stained linen apron over what appeared to be a major's uniform. He nodded to Kate as she stepped forward, then used the long curved knife in his hand to point at the body on the marble slab beside him.

"Here's the one you asked for," said the major. "She's been in the dead house, so she's nice and chilled." He turned to Echo and smiled. "My name is Dr. Sanger. Eugene Sanger. We keep the fresh ones in the dead house because that's where we store the ice."

The body on the table was that of a naked

woman, barely into her teens, brown-haired, with small, immature breasts and barely curving hips. A small strip of linen had been laid modestly across her pubic area. She appeared almost asleep, her eyes closed, her mouth relaxed. If it hadn't been for the gaping ragged wound in her throat, she would have looked quite peaceful. Her right foot was partially gone. It looked half eaten by small razor teeth. There was no blood.

"Who is she?" Kate asked.

"No idea. A prostitute certainly." Sanger cleared his throat self-consciously. "There's ample evidence of that."

"Where was she found?" Kate asked.

"Coal yard at the foot of Fourth Street and Tompkins, near the river," Sanger said. "She was buried in the cinders, but the rats had got to her." He pointed the heavy knife down at her foot. "A worker at the yard found her, and the police brought her here."

"How long ago?"

"Two days. She was fresh when she was brought in. Dead no more than a few hours."

"Cause of death?"

"I would have thought that was obvious." Sanger laughed.

"Not so obvious," said Echo, leaning forward to examine the girl's mouth. There was a wooden, velvet-lined case of surgeon's tools on the edge of the table by the dead girl's head. Echo selected a narrow pair of tongs generally used for removing bullets from wounds and pulled back the lips. They were neatly sewn together with strong gut, from the inside, like an embalmer would do.

"Good grief," murmured Sanger, "I never even noticed that."

Echo turned her attention to the girl's neck, pushing back a flap of ruined flesh on the girl's throat.

"Quite deft," remarked Sanger, raising an eyebrow. "Who is this young, er, man, Katherine?"

"My name is Van Helsing," Echo answered without looking up. She peeled back another scrap of pale flesh. Beneath it, almost obscured by the main tear in the flesh, were a pair of punctures about three inches apart. "Should you care to dissect the neck, I think you'd find the two punctures extend down into the main carotid artery," Echo said, standing upright. She pointed with the tongs. Sanger bent over, inspecting the wound.

"A reptile bite," he said.

"No," Echo said. "A man, of sorts."

Sanger turned to Kate, who was busy lighting another one of her cigars.

"She knows?" Sanger asked.

"I'm afraid so," said Kate. She blew out a cloud of smoke. "She followed one of them here from England."

"One of them?" Echo said, surprised.

"There's been murders like this one for the past few months, since Christmas," Kate answered. "Long before your man even arrived. This one is just the latest."

"We're trying to keep this quiet," said Sanger. "With the war going the way it is and the new draft ruling, a panic in Mr. Garvey's paper or Mr. Harper's magazine could throw the whole city into a frenzy. A million people rioting is not a prospect I enjoy contemplating."

"I still don't understand," said Echo. "The man who killed my father didn't fly here like some giant bird. He couldn't have been in two places at once."

"He wasn't," said Kate Warne. "We think there's more than one of them."

Echo stared, her eyes widening as the implications of what the Pinkerton agent was telling her sank in.

"Dear God," she whispered. "A breed apart."

The Vampyr followed Maddersly when he finally left Kit Burns's establishment several hours after the fight had ended. He'd watched as Gould and the pugilists' other friends toasted him with everything from tankards of beer to earthen bottles of imported Dutch genever water. Mounds of oysters were consumed along with the liquor, and by two thirty in the morning the fighter looked in worse shape than he had in the pit. By then most of his friends had taken whores upstairs to the rooms on the upper floors or, like Gould, were playing high-stakes poker in the gaming rooms above the saloon.

The fighter turned left after leaving the Sportsman's Hall and staggered up to Roosevelt Street, named for the prominent glass importer's family whose business had started there. At first it appeared that the man was making for the gaslit pleasures of the Bowery a few blocks away, but he turned again on Cherry Street, then abruptly turned into a narrow alley that ran between the high brick walls of a brewery and the tall gray planks of a fence around a livery stable. Horses whinnied and stamped at the disturbance, and somewhere a dog began to howl.

Enoch Bale stepped into the alley and reversed the heavy stick in his hand, putting the brass head at the lower end. The alley was totally dark, but shadows were where he lived, and it wasn't difficult to make out the whisper of the other man's breathing and to take in the absence of his receding footsteps. Maddersly was lurking no more than ten feet away, hidden in a doorway leading into the brewery's boiler room.

Without any pause the Vampyr strode ahead, seemingly oblivious, hearing the change in Maddersly's breathing. As he reached the doorway he swung the heavy end of the walking stick in a vicious arc, the brass wolf's head striking the tall man in the heart, doubling him over in pain. Something dropped from the man's hand. A pistol like the one he'd seen in Snatchem Leese's belt, except the cylinder of this one was plain steel. The Vampyr kicked it away with a booted foot and pushed Maddersly back against the brick wall. The horses in the livery yard were stamping and whinnying madly now, kicking in their stalls. The dog continued to howl.

The Vampyr dropped the walking stick and grabbed Maddersly by the throat. He leaned forward slightly and breathed in through his nostrils, taking in the scent.

"You are *Damphyr*," he said, his face no more than a few inches from the other man. "I smelled it on you in the rat pit. I tasted it on the night air. The black soulless stink of your kind."

"I don't know what you're talking about. You were following me," the man choked out. The Vampyr could feel the heavy muscles in the man's shoulders tensing. He was about to try to struggle out of Enoch Bale's grip. With his free hand the Vampyr reached down and grasped Maddersly's wrist, the sharpened, bone-hard nail of his thumb cutting into the ulnar artery and severing both the ulnar and radial nerves. Blood gushed. Maddersly screamed and the hand went limp. The Vampyr resisted the sensuous feeling of the man's rich warm blood flowing over his fingers and concentrated on the subject at hand.

"You are *Damphyr*," he repeated. "A creature of halves, neither one thing or another. A donkey trying to imitate a horse."

"I thought you were a thumper for sure, or a rope man after my purse." The fighter swallowed, his eyes flickering as the blood poured out of the long, deep incision in his wrist. "Please, take it. Two hundred dollars."

"I don't want your money," said the Vampyr. "I want answers to my questions."

"I don't know nothing about no Damphyr or whatever you call them, mister. I'm just a prize-fighter. I fight for Gould and his friends, that's all! I swear!"

"You lie," said Enoch Bale. "But not for long." Maddersly began to sag. The Vampyr's jaw slid and locked. He used both hands now to keep the man standing upright, supported by the wall. He whispered against the man's throbbing temple and into his ear, the fighter's terror almost palpable, like a fluttering bird in the grip of a cat. "Tell me what you know," he said, his lips sliding down the man's cheek to the salty, sweat-stubbled throat above his collar. "Tell me what you know, and I'll give you quick release from all your pain and fear. I'll end it."

"You can't . . ." breathed Maddersly, sighing as the blood pooled around his feet.

"I can," said the Vampyr, the ivory-bright needles curving down. "And I will."

CHAPTER 14

It smelled as though they were in the middle of a scene from *Charlie and the Chocolate Factory*, which wasn't surprising since it was a chocolate factory, specifically the main plant of Sweet Something Chocolates in south Brooklyn. The factory was in a stand-alone two-story building at the corner of Gold Street and Front that had once been a small restaurant. The reception area was very high-tech, done in chrome and black with a marble counter and glass display cases filled with examples of Sweet Something products.

There seemed to be everything from chocolate bunny rabbits to foil-wrapped chocolate effigies of the Virgin Mary and something that looked suspiciously like a vaguely pornographic naked Elvis. A teenaged girl in what appeared to be a candy striper's uniform stood behind the marble counter with a completely insincere grin plastered across her pretty face. Behind her was a pair of double doors and behind them was the muffled sound of machinery.

"Hello and welcome to Sweet Something," said the girl. "What sweet something can I help you with today?"

"I'm a cop," said Slattery. "We're here about a murder. We'd like to speak to your boss."

"Gee," said the girl, her eyes widening.

"No, your boss," said Slattery.

"He's in the back," said the girl.

"Could you get him, please?" said Slattery. Carrie was looking at the displays. There were several examples of gold coins, but none of them was an 1863 twenty-dollar piece.

"I'm not supposed to leave my post," she said, her face looking worried.

"This isn't the Marines, kid; go get him," said Slattery. He flipped back his jacket and showed her his holstered SIG-Sauer automatic. "I'll mind the store." The teenager's eyes got even wider.

"Gee," she said again. She turned and fled through the double doors.

"The smell is making me sick," said Carrie.

"It's making me hungry," said Slattery. There was a Sweet Something coffee mug on the counter filled with chocolate swizel sticks. The detective took two and began to crunch his way through them. "Peppermint," he said. "My favorite."

Carrie pointed to the display case. "They make coins, just like the ad said."

"But not the one we're looking for."

"The ad also said they did custom work."

The double doors swung open, and a muscular bald-headed man with a battered face appeared. He was wearing a chocolate-smeared apron.

"My name's Joe Torrini," he said. "Sally said you were cops."

"I'm a cop; she's an archaeologist. My name is Slattery; she's Dr. Norton."

"What can I do for you?"

Slattery took a photograph of the 1863 coin out of his jacket and handed it to the chocolate maker, who looked at it briefly and nodded.

"Sure. The gold Liberty. It was a while back. He brought in a reproduction coin and we made a laser die from it. It was a short order. Ten thousand units, as I recall. It was for a fund-raiser."

"Who brought in the reproduction coin?" Carrie asked.

"A guy named Ryan Trusell," said Torrini.

"I know that name," said Slattery.

"He's Henry Todd Lincoln's campaign manager," said Carrie. "Lincoln's fixer."

While Henry Todd Lincoln occupied a penthouse apartment at 740 Park Avenue, perhaps the most prestigious address in New York City, Ryan Trusell, his campaign manager, preferred the relative anonymity of the Dakota. It somehow seemed fitting that Trusell, renowned as a political ax man and backstabber, should live in a building best known for its association with the assassination of John Lennon and as the setting for *Rosemary's Baby*.

Carrie had seen an article in the paper about a plan to clean the exterior of the landmark building, but she doubted that it would ever happen. Half the cachet of the old relic was its long list of famous residents, but the other half was its blackened, slightly sinister look in what was now the ultramodern center of Manhattan. Beyond that, a cleaning would cost millions of dollars and would probably be structurally bad for the masonry.

Ryan Trusell occupied a subdivided four-room piece of what had once been Boris Karloff's much larger apartment on the sixth floor, overlooking Central Park. It had a living room, a dining room converted into an office, a bedroom and a kitchen. There was an awful lot of dark wood paneling, Home Depot crystal chandeliers and heavy Victorian furniture that was brought over from England by the container load and sold as "important antiques" to unwary culture-desperate customers like Trusell. There were doilies and dusty-looking Persian carpets everywhere, and bad paintings of horses and battles from forgotten wars on expensively papered walls. It could have been the home of somebody's dowager aunt.

Trusell looked like an undertaker. He greeted them at the door wearing a three-piece dark blue pinstripe, a Harvard Veritas silk tie and expensive-looking tasseled shoes. He wore round horn-rims balanced on a long nose that mimicked his overlong chin. The cheeks were a little sunken, his forehead arched up into thinning mouse-colored hair swept straight back in shiny, gelled perfection. The eyes behind the glasses were like lumps of coal, and when he smiled a greeting, it looked as though the slight movement of his thin lips would crack his entire face like a boiled egg.

He led them into the small living room and gestured toward a sofa upholstered in black and yellow stripes that might have suited Carrie's grandmother. He lowered himself into a tall-backed armchair upholstered in the same fabric, tenting his fingers like an old-fashioned schoolmaster surveying a roomful of students. Carrie suddenly realized the role he was playing: it was a combination of Basil Rathbone and Jeremy Brett doing Sherlock Holmes. When he spoke he even had a faintly British accent.

"I've already been through this once with the other homicide detectives. I did what I could. I told them everything I know," he said, and offered up his sour little smile for the second time. "I'm a little confused. Am I a witness or a suspect, or neither one?"

"Right now you're nothing at all," said Slattery.

"I see," said Trusell, who clearly didn't. Carrie could see that the position was making him uneasy. He was obviously a man who liked to know more than his companions. A gossiping spider in the center of his web; a man who used whispered confidences and secrets like a soldier used a gun.

"You ordered ten thousand chocolate coins from a place called Sweet Something in Brooklyn—is that right?" Slattery asked.

"Quite so." Trusell nodded, the smile flickering briefly.

"They were stamped with gold foil imitating a twenty-dollar gold piece from 1863," said Slattery.

"Right again," said Trusell.

"Why?"

"Why what?"

"That particular coin. That particular date."

"For no particular reason," answered Trusell.

"You just had one lying around?"

"No. Mr. Lincoln did. It was also the right size for the party favors I wanted."

"A fund-raising dinner."

"Yes." The plummy English accent was slipping a little bit. Trusell was getting irritated.

"For the mayoralty campaign."

"Yes. What else would Mr. Lincoln have to raise funds for?"

"Why a coin?"

"Because it's known as the Liberty piece, which was the theme for the dinner."

"Dinners need themes?" Slattery asked.

"Get to the point, Detective; what are you accusing me of?"

"During the last three months a number of homicides have occurred in Manhattan in which the victims had recently ingested your gold coins, foil and all. Your fund-raising dinner was fourteen weeks ago, two weeks before the first murder."

"And what does this have to do with me?"

"I have no idea. You were the one who ordered the coins."

"So?"

"It's an obvious connection."

"There are a dozen different explanations for the facts as you have presented them," said Trusell.

"Sure, and Eskimos have a hundred different words for 'snow,'" said Slattery. Carrie smiled but kept out of it. In the first place there was no such thing as Eskimos; in the second place there was no single Eskimo language; and in the third place, given the fact that Eskimo was a polysynthetic language, there were actually tens of thousands of words or word connections for "snow" in the dozen or more Inuit languages, but she didn't think that was the point Max was trying to make.

"Again, what's your point, Detective?" Trusell sighed.

"The coins originated with you. Whoever fed the coins to these people before they died felt they had some significance, just as you did."

"I still don't see what you're getting at," said Trusell.

"There are no coincidences in homicide. There are no mysteries like in an Agatha Christie story. There are only connections. It's a complicated form of connect the dots. You're the first dot."

"How exciting," quipped the campaign manager. "I've never been a dot before."

"How were the coins distributed?"

"I'll repeat what I told your colleagues. Every guest had one at his assigned dinner placement. There was also a large punch bowl filled with them at the entrance to the ballroom, and they were included in the gift bags everyone was given on the way out."

"How many were left over?"

"I wouldn't have the foggiest notion."

"Where would the leftovers have been taken?"

"If they weren't thrown into the garbage, they would probably have been taken to campaign headquarters."

"Where's that?

"The Graycliff."

Carrie nodded to herself. In the heart of Wall Street, the old McKim, Mead and White building had been a landmark New York City hotel for a hundred years, surviving the 9/11 disaster where other, much larger concerns such as the Regent Wall Street had failed. It had also been LinCorp's flagship piece of Manhattan real estate right from the start.

"The hotel?"

"Yes. The entire no-floor."

"No-floor?"

"It's an old-fashioned hotel. The thirteenth floor doesn't exist on the elevator buttons. It goes from twelve to fourteen. The thirteenth has several corporate suites and conference rooms. It's only accessible by a special key."

"So the coins would be there?"

"They might be. As I said, they may simply have been thrown in the garbage."

"I'll need to talk to Mr. Lincoln about this."

"He's a busy man."

"So am I. So was Jack the Ripper. I'm sure the future mayor would like to help out New York's Finest."

"I'm sure he would too," said Trusell, the smile flickering again. "But what would that have to do with you and your shy lady friend here?" he added. He glanced at Carrie. "You haven't said a word, dear."

Carrie frowned at his condescending use of the word "dear." She didn't think that kind of man still existed in the twenty-first century. "I was wondering about that picture on the end table," she said. The photograph was in an ornate pewter frame and appeared to be an old, faded daguerreotype of a bearded man in military uniform. "Civil War, isn't it?"

Trusell glanced at the picture. He turned back to Carrie and shrugged nonchalantly. "I have no idea. Most of the things in this apartment are heirlooms. Trusells have lived at the Dakota since it was built." He paused, then stood. "Now, if you'll excuse me, I have a great deal of work to do."

"Fine," said Slattery, levering his bulk upright. "I'd like that interview with your boss as soon as possible," he said. Carrie stood up as well.

"I'll see what I can do," murmured Trusell.

Carrie crossed to the picture and picked it up. Trusell watched her.

"A relative maybe?"

"As I said, I have no idea," answered the man. Carrie put the photograph down. She'd seen what she wanted to see. Trusell showed them out of the apartment, and they climbed into a waiting elevator.

"Little piss pot," grunted Slattery as they slid slowly downward.

"Powerful little piss pot," answered Carrie.

"What was that with the picture?" Slattery asked as the elevator bumped to a stop.

"I'm not sure," said Carrie.

"He was trying to sound casual, but you asking him caught the little twerp off guard. His Adam's apple was going a mile a minute there."

"I saw." Carrie nodded. They walked across the old-fashioned lobby and went out into the main interior courtyard.

"You recognize who it was?"

"No, but there were three stripes of gold lace on his uniform coat, which makes him a line officer, a captain of a ship in service. Shouldn't be too hard to find out who he is."

"You know a lot about that kind of thing?"

"You pick things up. The Civil War has always been a bit of a hobby with me."

"You think it's connected to our bog guy?"

"Could be."

They reached the main entrance archway, the place where John Lennon had been shot down. There was the sound of a cell phone ring tone: "Aquarius." Slattery dug in his pocket and pulled the phone out, scowling. "Stephen King was right about these damn things." He flipped it open and clapped it to his ear. "Slattery." He listened silently for a long time, then closed the phone and slipped it into his pocket.

"I'm really getting too old for this."

"What?" Carrie asked.

"That was Diddy," said the grizzled cop, referring to their young assistant. "He says the phones in the office are bugged. The whole place is. The computers too. He wants us to meet him at Nancy Whiskey's."

" 'Aquarius'?" Carrie grinned.

"It's a remix."

CHAPTER 15

Enoch Bale walked slowly through the maze of rooms that made up the second floor of Phineas T. Barnum's American Museum, the tip of his heavy walking stick lightly tapping at the varnished oak floor. It was midafternoon and rich sunlight came through the regularly spaced casements that looked out onto Broadway, illuminating broad wedges of dust motes hanging in the air, turning the light almost to a solid thing and making the bizarre exhibits on display look even more unreal in the strange, honey-colored light.

He'd seen places like this in London and in other European cities: cabinets of curiosities that called themselves museums but were really nothing more than naturalists' collections and the occasional physical aberration preserved. None of them were a match for Mr. Barnum's grotesquerie, five full stories of the strange, the out of place and the bizarre, all presented with the gaudy exuberance of a nightmarish traveling carnival.

Enoch Bale had come to the place less than an hour before, yet already he and the chattering horde of men, women and children swarming up the broad stairways and down the case-lined corridors and chambers had seen everything from waxworks of the famous Siamese Twins, whose numerous sons were now apparently fighting for the Confederacy, a one-hundred-and-twelve-pound rock crystal from Mexico, reproductions of the Czar's crown jewels, the full-sized state carriage of the late dowager Queen of England complete with waxwork footmen and six stuffed horses, a badly manufactured "Feejee Mermaid" that was clearly the skeleton of a large fish fused to the torso of an orangutan and the skull of a monkey, a headless mummy from Thebes and any number of animals, from a massive stuffed boa constrictor artfully wrapped around the slightly understuffed body of a snarling tiger to an armadillo and a perfectly ordinary-looking sheep. There were things in bottles floating in murky liquid, things hanging from the ceiling, things in glass cases and things tacked onto the walls. They all had one thing in common: they were dead, although apparently there were live animals in the basement, including several porpoises and a caged Bengal tiger.

"O day and night, but this is wondrous strange," said a pleasant voice beside him. The Vampyr turned. The man who'd spoken was somewhere in his early thirties, and well dressed. As he swept off his silk top hat he revealed hair thinning in

front and a little too long at the neck. He had a
long patrician nose, a wide mouth and a strong
chin. The eyes were dark and intelligent, with
small laugh wrinkles at the corners. He was carrying a copy of the museum's guidebook in his
left hand.

"All that lives must die, passing through nature
to eternity," replied the Vampyr.

His companion smiled, his face brightening.
"Ah! Good man! You know your *Hamlet*." He took
a step back, replaced his hat upon his head and
pushed his hand between the buttons of his ornate
brocade vest like some grand Napoleon. "Though
this be madness, yet there is method in't," he in-
toned dramatically.

"Certainly there's method for Mr. Barnum," answered the Vampyr. "At a quarter of a dollar a
time, I'd say he was doing rather well, all things
considered."

"Have you seen the child automaton?" the man
asked, taking off his topper once again. "The veri-
table Lilliputian Monarch?" He waved the guidebook airily.

"Indeed so," said Enoch Bale. "And the bust
of Leo the Tenth and the flag purported to be the
one George Washington carried across the Delaware River." He smiled. "I've always wondered
at the importance attached to that. As I recall,
there were only twenty-four casualties at the Battle of Trenton, not including the two men who
froze to death. Certainly not on the scale of a
Waterloo."

"A student of Shakespeare and of history, but not an American, I'd be bound," said the dark-haired man. "The crossing of the Delaware was the worm turning, the new leaf, the dawn of another day. It gave the failing Continental army the boost it needed to defeat the British once and for all. It is the essence of patriotism." The man paused, extending his right hand. It was gloved, as was the Vampyr's. "Booth, sir. Edwin Booth."

The Vampyr clicked his booted heels together and gave a short military bow. "Lord Enoch Bale," he said, "Conte de Parma and Viscount of Orange Nassau." The Vampyr had discovered that Americans seemed inordinately impressed by titles, even the most obscure ones.

"Italian?"

"Dutch," murmured the Vampyr.

"Bale. The only Bale I knew was Irish."

"Quite so," said the Vampyr. "On my father's side. He was one of the exiled Irish in Spain, which is where he met my mother, the dowager Contessa."

"I see," answered Booth, who obviously didn't. He paused and the Vampyr saw a slight shift in the man's eyes. "I thought I might have seen you before."

"Perhaps. I enjoy walking, especially in the evenings." The Vampyr knew precisely where the man had seen him before but said nothing. He hadn't noticed anything peculiar earlier in the day, but it was now clear that he had been followed.

"Your work doesn't interfere with outings like

this?" Booth asked, waving the guidebook around again.

"I have no work, unless you count dabbling in stocks on the exchange an occupation."

"Perhaps that's where I've seen you," said Booth.

"Perhaps," said Enoch Bale. "I'm usually there in the mornings."

"You have a seat on the exchange?"

Enoch Bale shook his head. "I trade through Murray and Brand," said the Vampyr.

"A currency man, then."

"Gold in particular," the Vampyr answered. The other man's eyes lit up.

"That settles it; you must meet my friend Jim."

"Jim?" the Vampyr asked.

" 'Diamond Jim' some call him. Jim Fisk. He works for Daniel Drew."

"I thought Drew was railroads," said the Vampyr.

"He is that," said Booth, his smile widening. "But then Daniel Drew is anything he wants to be."

"Like the young Mr. Gould," said Enoch Bale, watching Booth's expression closely. The other man's eyes hooded for an instant, but an instant later the friendly expression was back on his face.

"The wily Jew." Booth chuckled.

"Gould is Jewish?"

"No, he just acts like one." Booth laughed outright. "He loves money like a shylock—that's sure enough." The long-nosed man struck his pose again, pressed the top hat to his chest and cleared his throat. "Hath not a Jew eyes? hath not a Jew hands, organs, dimensions, senses, affections, passions? fed with the same food, hurt with the same weapons, subject to the same diseases, healed by the same means, warmed and cooled by the same winter and summer, as a Christian is? If you prick us, do we not bleed? if you tickle us, do we not laugh? if you poison us, do we not die? and if you wrong us, shall we not revenge? If we are like you in the rest, we will resemble you in that. If a Jew wrong a Christian, what is his humility? Revenge. If a Christian wrong a Jew, what should his sufferance be by Christian example? Why, revenge. The villainy you teach me, I will execute, and it shall go hard but I will better the instruction."

It was a long speech, perfectly and professionally recalled. A number of people in the crowd had paused to listen and applauded as he completed the quotation. He gave a deep, dramatic bow, then straightened. "Gould," he said, snapping his fingers. "Now I know where I've seen you. You were at Kit Burns's place last night. The prizefight between Sheehan and Maddersly."

"You have a good memory," said the Vampyr. "For faces and for Shakespeare."

"I had better," said Booth. "Memory's my profession."

"An actor?" Enoch Bale asked.

"Indeed," said Booth. "Actor, theater manager and occasionally a gambler."

"Did you bet on Maddersly last night?"

"Of course! Win or lose, you never bet against Jay Gould; it's liable to get you into trouble." There was a long pause, Booth staring thoughtfully at Enoch Bale, the Vampyr staring back, waiting. The laughter and clattering of feet was all around the two men, but the silence that stood between them was like the last sustained note on a piano, fading, but still heard long after the melody had gone. Locked in a vacuum, sealed in a bell jar like one of Barnum's oddities.

"I have an idea," said Booth at last. "If you've seen enough of this place, we can go across to the Astor House and have a drink. Meet a few of my friends from room eleven."

"Room eleven?"

Booth put a finger to his lips. "It's a secret."

The two men left the hotel, crossed Broadway catercorner and walked up to the pillared entrance of the Astor House. Nodding to the uniformed doorman and removing his hat once more, Booth led the Vampyr up the short set of steps and across the immense marble lobby to the sweeping twin staircases that led up to the mezzanine. Bypassing the staircases, Booth went down the carpeted, gaslit left-hand corridor to the end, rapped out a signal knock on the polished oak door and then stepped through it without waiting for an answer.

The Vampyr found himself in the large sitting room of a parlor suite. It was set out with two overstuffed leather sofas, comfortable chairs and walls half paneled in some rich burled wood with deep green moiré silk above. At one of a pair of tables sat two men playing cards, the second filled with bottles of all kinds and a silver tray of heavy-looking crystal glasses. There was a fireplace in the corner, the hearth cold, and a mantel above on which rested an ornately enameled ormolu clock that was ticking very loudly. The carpet on the floor appeared to be a genuine Aubusson, and a gas chandelier twinkled expensively from the ceiling. There were two doors leading to other rooms, one opened, revealing an office beyond with a white-haired man seated behind a heavy partner's desk.

The man looked up as Booth and the Vampyr entered. He was wearing a gold framed pince-nez he kept on a chain attached to the waistcoat of his suit, which he removed briefly to examine the two men. His face was narrow, the jaw heavy and the lips thin. Below his left eye there was a thin curving scar that went from his temple to the side of his nose as though he'd been slashed with a knife, giving his face a slightly lopsided, sinister appearance. He stared at the Vampyr for a moment, then replaced the pince-nez and returned to reading the sheaf of papers on his desk.

Booth introduced the card players. "The burly fellow with the bags under his eyes and the expensive duds is Mr. James Fisk, and the little fellow with the smooth cheeks and the caterpillar on his upper lip is my younger brother John, also a thespian, recently returned from a tour of *Richard the Third* that took him to Indiana and back." Fisk glanced up, eyes bleary and uninterested. Booth's brother nodded, then looked back at his cards. "The hardworking man in the office there is the inimitable Thurlow Weed, maker of kings and presidents, whisperer of secrets, father of any number of plots and mischiefs." Weed looked up again, the tiny spectacles dropping from his thin nose of their own accord. He stared at the Vampyr again but spoke to Booth. "Edwin, you are a buffoon, albeit a talented one, but a buffoon nevertheless."

"Perhaps," said Booth, bowing lightly. "But whatever the case, may I introduce Lord Enoch Bale, the Conte de Parma and Viscount of Orange Nassau."

"My, my," said the younger Booth disdainfully, eyes still on his cards. "Another just off the boat in search of adventure." He looked up, casting a long glance at the Vampyr. "You have the look of a soldier about you, sir. Who will you be fighting for, Mr. Lincoln's niggers or old Dixie?"

The Vampyr stared back at the young man without expression, only noticing the smooth, slightly flushed skin of his neck and the blazing, angry eyes. There was passion there, and more than a hint of madness.

"Lord Bale," said the older actor, "has an interest in gold."

There was a curious silence. Fisk laid his cards on the table facedown.

"Indeed," said Thurlow Weed, pushing back his

chair and standing up behind his desk. "A different kettle of fish, Edwin, a different kettle of fish altogether." The tall man with the scar beneath his eye came out from behind the desk and approached the Vampyr, hand extended in greeting.

CHAPTER 16

Echo Van Helsing had arrived back at the hotel very late. Returning to her rooms, she found a note from Matthew saying that he was traveling with his new cricket-playing friends to somewhere called East Hampton on Long Island, where they were to have a match. He expected to be gone for several days and hoped it would not be an inconvenience. Rather than being inconvenienced, Echo felt relieved that her little brother would not be caught up in the terrible events that seemed to be unfolding.

She undressed, put on her nightdress and fell into bed, exhausted and horrified by the thought that Draculiya might not simply be an aberration but the terrifying avatar of a whole race of beings. Her father had thought the Vampyr virtually ageless, created out of some hideous witch-borne incantation lost in time, an anomaly without ancestors or heirs, but according to Kate Warne he was merely one of many who had been preying on people like wolves on sheep and had been doing so for a very long time.

Sleep refused to come, tired as she was, so she got up and walked over to the windows. Her mind filled with images from the day she went to the window and stared out across the city's roof-tops and chimneypots. Somewhere out there was the creature that had murdered her father as well as his cohorts, the creatures that had savaged the young woman she'd seen on the cold slab in the Bellevue Hospital death house. Standing there, fa-tigue dragging at her like heavy weights upon her shoulders, she realized that even if she found Dra-culiya, the job would not be done.

Finding the creature would not be proof of what he and his fellow beings really were, and without that proof and its declaration from the very roof-tops she looked out upon, there would be no way to bring about the desperately necessary complete and absolute extermination of Draculiya and his wretched kind. Weeping softly, she returned to her bed and this time sleep finally came, dreamless, bleak and utterly dark.

She awoke, restless and uneasy, to the sound of rapping at her door. It was Kate, looking as though she'd slept the clock round, a cigar fuming between her teeth and carrying a heavy-looking portmanteau that she plumped down on the sofa in the outer parlor of the suite. She was wearing a plain black suit today, with a shiny black silk half-topper on her head. Clutching her nightdress around her, Echo stared blearily at the Pinkerton agent.

"I know it's not the thing to say in polite company, but you look like hell, Miss Van Helsing." Kate puffed broadly on the cigar, and the blur of smoke that began to fill the room made Echo feel slightly nauseous.

"What time is it?"

"Past noon. Time to be up and about. There's been another killing."

"What?"

"Your nasty friend's been at it again. Him or one of his friends. A man this time. Maddersly, the prizefighter. The Metropolitans found him in an alley by the Bernheimer Brewery. Or at least most of him. He'd been beheaded, rather gruesomely, and one of his wrists had been slashed down to the bone. They found the head spiked to an iron fence a block farther on."

"Dear God," whispered Echo.

"I doubt God had much to do with it." Kate snorted. "The coppers think it was for the money since his pockets were turned out, but it was our man all right." Kate dropped down on the parlor sofa and pulled open the portmanteau. She began pulling out articles of men's clothing. The clothes were all dark colored and plain except for a starched white shirt. "I've brought you another suit to wear and a fresh shirt. Get yourself dressed; I want you to meet a friend of mine."

"I have to bathe."

"Then hurry it up," said Kate. "I'll fetch us some lunch while you're doing it."

It was almost two o'clock before Kate Warne and Echo Van Helsing left Sturtevant House. Kate had hired a gig from a nearby livery stable, which was waiting by the curb. She tipped a coin to the waiting black boy holding the bridle under the watchful eye of one of the hotel doormen and climbed up into the driver's position. The boy offered his cupped hands to Echo, who stepped up into the passenger seat beside Kate. The Pinkerton agent twitched the reins and clucked to the dappled pony standing between the throughbraces. With barely a glance over her shoulder at the traffic moving up and down the avenue, she expertly turned the little carriage about and almost immediately had them heading south toward the lower part of the city.

Echo shifted, still not entirely comfortable in her trousers and feeling very exposed in the narrow seat. Thankfully her bust was small enough to be easily bound with a length of muslin Kate had brought for just that purpose, but Echo still felt sure that someone would soon see through the disguise. She said so to Kate, but her companion only laughed.

"Worried about being taken for a *femme Damnée*? This is New York, Miss Van Helsing. No one notices anything beyond their own noses unless it will make them a dollar, most would be too discomfited to mention it if they did notice and, most of all, Miss Van Helsing, nobody really gives a damn." She shook the reins to hurry the dapple gray a little more, then patted Echo on the shoulder. "It's the most important thing I've learned since joining the agency; people see what they want to see. Look like a young man about town, and that's exactly what the rest of the world will see."

They moved down Broadway, the small horse trotting energetically around slower vehicles. They eventually reached Union Place, a pretty square surrounded by a high wrought-iron fence and an enclosing fence with a large bronze statue of a man on horseback in the center. Someone had set the pole of an immense American flag in the figure's outstretched hand. The park was surrounded by hotels, grand-looking row houses and a variety of commercial establishments.

"George Washington," said Kate. "He's supposed to be pointing toward the enemy, but he's actually pointing at Wall Street. Wise fellow. He knew who the real enemy was."

They drove around the park and its parade ground and continued south along University Place, narrower than Broadway by far and lined with hotels, office blocks and manufactories of one kind or another. They finally came out on another, much larger square or parade ground, fixed at the near side with an enormous stone building, towered and turreted like a castle but with a looming arched front in the way of a cathedral, complete with a great window of stained glass. To Echo it looked very much like a much larger though somewhat less ornate version of King's College Cambridge, a place where she'd once gone with her father when they were in England.

Echo stared as Kate guided the gig around to the far side of the great gray building. "What is this place?" she asked.

"The University of New York," said Kate. She pulled back on the reins, drawing the gig to a halt. She swung down from her seat and tied the reins to an iron ring post by the curb. Scores of young men trotted along the sidewalk, all dressed identically in dark, serious suits and wearing top hats that served to make them all look like junior clerks in a countinghouse. They moved in groups, heads together, discussing matters of utmost importance as though the fate of the world might hang on each and every word.

Echo found herself smiling; it was the same the world over, the sight repeated in Oxford or Cambridge or Leiden or Paris, the same furrowed brows, the same restrained excitement, and all of it with an overwhelming sense of the dramatic as though the students were all being watched by some omnipotent professor, some Socrates or Plato who was observing them and judging their every pearllike opinion. It was also plain from looking at them that she and Kate were dressed almost identically.

The two women walked down a stretch of graveled pathway toward a pair of narrow doors just as they burst open and another chattering group

of students appeared. Kate and Echo stood aside
and let them pass, then went up the three short
steps and in through the doors.

Echo found herself in a dark foyer. A long,
gloomy corridor led off directly ahead, and there
was a narrow, winding iron stairway to their
right. Echo could hear the faint booming sounds
of laughter and running footsteps in the distance.
Kate headed up the iron stairway, with Echo on
her heels.

They climbed up several floors, then followed a
long passage flanked by closed doors and small
rooms to a second circular stairway even narrower
than the first. They climbed again and eventually
reached an empty stairwell fitted with a single
door. Slightly out of breath, Echo stood beside
Kate Warne as the Pinkerton detective knocked.
At first there was no answer. Kate knocked again.
The knock was followed by a long silence and
then the muffled sound of a man's voice.

> Once upon a midnight dreary, while I pondered,
>   weak and weary,
> Over many a quaint and curious volume of forgot-
>   ten lore,
> While I nodded, nearly napping, suddenly there
>   came a tapping,
> As of some one gently rapping, rapping at my
>   chamber door.
> " 'Tis some visitor," I muttered, "tapping at my
>   chamber door—
> Only this, and nothing more."

Kate smiled and cleared her throat, then spoke in response:

> Ah, distinctly I remember it was in the bleak December,
> And each separate dying ember wrought its ghost upon the floor.
> Eagerly I wished the morrow;—vainly I had sought to borrow
> From my books surcease of sorrow—sorrow for the lost Lenore—
> For the rare and radiant maiden whom the angels name Lenore—
> Nameless here for evermore.

An instant later there was the sound of a key turning in the lock and the door opened. Echo found herself looking at a very short man dressed entirely in black. He had stringy brown hair that reached to his shoulders and a narrow face that looked more like a skull with a thin layer of parchment stretched over it. The hair, oddly, had a streak of white in it two inches wide and only on the left side. A silk ribbon tie jerked and danced beneath a yellowed cardboard Pembroke collar and an Adam's apple that bobbed up and down like something alive. He looked to be in his early thirties.

The eyes in their deep sockets were a strange gray-blue color, and one shoulder twitched every few seconds as though he was shrugging something away. His long fingers were ink stained and twisted and turned as though they were beings apart and trying to escape from the young man's thin, skeletal wrists. Echo had seen saner-looking people in Dr. Seward's asylum at Carfax, that gruesome place where the insect-eating lunatic Renfield was imprisoned. Renfield, once Draculiya's companion.

"Katie!" said the man, grinning widely and making his face even more skull-like. "And a friend as well!"

"Percy Dunninger, meet Miss Echo Van Helsing. Echo, this is my particular friend Percy."

"Charmed," said the excruciatingly thin man. "Do come into my chambers."

Kate and Echo stepped into the room beyond the door, which Dunninger carefully locked behind them. The room was tall and octagonal, and any windows had long ago been blocked by the oak bookcases that stood around the walls. At one angle of the octagon there was a small stage, complete with curtains and a canvas backdrop painted with a bucolic country scene of hills and trees and grazing cows and sheep. It looked old.

Around the miniature stage there was a balustrade-like barrier that would have been at home in a courtroom. To the left, taking up another angle of the octagon, was a blackboard. In an alcove there was a single long table set out with half a dozen chairs and a small desk, and behind the table there was a narrow cot. A single, very ornate candelabra dangled on a chain from the ceiling, and eight identical gas jets flared in sconces on the walls around the room. High in one corner a large stuffed raven was perched on the moldings, staring down at them, its single visible glass eye like a glittering speck of shiny coal.

The rest of the room was filled with an impossible clutter of dusty junk that seemed to include everything from a gigantic bat modeled from sticks and paper that hung from the ceiling next to the candelabra to some sort of large steam-driven device of wheels and gears that thankfully appeared to be inert for the moment. Directly under the candelabra was a small, delicate-looking games table covered with a green cloth. In the middle of the cloth a silver tea service sat on a tray. Four plain chairs had been arranged around the table. Dunninger graciously pulled out a chair for Echo and then one for Kate before seating himself.

"How have you been keeping?" Kate asked.

"Quite well, quite well," said Dunninger, his smile fixed. "Never too old to learn, as Mr. Morse often told me."

"Mr. Morse?" Echo said.

"Samuel," offered Dunninger.

"The telegraph," explained Kate.

"I built it," said Dunninger.

Echo was confused. "Samuel Morse, the man who invented the telegraph? Morse code?"

"I built it," Dunninger repeated.

"But you just said—"

"Morse *invented* it, but he was no mechanic, I assure you," explained the strange-looking man. "I *built* it for him."

"You're an engineer?"

"A bit of everything," said Dunninger. "Ask Katie." He smiled. "Mixed paints for my friend Winslow, helped Mr. Draper with his photographic device, drilled the barrels for Mr. Colt's revolver, cut nibs for poor old Edgar Poe, may he rest in peace." At this Dunninger glanced up at the raven roosting on the corner molding. It squawked loudly, its beak jerking open, and began to speak in a sinister, scratching voice:

> Then this ebony bird beguiling my sad fancy into smiling,
> By the grave and stern decorum of the countenance it wore,
> "Though thy crest be shorn and shaven, thou," I said, "art sure no craven,
> Ghastly grim and ancient raven wandering from the Nightly shore—
> Tell me what thy lordly name is on the Night's Plutonian shore!"
> Quoth the raven "Nevermore."

Kate burst out laughing at the demonstration, but Echo just stared at the large black bird, awestruck and horrified. "How is this possible?" she whispered. "Surely the creature is dead!"

"As a coffin nail," said Dunninger. "The bird is a clockwork automata, of course. Squawks like that every twenty minutes or so until it winds down. A foolish trick I learned from Mr. Heller a few years back. Common enough among the quack spiritualists that seem to haunt some of New York's most esteemed parlors these days."

"Mr. Heller?"

"Robert Heller the magician. I was briefly his *engeneur*."

"Ingénieur? His engineer?"

"*Engeneur*. French word. He described the illusion he wished to create, and I provided the necessary technical expertise. Like this." He laid his hands flat out on the table an inch or two away from the silver tea set. Suddenly the tray and the tea set began to shake and rattle all by themselves, making a fearful clatter. High above them the perching raven began to cry mournfully, and a strange, otherworldly vapor rose up around the table. Finally the table itself began to rise and heave back and forth a few inches in the air. Then, as suddenly as it started, the strange incidents came to an abrupt stop. During the whole process, Dunninger's hands never moved off the table.

"The spirit vapor is actually a release of a vessel of carbon dioxide hidden within the table, based on the experiments of Thilorier some thirty years ago. The shaking is a clockwork mechanism similarly hidden within the table and operated by a switch close to my knee. The raven quoting Mr. Poe's poem is nothing more than simple ventriloquism."

"And the levitating table?" Echo asked, fascinated.

"The simplest of all." The thin man raised his arms and showed her the two long metal struts hidden within his sleeves. "The armatures fit into slots in the table's edge and support its weight easily. All simple tricks, easily explained."

"This is marvelous!" Echo laughed. "You should be on the stage!"

"I think not, Miss Van Helsing." He flushed. "I am something of a private man and no performer. The university is my life."

"You teach here?"

"I've been a student here for more than thirty years," the thin man answered.

"He means it," put in Kate. "He was born here."

Echo stared. "Born here?"

"There is some thought that my father was one of the convicts from the penitentiary at Sing Sing used for labor to build this place and that my mother was a housemaid," explained the strange-looking man. "I was a foundling." He smiled grimly. "Personally, I think my origins might have been a little more elevated."

"I'm sorry?" said Echo, not understanding.

"He means that his mother may well have been one of the university housemaids but his father was more likely one of the professors or one of the students." She grinned at Dunninger. "The other possibility, and more to the point, I think, is that a student was the father, and the mother was wife or daughter to one of the professors."

"An anonymous trust was established for my

upbringing and education," said Dunninger. "The trust was in the care of a certain professor of law who was in turn the protégé of a certain wealthy family in the city, the name of which is writ large on Wall Street and elsewhere in the business of much larger trusts." Dunninger cleared his throat. "Not that it matters. This building and the knowledge it contains have been mother and father enough for me."

Echo had no idea what Dunninger was talking about, but Kate seemed to. "What has Kate told you of my problem?" she asked, changing the subject away from Dunninger's supposed origins.

"Something to do with vampires, as I understand it."

"You believe in their existence, then?" Echo asked, surprised.

"Vampires are a myth," said the man without equivocation.

"Then how can you help me?"

Dunninger waved his hands around the room. "Once upon a time this was the meeting room of a secret society at the university called the Euclidians. Do you know who Euclid was?"

"A Greek mathematician and philosopher," answered Echo promptly, feeling slightly patronized.

"Indeed," nodded Dunninger, "but more importantly he was the man who first began to theorize in terms of logic. The society believed in the essential purity of logic as applied to all things in life, not just mathematics. I was one of the founding members. You might be surprised to know that

Mr. Poe was as well. Here at the university, in fact, we were often known simply as the Ravens, in his honor."

"What does this have to do with vampires?" Echo asked a little testily. "Especially when you say you don't believe in them."

"I said nothing of the sort, Miss Van Helsing. I merely said that the vampire was a myth."

"Isn't that the same thing?"

"What is a myth?" Dunninger responded.

Echo shrugged. "A legendary narrative. Usually of heroes."

"And generally a fact disguised as a fiction. A parable based on some element of truth, yes?"

"I suppose."

"And magic?"

"What of it?"

"A truth or a lie? A fiction or a fact?"

"Neither. Both. Religion, I suppose," answered Echo. Talking to the strange man was both irritating and exciting. She could almost see the seething mass of ideas exploding like flashes of brilliant lightning behind the death-mask face. He was hard to keep up with, but she'd had practice with her father.

"Religion indeed." Dunninger smiled. "And when is religion mistaken for magic?" He replied rhetorically. "When it is misunderstood. To send a message along a wire, to kill a man at a distance from a bullet that moves too fast for the eye to see, to catch lightning in a bottle like the venerable Mr. Franklin. Joan of Arc was burned at the stake for less than that. Galileo was branded a heretic and imprisoned for stating the obvious. For myth mistaken for magic, mistaken for fiction, mistaken for simple, foolish fear. The passage of time renders most magic or heresy no more than commonplace information."

"Do you believe in vampires?"

"I believe in their possibility," said Dunninger, "since I believe that all things are possible. I believe in the simple logic of their existence. Kate tells me that something like the mythological creature from the old tales is here in New York. Who am I to dispute her word? All is evidence, all is logic. Give me the facts and not the mythology, and we'll find your fiend."

"How?"

"Who has he killed, where has he killed and how often?"

"Prostitutes, beggars, down-and-outs. Two flower sellers, a snatcher, an in-and-out playing the sweep game, a boatman, a sally boy and last night a prizefighter. Mostly in the Fourth Ward. At least one that we know of, a prostitute found in a coal tip a few days ago, had her mouth sewn shut with a professional embalmer's stitch. In all, thirteen identical killings since Christmas." Echo glanced at Kate. She hadn't known there had been so many.

"Identical how?"

"Puncture wounds in the carotid artery," said Echo. "Disguised by tearing of the throat."

"Tearing?"

"Savage," said Kate Warne, a sour look on her face. "Like an animal. According to Dr. Sanger at Bellevue Hospital, there was a great deal of blood loss, but not from the major throat wound. The blood had been siphoned away earlier."

"Before?"

"Yes. He said that if he didn't know better he'd have thought the victims had been drained with an embalmer's cannula."

"Could that have happened?"

"Highly unlikely," answered Kate. "From what I understand, that sort of thing takes a great deal of time and equipment."

"Or a vampire's fangs," said Echo firmly. "It was my father's opinion that the Vampyr's eye-teeth are created much like those of a serpent."

"A hinged jaw and hollow fangs for the injection of venom?"

"Yes," said Echo. "It was also my father's opinion from his research that the Vampyr was capable of injecting some sort of laudanum-like secretion that calms the victim before the blood is drained."

"You seem to infer some vampire in particular," said Dunninger slowly, glancing at Kate Warne, who shrugged.

"I am," said Echo. "His name is Count Vladislaw Draculiya, supposedly a Prince of Walachia."

"You think he is in New York?"

"I know it. I followed him here after the death of my friend and of my father."

"Kate?"

"Echo's father was a scientist. A vampire

hunter, by all reports. And well known. He was murdered in London under mysterious circumstances. If Draculiya is a vampire, he is one of many."

"They would seem to be a breed of singular method and habit," said Dunninger. He smiled pleasantly and leaned back in his chair. He took out a small clay pipe and a box of Barber Diamonds, then lit up, puffing clouds of smoke toward the candelabra over their heads and staring at the ceiling as though for inspiration.

"He must be found, and soon, before there are any more tragedies like the death of my father," said Echo.

"Not to mention thirteen others," murmured Dunninger. "We mustn't forget them."

"But how do we find him?"

"Begin at the end and work our way back to the start, I should think," said Dunninger.

"Bit over my head," said Kate. "You'll have to explain."

"Logic, Katie, my dear. We use simple logic." The thin man with the skull-like face sat forward in his chair again, the pale blue eyes flashing with a mixture of madness and excitement. "Simple logic and the friends of Euclid. What could be better than that?"

There was a croaking screech from the raven sitting high above them.

"*Nevermore!*" said the dreadful bird.

CHAPTER 17

Diddy was waiting for Carrie and Slattery at a dimly lit table in the back of Nancy Whiskey's. It was late afternoon now, and the after-work crowd was straggling in. A pair of TVs was showing rugby games, the shuffleboard tables were doing business and AC/DC was pounding out "Safe in New York City" on half a dozen speakers spread around the pub, ringing off the brown tin ceiling as Max and Carrie came through the door. Diddy looked both nervous and excited. Before he had a chance to say anything, Max whistled up a waitress and ordered double orders of wings and rings and a pitcher of St. Pauli Girl.

The food and beer arrived. Max poured everyone tall glasses of the ice-cold beer, then bit into one of the onion rings. "Talk."

The noise level in the pub meant that they had to lean forward to hear one another, but the blaring of the televisions, the music and the cheering sections around the shuffleboard players also ensured a level of privacy.

"You might not notice it unless you worked around computers a lot, but right from the start I had a feeling. Little jumps and jerks in the programs, lags that shouldn't have been there. The ghost in the machine. You know what I mean?"

"No," said Max flatly. "I have no idea what you're talking about." He took another onion ring and dipped a chicken wing into the accompanying bowl of barbecue sauce. He chewed through the onion ring and started on the wing.

"Think of it in terms of the echo you used to get on old-fashioned phone taps," said Diddy.

Max sucked the meat off a wing and started on another. "Okay, now I'm with you."

"It was that kind of feeling. So I ran a few checks. Then I ran a few more. I found Spector CNE on all the computers in the office, and Net-Vizor as well."

"Which means?"

"Which means someone's monitoring and recording everything that we do on every computer in the office."

"Who?"

"I'm working on it," said Diddy. He tried one of the onion rings and took a tentative sip of beer.

"Anything else?"

"The phones."

"What about them?"

"They're being monitored. There's some kind of

CO/REMOBS activity on both the phone lines and the cable for the Internet."

"Say what?" Max asked.

"CO/REMOBS," said Diddy. "Central office remote observance. Somebody's actually tapped into the local switching computer at the phone company and is redirecting all the calls to some remote location, where the conversations are monitored or recorded or both."

"Take a lot of pull," said Max, chewing thoughtfully on another wing. Carrie gave up, took one off the plate and dipped it into the blue cheese dressing.

"Like LinCorp?"

"They own the cable company we're using for the Internet hookup," said Diddy.

"So they're watching us," said Max. He signaled to the waitress for another pitcher of St. Pauli Girl.

"Literally." Diddy nodded.

"Cameras?" asked Carrie.

"Everywhere," answered the young cop. "Wireless pinholes in every room."

"What kind of range are we talking about?" Max asked.

"With LinCorp's resources? Almost infinite. They could be watching us from Rangoon if they wanted to."

"Any way to find out?" Carrie asked, taking an onion ring.

"It would take time, and they'd probably be able to figure out what we were doing."

"The question," said Max, vacuuming up another wing, "is why they're doing it in the first place." He dropped the stripped bone into the bowl provided for the purpose and switched to onion rings for a while, thinking it through. "We find a mummy from the Civil War, and that gets everyone's gonads into a sheepshank?" He shook his head. "Doesn't make any sense."

"It's a multimillion-dollar project. We know what happened at the African Burial Ground."

"A park where they wanted a building," said Diddy.

"Maybe LinCorp's thinking the same thing."

"Too late for that," said Max, shaking his head. He batted crumbs off his tie with a paper napkin and went back to wings. "They would have snuffed this thing out by now. Bribed you maybe, shut you down for a day or two and brought in the backhoes for a bit of smoothing over. Who knows? But they could have done it."

"Maybe they're worried about the other guy," said Carrie.

"What other guy?" Slattery asked, licking sauce off his fingers.

"The brother other guy," said Diddy. "Mr. James Washington Stone."

"Now, there's a thought," said Slattery, leaning against the back of the chair. Stone was the Spike Lee of the documentary. His first film, *White Nigger*, done while he was getting his doctorate at Columbia and based on the O. J. Simpson trial, had put him in the spotlight, and a series of other critically acclaimed race-related films had kept him there. The year before, he'd won an Oscar for *Black Is a Country*, a biography of Amiri Baraka, the sixties' radical and beat poet once known by the name LeRoi Jones. On the strength of the Academy Award, he'd launched a mock campaign against Henry Todd Lincoln that had quickly morphed into a groundswell of support, and now the two men were in what was quickly becoming a dead heat.

"They're trying to bury this until after the election?" Carrie said. She picked up another onion ring and dipped it into the blue cheese.

"Bad pun." Diddy smiled.

"That's disgusting," said Max.

"A cover-up?" Carrie said.

"No, dipping an onion ring into blue cheese dressing."

Diddy tried the same thing. "Not bad." He nodded.

"You're both disgusting."

"But are we right?" Diddy asked.

"LinCorp covers up the body of the dead Civil War sailor because it obviously has something to do with the New York Draft Riots of 1863," said Carrie. "There's no doubt Stone would get a lot of publicity even without—" She paused.

"Without what?" Diddy asked.

"There's been a series of murders over the last three months," said Max. "All the bodies have had their lips glued shut and all of the bodies had recently eaten a chocolate coin in a gold foil wrapper. The coins were replicas of an 1863 Liberty gold piece."

"How many murders?"

"Eight."

"So there's already a cover-up," said Diddy. "A serial killer on the loose without the *New York Post* doing front-page headlines?"

"I think One Police Plaza is treading carefully. Lincoln is very pro-cop. If he's elected, there's going to be a lot more of New York's Finest on the beat. He's promised all the SWAT guys Hummers, among other things."

"It still doesn't explain why they bugged everything in the office," said Carrie. She headed toward the blue cheese dressing with one of the fat, crunchy onion rings, but a look from Max stopped her. She opted for a sprinkle of salt instead.

"They think we're going to find out something," said Max. "They want to find out about it before anyone else."

"What could we find?" Carrie asked. "The guy's been dead for a hundred and fifty years."

"The chocolate coins, remember?" Max answered. "There has to be a connection."

"A coincidence?" Diddy suggested.

Max gave the young cop a frosty glance. "No such thing." He blew out a long breath, leaned back and closed his eyes. "The body's found in the basement of a LinCorp property. The body definitely dates from 1863. The body is African-American. He was apparently a crew member on the *Monitor*. The body had an 1863 Liberty gold piece in his gut. Chocolate 1863 Liberty gold pieces were found in the stomach contents of eight present-day homicides. LinCorp obviously sees a connection or a threat, because they've got us bugged." He opened his eyes. "When's the election?"

"Two weeks," answered Diddy promptly. "July thirteenth, to be exact."

"When were the New York Draft Riots?" Max asked.

"July thirteenth," said Carrie. "To be exact."

"No coincidence," said Max. "This is really beginning to stink."

Then Carrie's cell phone twittered and everything changed.

CHAPTER 18

The Assassin's Club was located on Sixteenth
Street, just off Fifth Avenue, east of Union Park
and midway between the university on Washington Square and Madison Square Park. The building itself was a huge Italianate mansion in brick
built by Alexander Jackson Davis more than thirty
years previously for a stock trader who had bank-
rupted and then committed suicide after losing
everything in the British Railway bubble of 1846.
It was approached by a semicircular drive of
crushed stone, bringing visitors to a long, multi-
columned porch bracketed by a pair of soaring
towers topped with copper-sheathed cupolas. At
night gaslights lined the drive and brightly lit the
dramatic entrance.

Fu Sheng drove the rented hansom up the drive,
the iron-bound wheels crunching heavily on the
gravel. He pulled up the pair of matched black
horses in front of the looming building and
dropped down from his position above and be-

hind the carriage cab. He opened the door for his master and stood to one side as the Vampyr stepped down onto the ground.

Enoch Bale breathed deeply, taking in the heavy, sweet scent of the lilac tree planted in the center of the half-moon lawn in front of the mansion. He was dressed formally in a black tailcoat covered by a European-style cloak that fell to his ankles. Beneath the tailcoat he wore a white silk waistcoat with pearl buttons and a white silk shirt with onyx studs. At his throat he wore a cream-colored stock, and his military-style trousers had the appropriate lack of side-seam ribbons and creases. His boots were black and his gloves were white. On his head was a silk top hat. He'd left his stick behind; the brass-headed knobkerrie would have been out of place in such an environment.

"The lair of the wolf," said the Vampyr, glancing up at the large house.

"Yes, master," said Fu Sheng uneasily. "A dangerous place."

"Perhaps," the Vampyr answered with a faint smile. "But we've been to dangerous places before, haven't we?"

"Yes, master, that is the truth." Fu Sheng nodded. Instinctively his hand fell to his waist and touched the butt of the Pocket Police revolver jammed into his belt and hidden by the fall of his short jacket.

"Is there anything more about this Adam Worth?" the Vampyr asked.

"He is nearby, master; that is all I know."

The Vampyr coughed harshly, dragging out a handkerchief from the pocket of his tailcoat. He patted his lips and the square of silk came away spotted with blood.

"The flux, master?" Fu Sheng asked, concern in his voice. "So soon."

"I'm afraid so," said Enoch Bale. It was the only disease common to the Vampyr breed: *verruca necrogenica*, or "corpse disease," sometimes known as gravediggers sickness or anatomists consumption, an ancient form of tuberculosis that Enoch Bale knew would eventually put him into a deep, dreamless sleep that could last for decades before it ran its course. It was his only weakness.

"If the sickness worsens, I will take care of everything," said the Vampyr's Oriental companion. "You can depend on me, master. I've already found the medicines. I will not fail you."

"You are a good friend, Fu Sheng."

"Shall I wait?"

"No. See if you can find out anything more of Adam Worth. Anything at all. I'll find my own way home. It's not far."

"Yes, master." The Chinaman nodded. He swung himself back up into the driver's seat of the hansom, flicked the reins and disappeared down the curving drive and out onto Fifth Avenue. The Vampyr stood quietly for a moment, enjoying the simple pleasure of the night, then climbed the front steps and went forward to the large oak and glass doors.

The doors swung wide even before he had a

chance to knock. He was greeted by two black footmen dressed in satin uniforms and wearing old-fashioned wigs in the manner of the French court a hundred years past. One took his cape while the other took his hat and gloves. They bowed, then moved off.

The Vampyr examined his surroundings. The lobby was an immense circle with an upper gallery and a sweeping spiral staircase. A massive crystal chandelier hung from a white-domed ceiling high overhead. The huge cascading fall of leaded glass was lit from within by at least a dozen mantled jets of quietly hissing gas. The overall impression was of an ostentatious display of luxury for its own sake. Enoch Bale's attention was taken by the floor beneath his feet. It was made up of marble tiles in a Greek motif, three horrific women's heads, hair made up of writhing snakes, orbiting a male face set into an idealized sunburst. Everything was done in reds and blues and gold.

A man appeared from a doorway to Bale's left, dressed almost identically to the Vampyr except that instead of a folded silk stock he wore a black cravat, loosely tied. It was Gould.

"You must be Lord Bale, Weed's new acquaintance. Welcome. I'm Jason Gould. My friends call me Jay." He noticed his visitor's interest in the ornate flooring. "The previous owners had a classical bent," said the gaunt, dark-haired man with the piercing eyes. "The three Furies circling their sworn enemy, Helios, the Sun."

"The Eumenides." Enoch Bale nodded. "The female personification of all the forms of vengeance"—he pointed them out one by one— "Alecto, the Unceasing, Megeara, the Grudging, and Tisphone, Avenging Murder, the most powerful of the three. Hair made up of serpents like the Gorgon, with the wings of a bat and the body of a dog."

Gould let out a short, barking laugh. "You sound as though you know them personally," he said.

The Vampyr shrugged. "I've run into them on occasion."

"Well, forget about them for the moment. Come and join the party." Gould gestured toward the doorway he had just come through. He stepped forward and took Bale by the elbow, leading him. For an instant the Vampyr tasted the faint waft of fading bergamot and wormwood once more. He hesitated briefly, and Gould turned and stared.

"A problem?" Gould said.

"Not really," said the Vampyr. "It seems strange; you act as though you know me."

"Don't I?" said Gould. "I saw you at Kit Burns's place last night. You seemed interested in poor old Maddersly, my late prizefighting friend."

"Late?"

"Someone blew him down after the fight in a Kraut Town alley." Gould stared at Bale. "Cut his throat with an ax—that's what the Metropolitans say. Almost carved one of his mitts off at the wrist as well." Gould's eye glittered fiercely for an instant, then dimmed. "I'd like to meet the man who could do that. Yes, I would."

"And if you did?" the Vampyr prompted.

Gould paused just at the door to the main salon. "We'd have to see, your grace, we'd have to see." The pale young man smiled coldly at Bale, then threw open the door. "But for now, let me introduce you to my friends."

The main salon of the house was as imposing as the lobby. The room was very large, with tall windows on two sides, each window covered by a pair of thick velvet curtains in deep blue fringed with gold. The oak floor was almost entirely covered with an enormous French Savonnerie carpet with an intricate design of lattices and cartouches interspersed with dozens of fantastic flower and plant motifs all done in pale blues and grays and greens, the silk wallpaper repeating the same designs in various shades of red. The walls were hung with large paintings, mostly hunting scenes or depictions of great battles, one or two of which, ironically, the Vampyr saw, he had fought in once upon a time. The ceiling was framed by gilded plaster moldings, and the ceiling itself was coffered in rich, exotic woods. Half a dozen gas chandeliers almost as large as the one in the lobby lit the scene brightly. More of the bewigged and uniformed black servants wandered about carrying trays of food and drink. In the far corner of the room, six black men in white tailcoats and trousers played light airs on stringed instruments. It sounded like Purcell.

"The design of the room is based on Crockford's in London," said Gould proudly. "You know it, I'm sure."

"I've been there once or twice." Enoch Bale nodded. He wondered whether Gould knew that William Crockford, the club's owner, had once been a fishmonger and a small-time bookmaker and swindler.

In most other houses, a salon like this one would have been filled with rich furniture: comfortable chairs and couches, ornate tables and place settings. Here, however, the room was furnished as a gambling club of the first water. Standing in the doorway with Gould, the Vampyr could see virtually every possible game of chance being played. There were two faro tables in operation, several large tables offering ongoing games of poker, pontoon and piquet, a high-sided hazard table with at least a score of spectators cheering on the dice thrower, and even a table with a French roulette wheel.

"The Devil's game," commented Gould.

"I presume you refer to the fact that the numbers on the board combine to make the number of the Beast," replied Bale.

"You've played before, then?" Gould asked.

"I rarely play games which I cannot win, Mr. Gould," the Vampyr answered. There were at least a hundred people in the room, most of the men dressed as he was in formal evening attire, although some were dressed in military attire. The women were all beautiful, extremely well dressed in the latest fashions from the Continent, and all seemed quite young. The Vampyr quickly observed one other thing and commented on it. "I see no plaques or tokens for the games," he said.

"We don't use them," said Gould. "Only specie. Twenty-dollar gold pieces, to be exact. Double eagles. The eagle has become the club's symbol."

"A gentleman's tailor might not approve," answered Bale. "A lot of coins to carry around."

"We provide them," said Gould. "No one plays here without a letter of credit from his bank or a reference from one of the members."

The two men moved through the room, pausing here and there to watch the play for a few moments before moving on. Gould introduced the Vampyr to a number of men, mostly traders on the exchange or important bankers. There were a few businessmen, including A. T. Stewart, who owned the huge "Marble Palace" Department store on Broadway, Moses Taylor, the sugar importer and Abiel Low, a leading figure in the China trade.

"We call them the Pine Street Boys," said Gould quietly. "They made all their money from King Cotton, and they want to keep it. They had their way, the capital of the United States would be in Mobile or New Orleans, not Washington."

"They support slavery, then?"

"They support money, my friend. Slavery is incidental. Black, white, Chinee, Jew or Mohammedan, we're all slave to it, for money is wealth, wealth is power and power is all. Only life and death are free, which is why they both come so cheap."

"An odd philosophy," said Bale.

"It's stood me in good stead," said Gould. "The war, for instance—everyone said it would be the death of this city. Without cotton to sell, what have we got?" He laughed. "Guns, bombs, bullets, boats, iron, coal, that's what, and plenty of cotton besides, smuggled to us so we can make uniforms for Lincoln's army to get all covered with blood so they'll buy some more. Believe me, your lordship, war's good for business no matter who wins it."

"Wars end," said the Vampyr.

"Then we'll just start another one," said Gould, the glitter in his eye again. "Wars are dependable, and one way or another the world wouldn't be what it is without them."

The Vampyr shrugged; he hadn't come here to get into political or philosophical discussions about either war or slavery; he'd seen enough of both in his time. Two things that the thin, dark man had said were true, however: wars never really ended and slavery came in every color of the rainbow.

"The women are very young," the Vampyr commented. So far he'd been introduced to none of them.

"That's because none of them are wives," laughed Gould. "This is a gentleman's club, my lord; married women are not allowed through the doors. The women here are as much for decora-

tion as the drapery." He paused for a moment.
"Just like the little Sambos in their wigs, if your
tastes lean in that direction," he added. "Do your
tastes lean in that direction, my lord?"

"My tastes are otherwise," answered Bale, "and
are entirely my own business."

"No offense, my lord, I hope," said Gould
stiffly. "I don't mean to pry."

"No offense, Mr. Gould, I assure you." The
Vampyr smiled.

Gould plucked a thin flute of champagne off the
tray of a passing servant and offered it to Bale.

The Vampyr declined. "Too early for me," he
said. "I don't drink until much later." He smiled
pleasantly at his host. "It helps me to sleep."

"You have trouble sleeping, my lord?" Gould
asked.

"I am something of a night person, I must
admit," the Vampyr answered. "Not greatly sociable, I'm afraid." Bale was becoming tired of the
man's attentions and his intrusive prattle.

"Then I should feel honored that you came at
all," said Gould. They'd reached the hazard table
and paused again.

"This isn't really hazard," said Bale as he saw
how the game was being played. "The main is
always seven." The shooter at the table was an
immensely fat man who huffed and puffed as he
played, flinging the ivory cubes down the table to
the back of the pit as though he was angry at
them. There were three or four stacks of bright

gold coins on the felt of the table in front of him and more scattered on the betting lines around the table. At least a dozen men were wagering along with the fat man and calling out their encouragement.

A woman stood beside him wearing a pinch-waisted low-cut gown in dark red that matched her auburn hair. Her skin was as white as milk, and when she bent to blow on the dice in the man's pudgy hand, the Vampyr could plainly see the delicate structure of the vertebrae in her neck.

"It's called *crapaud*, or craps," said Gould. "French. A nigger's game from New Orleans. Would you like to play?"

"No, thank you," said the Vampyr. He suddenly felt faint, and the taste of ashes rose in the back of his throat. He'd come to this place hoping to find a nest of Damphyr and instead he'd just felt the dark presence of something much more powerful. Regaining his equilibrium, he looked around, but the taste in his throat and the deep, shaded presence he'd felt for a brief instant were gone. One of the Nine here, in this garish place? It didn't seem possible, but the tugging nausea that wrenched at him was unmistakable. There was another of his kind nearby, not in this room, perhaps, but very close.

"Perhaps I'll have that drink now," he said. Gould nodded and turned away to find a servant. The Vampyr lowered himself carefully into a plush chair set by the wall, tasting blood in his mouth. He took out his handkerchief and held it to his lips. There was a sudden roar from the hazard table.

"Snake eyes!" The fat man groaned.

CHAPTER 19

The commuter aircraft slid downward through the crosswind like a wounded duck. Carrie glanced nervously out the window. A few thousand feet below her, the long, sausage-shaped bodies of dark water pointed like a gigantic splayed handprint toward the more distant blue of Lake Ontario. No wonder they call them the Finger Lakes, she thought. Rain was beginning to spatter against the oval window. The weather outside didn't look good.

Beside her Max Slattery was gripping the edges of his seat, white-knuckled. The Jetstream turboprop was designed to transport nineteen passengers in relative comfort, but they hadn't figured on carrying large, terrified New York police detectives like Max. Much more turbulence and Carrie was sure he'd rip the seat rests out with his bare hands.

"So," he said, sounding as casual as a man could through tightly clenched teeth. "Tell me again about how the Russian symphony conductor from Detroit with the unpronounceable name and his drug addict daughter fit into all of this." They hit an air pocket. The engines screamed for a second and the small airplane dropped like a brick. Max squeezed his eyes shut and a long bead of sweat emerged from his receding hairline and headed south. Carrie started talking as quickly as she could, hoping to distract Max from either a heart attack or a screaming anxiety surge.

"The drug addict's name was Nina Gabrilowitsch. She overdosed on barbiturates in LA in 1966. It was probably intentional. She was the daughter of Ossip Gabrilowitsch."

"The Detroit Symphony conductor."

"Right. Anyway, her mother was Clara Clemens."

"Mark Twain's daughter," Max ground out.

"One of several, but the only one to live long enough to marry and have children. Her mother, Olivia Clemens, was a Langdon from Elmira, and the Langdons' neighbor was Thomas Beecher, the brother of Harriet Beecher Stowe, the woman who wrote *Uncle Tom's Cabin*."

"I think I'm going to be sick," muttered Max. They were dropping down noisily and the rain was steady now, coming in gray sheets.

"Please don't," said Carrie. "Anyway, Jervis Langdon, Olivia's father, was a firm abolitionist and supporter of the Underground Railroad—literally, since he was part owner of the actual railroad that ran through Elmira. That's the connection with Barnabus Coffin, our murdered bog man. He was a runaway slave who was helped to escape by a friend of Jervis Langdon's named John W. Jones. Jones, as well as being part of the Underground Railroad, was an ex-slave who made his living by burying the dead Confederate soldiers from the Elmira prisoner-of-war camp. He was paid two dollars a corpse and apparently got quite wealthy by the standards of the day. They ran almost thirteen thousand prisoners through the camp, and close to three thousand died. Jones buried all of them. Whole lot of digging going on."

"Ha-ha. Get to the point." Max's eyes remained resolutely shut.

"I'm getting there. Like I said, Jones and our bog body knew each other, and they also knew the Arnots, who were vaguely related to both the Langdons and the Beechers. The Arnots were also involved in the smuggling of runaways both before and during the war."

"And all of this concerns us how?"

"It turns out that Katherine Arnot, Olivia Langdon Clemens's cousin, was the maiden name of Kate Warne, the famous Pinkerton agent and Civil War spy who once saved Lincoln's life by uncovering an assassination conspiracy."

"I'm getting dizzy."

"Almost done. When Will Croaker phoned me from the Museum of Natural History, it was to tell me that he'd recovered a letter folded twice and hidden in Barnabus Coffin's shoe. The same lack of oxidization that preserved the body preserved the letter almost intact. The letter was from John Jones, the grave-digging ex-slave, acknowledging receipt of Kate Warne's journal and promising to pass it on to Olivia, Kate's cousin. This was before she'd married Mark Twain.

"Diddy did some research on the New York Public Library computers and found a vague reference to the journal in a collection of uncataloged documents and Mark Twain ephemera from the Samuel Clemens estate via the drug-addict granddaughter, Nina Gabrilowitsch. Apparently she left a trunk full of stuff behind that wound up in the hands of a retired researcher from the Center for Mark Twain Studies at Elmira College, a woman named Betsy Jones Arnot, who now lives in a little village called Erin a few miles out of town."

There was a heavy thumping sound from directly beneath them and Max froze. "Aw, jeez, we're all going to die," he moaned.

"No, we're not," said Carrie. "We just landed."

Max finally opened his eyes again.

The Elmira Corning Airport was a medium-sized two-runway regional facility with a low-ceilinged generically modern interior that was trying very hard to look sophisticated. They stopped for a late breakfast in the airport's DC2 restaurant, a bleakly trendy space with an old radial engine complete with wooden propeller bolted to the wall and a wood and aluminum bar that was meant to look like the trailing edge of a wing. The airplane-parts motif inspired twenty minutes of grumbling from Max, and after picking at his food and getting a couple of giant-sized coffees to go, he led the way to the Alamo counter, where they rented a full-size Pontiac Grand Prix that the grizzled cop insisted on driving even though he was clearly still in a state of semishock after the flight from New Jersey.

"We should have driven here in the first place," he said, climbing behind the wheel. He started the engine, flipped on the wipers against the steady drizzle and buckled up.

"In this weather it would have taken us five or six hours," said Carrie, settling in beside him.

"It was a two-hour drive to Trenton and a ninety-minute flight, so what's the difference?" grumbled the cop as he wheeled the car out of the parking lot. "Why couldn't you have picked an airline that flew out of Teterboro or Newark or somewhere halfway civilized? New Haven, even."

"It was short notice." Carrie laughed.

"Tell that to my cardiologist," said Max. "You can fly back if you want to; I'm driving."

They left the airport complex and headed out onto the Southern Tier Expressway, following Interstate 86 into the rolling hills of northeastern New York's Finger Lakes District. Bypassing the city of Elmira entirely, they took the 223 exit and continued east, following Newton Creek and the signs according to the instructions Betsy Jones Arnot had given Carrie on the telephone.

"There's the Old Scotchtown Cemetery," said Carrie, pointing to a scattering of stones among the trees behind a low iron fence on their right.

"If we go past the trailer park we've gone too far." She spotted another sign. "Fairview Road, that's it. Turn right."

Max did as he was told. On their left a pine- and cedar-shrouded hill rose steeply, while on their right was the sloping bottomland of a little valley that led down to the town of Erin itself, no more than a church steeple and a huddle of build- ings at a crossroads a mile or so away, barely visible through the gloomy drizzle.

"*Sleepy Hollow* time," said Max irritably as he guided the big car down the narrow strip of road. There was another small creek running beside them, the banks of the little stream fringed with cattails.

"*Sleepy Hollow's* on the Hudson," said Carrie. "This is more like *Deliverance* or *The Village*."

"That piece of crap," said Max. "Blind people running around through the woods, and monsters with bunches of twigs strapped to their backs run- ning after them. Stupid."

"That was *Scary Movie 4*."

"Equally dumb."

"Agreed." She saw the sign for Wheaton Road and Langdon Hill. "Turn right here. Last house at the top, just before another crossroads. The mail- box says Harvest Home."

"Funny name," commented Max.

"It's a pagan fertility rite," said Carrie. "Human sacrifices for good crops, that kind of thing."

"Right," said Max. "You're on a roll, Trixie. Mummies in the basement, lips sewn shut, slit throats, serial killers past and present, and now we're doing a Stephen King story. What's next?"

The house, when they found it, was refreshingly ordinary: a straightforward, simple Cape Cod in a pasturelike meadow at the end of a short driveway, looking lonely in the steady rain. There were window boxes planted with pansies. A burgundy Ford Focus hatchback with a mismatched hood was parked in front of a carport along with a boat covered in a blue plastic tarp. A set of yellow wooden ducks with most of the paint peeled off marched across the front lawn.

"Very sinister," said Carrie. Max pulled up behind the Focus. They climbed out of the rental and ran toward the front door. It opened before they reached the house, and a small black woman in jeans, a woolly cardigan and sneakers ushered them inside and out of the rain. She had permed, iron gray hair, intelligent brown eyes behind a pair of round steel-framed glasses and a smile that revealed one old-fashioned gold-capped incisor. The entire house smelled like fresh coffee and Toll House cookies. Max took a deep breath and smiled broadly.

"You must be Hansel and Gretel," said the old woman. "Come on inside."

The house was small and simply laid out. A small entrance hall led to a back kitchen and a bathroom. There was a single bedroom on the right and a living room and dining room on the left, separated by a fieldstone fireplace built against the side wall. A banked fire burned warmly in the big open hearth. Coffee things and a plate piled high with cookies sat on a small table in front of the fire. It reminded Carrie of the fireside set from an old bass-fishing show she remembered watching as a child. Except for the dining room, the walls were lined with handmade pine shelves crammed with books. A plain desk in front of the window in the living room held a flat screen computer monitor. Unless it was lurking in the bedroom, there was no television visible anywhere in the house.

The elderly woman sat them down in comfortable upholstered chairs in front of the fire, poured coffee and offered cookies. Carrie took the coffee and declined the cookies for the moment. Max took both.

"It's an awful story when you think about it," said Betsy Arnot, sipping her coffee. "Especially when you consider that it's a fairy tale for children. Impoverished father is convinced to abandon his children by their heartless mother. The children run into a cannibal witch who fattens up the boy and enslaves the girl. The girl burns the witch alive in her own oven and the children return home to find that their mother has died in the meantime. No moral, no lesson learned; just a thoroughly unpleasant story that would scare the hell out of most kids." She shook her head. "They ban Harry Potter and Huck Finn, but you never hear people raise a peep about Hansel and Gretel." She glanced at Max. "You like the cookies?"

"Wonderful." He nodded, reaching for another one.

"I thought I'd bake a batch to catch you off guard," she grinned. "Make me look a little less like the wicked witch."

"I thought you were retired," said Carrie with a smile.

"Six of one, half a dozen of the other," said the old woman. "Like most things, it's all a matter of perception." She paused for a moment. "Like the letter you found," she added. "Did you bring a copy?"

Carrie reached into her bag and took out the digitized scan Will Croaker had made for her at the museum. It was twice the size of the small, folded original, and the museum technicians had enhanced the image to make it more readable. She handed it across to Betsy Arnot. The old woman took it and tipped her glasses up onto her forehead. She examined the scan carefully, then nodded.

"That's Johnny Jones's handwriting," she said. "Neat and precise, just like everything else he did. He could dig a grave by eye perfectly, you know, six by three by six, every time, each one spaced exactly the same distance from the one next to it. The records he kept were so precise that the U.S. government declared Woodlawn in Elmira a national cemetery, just like the one in Arlington. Not bad for a cotton-chopper slave from Leesburg, Virginia."

"I'm still not exactly sure what the relationship was between Jones and Kate Warne and why she'd entrust her secret journal to his care," said Carrie.

"They were neighbors. My great-great-grandfather worked for the Arnots when he first came up from the plantation in Leesburg in 1844. He share-cropped a piece of land owned by them, which he eventually bought. He and Kate were both in their mid-twenties then, Kate a little younger than he was. They became good friends and stayed in touch even when Kate left for Chicago with her new husband. Then her husband died and she went off to work for Allan Pinkerton." The old woman paused. "How much do you know about Kate?"

Carrie shrugged. "Not a lot. She was a widow. She was the first female private detective. She was instrumental in saving Lincoln's life. As far as I can tell, there isn't much more than that on the record."

"She wanted it that way," said Betsy Arnot. "Kate was a very private woman. That's part of the reason she kept her journal secret. There was a rumor for years that she was a lesbian, since she preferred to wear men's clothes and she was quite plain, but the truth is she was Allan Pinkerton's mistress right up until the day she died. She's buried next to him in the Pinkerton family grave-yard."

"I still can't see what any of this has to do with our bog body," said Max.

"My ancestor didn't just record the names of Confederates he buried," said Betsy Arnot. "He also recorded the names of slaves he helped on the Underground Railroad. One of them was Barnabus Coffin. Coffin had worked the Mississippi paddle wheelers as a slave; my great-great-grandfather suggested that he join the Union navy, which he did. That's how he wound up on the USS *Monitor*."

Max frowned. "I'm more interested in how he wound up in a sewer on Minetta Lane in Manhattan with his throat slit and a gold coin stuffed down his gullet."

"And how Kate Warne got involved with him," added Carrie.

The old woman stood up and went to her desk under the front window. Outside it was still raining, the downpour drumming comfortably on the roof of the little hilltop bungalow. Betsy Arnot took a key out of the pocket of her jeans and opened one of the desk drawers. She carefully removed a bound volume in an archival plastic sleeve and brought it back to the table. She eased the book out of the sleeve. It appeared to be covered in some sort of soft leather binding.

"Deerskin," said Betsy. "Fancy bookbinding was a hobby of my great-great-grandfather's. The diary was a Christmas gift from him to Kate." She eased the thick volume open. Carrie bent forward, examining it without touching the pages. It was written in faded sepia-colored ink. Block-printed neatly, an unreadable chaos of letters and numbers.

"Code," said Carrie.

"Pinkerton railroad cipher," said Betsy. "The agents used it for security when they sent telegrams to each other."

"Can you read it?" Carrie asked.

"Yes," said the old woman. "I translated it years ago."

"Well?" said Max. He bit into another Toll House cookie.

Betsy Arnot smiled, her gold tooth gleaming in the dancing firelight.

"What do you know about vampires?"

CHAPTER 20

"Of course it's the Chinaman," said Percy Dunninger, squeezed in between the two women on the padded seat of the gig. They were clattering south down the gaslit length of Broadway, threading their way through the thinning evening traffic that moved up and down the broad avenue.

The lanky scholar had sat in the strange octagonal room at the university for hours listening to everything Echo Van Helsing knew about the man called Count Draculiya, occasionally prodding for details and twice leaping up to make the two women tea.

In the end he'd gone to his cot in the corner and laid himself down for the better part of an hour, going into what he described as a "logic trance." Her father had the same habit, although he'd referred to it as "resting his eyes." Based on the faint snores Echo heard, it sounded more like a nap. Eventually Dunninger had risen, insisting that it was imperative that they head down into the city on the instant.

They crossed Spring Street, swerving to avoid an upset cart of nail barrels unloading at a dry goods store on the corner, then continued on past the opulent Saint Nicholas Hotel on the right, and Minstrel Hall on the left. "The last duel with swords was fought at the Saint Nicholas," commented Dunninger mildly, pointing out the building. "It's the headquarters of the New York Chess Society as well. Odd juxtaposition of facts, don't you think?"

"How can you be sure?" Echo asked.

"About the duel or the chess society?"

"About the Chinaman." Echo sighed.

"Ah yes, the Chinaman," said the scarecrowlike man, nodding, his Adam's apple bobbing. "Well, that's simple enough, really. Just logic. You told me this Dracula or whatever you call him is wealthy, that he carries about his fortune in jewels, then sells them to establish himself. You also know he banks at Irving's, probably invests in the exchange and is a murderer. None of those things is particularly uncommon in this city. Many here are wealthy, many bank at Irving's, even more trade on the exchange and there are enough murders in this place to satisfy the needs of a dozen cities. There is nothing you see that is . . . particular about your information. Hence the Chinaman."

"Hence how?" Echo asked as they rode past a vacant lot. The waste ground was lit with torches, and somebody was giving a speech in a loud voice as he stood on a makeshift stage. A child in an ornate green uniform was beating a bass drum loudly. A large banner said STOP THE DRAFT. The speechmaker sounded angry.

"Turn left!" shouted Dunninger, plucking at the sleeve of Kate's jacket. She swerved in front of an omnibus rattling in its rails up Broadway, causing the team of horses pulling it to rear and bolt. The gig barged into the side street, passing into the shadow of the enormous tabernacle building on the corner. In an instant the bright lights of Broadway disappeared and quickly a stench arose that was almost overpowering: rot of every kind, human filth, animal waste and flesh, grease smoke from several tanneries, the brewery breath of sour hops, all mixed with the dry taste of ashes in the mouth and stinging cinders in the eyes.

"Dear God," whispered Echo. "Have we stepped into some sort of Hell?"

"Not far from it, I think." Kate laughed, slowing the pony and picking her way more carefully through the dark. "Welcome to the Sixth Ward!"

In the gloom Echo could see every kind of decay—the bloated corpse of a ravaged cow, a group of feral swine tugging at its leathery remains while rats swarmed madly under its curving ribs, equally feral and vicious dogs leaping at the rats and from everywhere above the loom of sagging buildings, mostly wood, barely painted if at all, most terribly tumbledown, doors gaping, windows roughly covered with boards, faint candlelight flickering within.

"Don't slow any more," warned Percy Dunninger, eyes flickering left and right. Everywhere it seemed that shadows twitched and moved just on the edge of vision. There were other animals in this place more dangerous than gnawing rats and savage dogs.

They emerged finally in a broad square, abandoned now, but from the smell and the look of it, the place was some sort of open-air market in the daylight hours. At Dunninger's instruction they turned to the right and made their way up a street so narrow and so abruptly curved, it looked like little more than a cul-de-sac, a tightly constricted canyon of tall, narrow tenements lurking in utter darkness, the gaping, waiting belly of a snake. The smell was different here, a sweet and bitter mixture of aromatic smoke and peaty earth. The rich, mysterious scent of a ship long at sea, its cargo of exotic spices mixed in brine, infused and embedded in the vessel's very planks and beams.

"Now even I'm lost," said Kate, whispering in the dark even though there was no obvious reason for quiet. The street was empty. Nothing moved. No light shone. It was deserted. Ghostly. But the ghosts had eyes. They were being watched. "Where the hell have you taken us, Percy?"

"Doyers Street," replied Dunninger. "Chinee Town."

Kate slowed their pony to a bare walk as she guided the gig around the sharp angle of what was really little more than a widened alley. Unlike on most of the nearby streets, none of the buildings had any signs; there were a few obvious storefronts, curtains tightly drawn, but nowhere was there any indication of what went on behind the rows of darkened windows above.

"I didn't think there were enough of them here to have such a thing," said Kate.

"More than you might think. City hall says there's fewer than a hundred in the whole city, mostly sailors in the flops down on Cherry Street, but that's just what the Chinee want you to think. Truth is, there's a lot more than that, mostly labor that snuck off the railroad when they found out they weren't getting the same pay as their Irish brethren but doing twice the work and no whiskey besides." Dunninger laughed darkly at his thought. "Even the nigger must have his nigger. The Chinee seems to fit the bill." The thin man held up his hand. "Stop here." Kate pulled the gig to a halt.

"How do you know all this?" Echo asked.

"I told you, Miss Van Helsing; I'm a student. New York is my teacher." He dropped down onto the sidewalk and held his hand out, helping her down from the small carriage.

There was a water trough by the curb with a hitching post beside it. Kate tied the reins to the post ring and let the tired pony drink. "Shouldn't someone stay with the gig?"

"No need. These people are not thieves; no one would dare risk the enmity of the Low Gui Gow."

"Pardon?" Echo said.

"The Low Gui Gow," said Dunninger, pronouncing the words carefully. "A tong, or benevolent society. In this case a thoroughly criminal one, I'm afraid." He waved them forward. In the darkness Echo saw a narrow wooden stoop with three steps. Above it was a plain door. In the center of the door there was an iron knocker depicting a fearsome demon with a single eye painted deep red.

"Len Yo Wang," said Dunninger. "The Chinee god of Hell. Ugly fellow, don't you think?" He rapped the hinged knocker hard, three times in quick succession, then twice more, slowly. There was silence for a long moment, and then there was the sound of a bolt being withdrawn.

The door creaked open an inch or so. "Chu Sing," Dunninger said. The door opened wider and they were ushered into a small foyer that smelled heavily of sandalwood. Smoke hung in the air like fog. The door closed behind them, the bolt was thrown and a large shuffling figure in a long, dark-tinted robe scuttled away, slippers whispering on the matting that covered the floor. A single gas flame sputtered in a sconce on the far wall of the vestibule.

On the left was a cagelike enclosure, barred with iron rods. Inside the narrow booth was a raised table containing a lacquer tray filled with a number of utensils: a small lamp, miniature scissors for trimming the lamp's wick, a sponge in a bowl made from a polished oyster shell, several small boxes painted with Chinese characters, a long needle fitted with a pearl tip leaning on a tiny block of discolored wood and a foot-long *yen tshung* pipe, its ivory stem blackened with years of use. Beside the pipe on its own small tray was a silver *yen ngow*. A bowl scraper. It was an opium smoker's layout, the tray usually arranged so that two smokers could use it simultaneously.

Beside the tray, leaning with his elbow on a bright blue satin pillow, was a man wearing a plain black cheongsam that came to his ankles and a matching black *jin* that covered his head. Slippers covered his white-stockinged feet. He was a Han, his salt-and-pepper hair tied in a long braid that fell below his knees. He was smoking another pipe like the one on the lacquered tray beside him. He drew steadily on the mouthpiece, exhaling trails of smoke through his nostrils, the pill of opium in the bowl of the pipe crackling and fuming as he sucked in the smoke. He nodded to Dunninger and Dunninger nodded back.

"This way," said the thin man. He led them through a calico curtain that covered the exit from the little vestibule. On the far side of the curtain was a long room, thirty feet by twelve, totally filled with several distinct layers of smoke that shifted and moved like swells on a gently undulating sea. At least a score of men and women occupied the room, all lounging on low, rough beds on raised platforms. The women were all Caucasian, the men mostly Chinese but in poor Western clothing. The only light in the gloom came from a dozen or more of the opium lamps, their wicks burning low. The pungent odor of the drug was suffocating.

Dunninger led them down a narrow, matting-covered aisle that ran the length of the low room. They reached the end of the cavelike chamber. Rickety wooden stairs led both upward and down. Below them in some basement chamber Echo could hear the sounds of voices speaking loudly in Chinese, laughter and the constant rhythmic crashing sound of mah-jongg tiles and the bony rattle of tossed dice. From the upper regions there was only silence.

"We go up," said Dunninger and led the way. They climbed into the darkness, emerging eventually in another vestibule. Instead of a cloth curtain there was a wooden door. Seated on a stool beside the door was the same servant who had let them into the front entrance to the building. Seeing them, the servant stood wordlessly and opened the door. Echo and her friends stepped into the room beyond.

The room was large, low ceilinged like the floor below and well lit from a mantled gas chandelier hanging from the ceiling. The room was lined on all sides with all manner of drawers, large and small, some glass fronted while others were plain, each one labeled neatly with small rectangles of red paper inked in strange Chinese characters. There were tables underneath the drawers set out with scales of several different kinds, glass beakers, Faraday burners, their jets turned low beneath both glass and metal vessels, and in one corner, with its own bright lamp, a beautiful and very modern-looking brass microscope of the type recently manufactured by Zeiss in Switzerland. The smells in the room were enough to overpower even the powerful fumes from the opium den below: chemicals in solution, powders, medicines, tinctures, all familiar to Echo as she stood staring.

"A laboratory!" said the young woman, strangely touched. She almost expected to see her father in the room.

Instead a small, white-haired man wearing old-fashioned but quite expensive-looking Western clothes looked up from the microscope. He groped around on the table for his spectacles and, finding them, hooked the gold wire stems around his ears. The man's face was clean shaven, smiling and very wrinkled. He was Chinese and clearly quite old.

"Dunninger," he said in cultured English. There was a hint of a British accent. "How very nice to see you. And with guests as well."

"Dr. Chu," said Dunninger, "these are my friends Mrs. Warne and Miss Echo Van Helsing. Kate, Miss Van Helsing, this is Dr. Chu Lo Sing."

"Van Helsing," said Chu Sing, frowning. "A relation to Abraham Van Helsing perhaps?"

"My father," said Echo.

Chu Sing's frown deepened. He bowed briefly. "I was sorry to hear of his recent passing," he said very formally.

"You knew him?" Echo said, surprised.

"I knew of him. He was a remarkable man. I read several of his papers while I was teaching at Cambridge."

"England?" said Kate Warne, looking even more surprised than Echo.

"Certainly not Cambridge, Massachusetts." The old man smiled. "Enlightened as the university there is, the only thing a Chinaman could do at Harvard would be the laundry, I'm afraid."

"You're a real doctor, then?" Kate said, dumbfounded.

"I could prescribe you bear bile as a Chinese apothecary would if you had gallstones," the old man said. "Or simply cut your gallbladder out with a scalpel in the Western way. I am expert at both, I assure you. A member in good standing of the royal colleges of both physicians and surgeons, as a matter of fact."

"I'll be damned," said Kate.

"Quite possibly." The Chinese doctor smiled. "But not by me." He shrugged eloquently. "To most people in this country a Chinaman is a laundryman, a servant or a railroad laborer. All of us are opium addicts and most of us would chop up your babies with cleavers given half a chance. In the country of my birth, most people think that Americans smell of rotting meat and rarely bathe." He smiled. "Personally I have never once chopped up a baby with a cleaver, but I do occasionally enjoy a bowl of *gajangkuk*."

"What's that?" Kate asked.

"Dog-meat soup," explained Dunninger, whispering.

Chu Sing stood up. "I was just about to have some dinner," he said. "Why don't you join me?" He saw the look of growing trepidation on Kate's and Echo's faces and smiled, holding up a small, placating hand. "No dog meat, I assure you," he said. He led them through a curtained archway into a small dining room beyond. They were served by an elderly man wearing the same sort of plain black cheongsam as the man in the iron cage on the floor below.

They sat at a plain wood table set with four places. There were a dozen bowls and dishes on the table, some containing recognizable meats and vegetables, others beggaring description. It all smelled wonderful and Echo suddenly found herself quite ravenous. The floor was covered with bamboo mats and the walls were paneled in dark wood. Once again light was introduced by means of a gas-jet fixture hanging from the ceiling.

Looking closely, Echo saw that the wood paneling of the walls was covered in faint Chinese characters a shade darker than the rest. She realized that the paneling was actually made from the sides of packing crates, stained and lacquered. She was beginning to understand that the building, indeed the very street outside, was a sham, as artfully disguised as the paneling, the plain and desperately tumbledown exterior hiding an exotic life within.

"Most of the street is like this," said Dr. Chu, seeming to read her mind as he seated himself at the head of the table. "The basements are at least two levels below ground and all the buildings are connected. You can enter a house on Doyers Street and exit three blocks away in an alley on Bayard. The floors within the buildings have been changed as well. From the outside you might think that this building is seven stories tall when in fact it is nine. The ceilings are a little low, but there is a great saving of space, and thus money."

"And tax," suggested Kate Warne with a smile.

"Quite so," said Dr. Chu. "The assessors from city hall simply count the windows. They're too afraid to come inside the buildings." He paused. "And so they should be." The old man deftly picked up something that looked suspiciously like a cat's eyeball in his chopsticks. He placed it between his teeth and bit down hard. Kate looked sick. "Not to worry," he said, grinning. "It's a fruit called *guiyuan*. It only appears to be an animal's eye." He paused. "Presumably you have come to discuss the *jiang shi* that has appeared in the city."

"*Jiang shi?*" Echo repeated, trying to imitate the slurred, sibilant pronunciation.

"It means 'stiff corpse' literally translated, or 'hopping dead man,'" said the old doctor. "The European name for such a creature is 'Vampyr,' I believe. The vampire."

Echo stared across the table at her host, dumbfounded. "How could you possibly know such a thing?" she gasped.

"In Carpathia, some hundreds of years ago, a great plague spread across the European continent and into Asia. It was a quiet plague, not like its gaudy and theatrical cousin, the Black Death. It was the White Plague."

"Consumption," said Echo, nodding. "But what does that have to do with the Vampyr?"

"A great deal, as it turns out," the Chinese doctor answered calmly. He picked up a small piece of carrot with his chopsticks and chewed thoughtfully. "At the time, with so many dying, coughing their lungs out, fading away, as it were, few people noticed a variant of the disease. It was termed *verruca necrogenica*, or 'corpse disease,' and was usually associated with grave diggers and the like."

"I still don't see the connection," persisted Echo.

"It is the only disease known to affect the *jiang shi*, or Vampyr, who is said to have originated in that part of the world. In ordinary men it causes a lesion on the skin that spreads like a chancre. In the Vampyr it first infects the lungs and eventually causes a deep and seemingly endless sleep. A catatonia that can sometimes last for years, decades even." The old man paused and smiled sympathetically down the table at Echo. "As I said before, child, I knew of your father, and more importantly I knew of his interests and how those interests led to his death."

"Murder," said Echo.

"Yes." Dr. Chu paused again for a long moment and there was an uncomfortable silence in the room. "Miss Van Helsing, among the Chinese here I am more than just a doctor. I am the Ah Kung, the Grandfather. People come to me for help and bring me information in return. I know much of what goes on in the Sixth Ward and beyond, whether it concerns my people or not. I know of the strange deaths which have been occurring for the past several months. Considering how your own father met his end, I concluded that you were hunting his killer."

"And this grave-diggers' disease or whatever you call it," said Kate. "How does that fit into all of this?"

"It is not such a leap of thought," the old man said. "Only yesterday a man of my race but one whom I have never seen before approached me for the dispensation of a number of herbs and specifics. Circumspect though the man was, there could be no doubt of his intentions; he wished to dose some-one infected with corpse disease, *verruca necrogenica*. The murders, Miss Van Helsing's name, the un-known man seeking my help in aiding someone with the disease. My conclusion was inevitable."

"Bravo!" Dunninger crowed. "A perfect demon-stration of Euclidian logic!"

The old man turned to the rail-thin man, shak-ing his head, his mouth turned down into a frown. He sighed heavily. "Be advised, Percival," said Dr. Chu, the tone of his voice suddenly dark and foreboding. "All of you. There is a place in the world of men where Euclid leaves off and madness begins. A place where demons like the *jiang shi* become terribly real. Step into that world and all the rules of logic and reality vanish."

"This Chinese man," said Echo insistently. "What is his name? Where does he live?"

"I know neither thing," said the old man calmly, "and would not tell you if I did."

"Then what help are you?" Echo cried out, pushing herself away from the table angrily.

"It is not part of my *yunqui*, my fate, to tell you these things," said Dr. Chu. "But there is no harm in telling you that this man will return here tomorrow evening to receive the medicines I have prepared for him. If this man should lead you to the one you seek, then that is his fate, and perhaps yours."

Kate Warne leaned back in her chair, fished in her pockets for a cheroot and a match, then lit up happily. She blew a cloud of smoke at the ceiling.

"Then we've got him!" The Pinkerton agent grinned. "We've got the bastard at last!"

CHAPTER 21

"Vampires? You've got to be kidding me," said Max Slattery. In the hearth the fire crackled and hissed pleasantly. Outside the steady rain had become a booming thunderstorm, complete with splintering flares of brilliant lightning. Betsy Arnot sat in her chair with Kate Warne's journal in her lap, her gnarled hands resting together possessively on top of the worn deerskin cover as though it was a family treasure, which perhaps it was.

"Not at all," said the old woman, eyes bright behind her old-fashioned glasses. "It's all very matter-of-fact and plainly written—more a series of notes and observations than what we might think of as a diary these days. It mostly concerns events between July first and July eleventh, 1863."

"Two days before the New York Draft Riots," murmured Carrie.

"Quite so," said Betsy Arnot. "The journal describes Kate's meeting with a young woman named Echo Van Helsing and their resultant search for what

Kate refers to as a Vampyr, a vampire. The name which keeps on popping up throughout the pages is Draculiya. The young Miss Van Helsing was sure this creature had murdered her father, a Dutch naturalist named Abraham Van Helsing." Outside lightning flared wildly, followed almost instantly by an earsplitting clap of thunder. Carrie almost jumped out of her seat. "Have a cookie," said the old woman.

"This is 1863?" Carrie asked. "The words 'vampire,' 'Van Helsing' and 'Dracula' are used?"

"Draculiya and Vampyr, with a *y*. Yes."

"Then it's a fraud," said Carrie firmly. She selected one of the Toll House cookies from the plate and took a bite. "Bram Stoker didn't publish *Dracula* until 1897. The characters were fictional. There was no Dracula or Van Helsing. They were a product of Bram Stoker's imagination."

"Tom Clancy the thriller writer is often credited as having said 'The difference between fiction and reality is that fiction has to make sense.' He's actually paraphrasing the real quotation by Mark Twain: 'Truth is stranger than fiction, but it is because fiction is obliged to stick to possibilities. Truth isn't.' "

"And just what does that have to do with the price of bread, if you don't mind me asking?" Max said.

"Dracula is what is referred to as an 'epistolary' novel; in other words, it's not a single narrative; it's a collection of notes, observations and diary entries, remarkably like the ones in Kate Warne's

journal." The woman's bright eyes twinkled behind her glasses. "And very much like Stephen
King's first published novel, *Carrie*."

"So what?" Max countered skeptically.

"In 1878, long after the Civil War was over, but
almost exactly twenty years *before* Dracula was
published, a famous British actress named Ellen
Terry and an actor named Henry Irving toured
Shakespeare in America, particularly New York.
Much as he loved his wife, Olivia, Mark Twain
became infatuated with Ellen Terry and they became close friends. Mark Twain also became
friends with Ellen Terry's and Henry Irving's
stage and business manager, a young Irishman
who fancied himself a writer. His name was Bram
Stoker."

"You're saying that Mark Twain gave Stoker the
idea for *Dracula*? That the vampire was real?"

Betsy Arnot nodded complacently. Lightning
flared and crashed. "Based on Kate Warne's journal, that would appear to be the case."

"How did Mark Twain get the journal if it was
delivered to John Jones?" Carrie asked.

"My great-great-grandfather had known Mark
Twain ever since he started spending his summers
in Elmira, writing in that little study the family
gave him on the old Quarry Farm property. One
day he mentioned the journal and the fact that it
was in code to Twain. He had an interest in such
things, and since Kate was long dead by that time,
my great-great-grandfather saw no harm in letting
Twain try to break the code. As soon as he saw

the cipher he recognized it and had no trouble decoding the entries."

"You know this for a fact?" Carrie asked.

"I do. Stoker discusses it in his correspondence with Twain."

Carrie stared, dumbfounded. "There are letters between Bram Stoker and Mark Twain?"

"Yes. The letters and the journal form the bulk of what was in the trunk that was sent to me from the lawyers handling the estate of Twain's only granddaughter, Nina Gabrilowitsch."

"Why haven't you ever published them?"

The old woman shrugged. "I've considered it over the years. I could almost certainly get a book deal out of it, or at the very least some sort of fellowship." She smiled. "My fifteen minutes of fame, I suppose."

"But you didn't," said Carrie.

"No," Betsy Arnot answered. "I suppose because I felt that the reputations of too many people were involved. Kate Warne's, for instance. Some of what is included in the journal verges on insanity if not something even more disturbing. Stoker would be branded a plagiarist at best, and it wouldn't have done Twain's reputation any service either; he was renowned for the love he had for his wife, and his relationship with Ellen Terry has always been a secret; who am I to break that confidence? Mark Twain is a national treasure. I didn't want to tarnish that image. I still don't." She smiled again. "Not to mention the fact that bringing all this to light now wouldn't do much for people's estimation of my own sanity. Old ladies shouldn't go around promoting the idea of vampires; that's a one-way ticket to the old-folks farm."

"Then why talk to us about it now?"

"When you called me on the phone you told me there was a connection to a series of killings in the here and now, killings just like the ones in New York in 1863. Kate Warne and Echo Van Helsing started something a century and a half ago. It's time we finished it."

CHAPTER 22

Midnight came and went, but the pace of activities in the main salon of the Assassin's Club seemed to increase rather than diminish with the passage of time. Jay Gould had long since left Enoch Bale to his own devices, and the dark man moved slowly around the room, joining groups of players for a few hands of poker, a run at one of the three very popular faro tables and even spending some time playing whist, a game he had much enjoyed back in his own land long ago.

As the hours passed, he carefully scanned the large room, assessing the people in it. By his estimation, perhaps a quarter of the men were Damphyr, at least by their dark auras and their quick, furtive glances, but to be a member of that bastard cult didn't seem to be a requirement for membership in the club; all that was required, it seemed, was wealth and the lust for it.

Initially he'd thought that the approach by Edwin Booth at Barnum's Museum had been to draw him into some sort of trap, but now he realized they didn't have the slightest idea that one of the Nine was among them. It seemed that here at least the Damphyrs' senses had been dulled by luxury and their own excesses.

Soon, just as it had been in Bucharest, Berlin, Paris and finally London, the whispers would begin, their crimes would become obvious and once again the hunt would be on. Centuries ago the *Vampyr-vadász*, the vampire hunters, were few and poorly organized, but their numbers, and more important, the numbers of those who believed in them, were growing; Van Helsing and his spawn were proof enough of that.

It was past two in the morning when Jay Gould reappeared and invited the Vampyr to join him and a few select friends for a final drink before departing. Gould escorted Bale out of the noisy and brightly lit main salon, then across the ornately tiled hall to the two-storied circular library in the tower. Partway across the large galleried hallway the Vampyr caught a sudden movement out of the corner of his eye and turned, his knees buckling with a sudden surge of nausea.

He was here. The Other.

The sense of him was almost overpowering, like a shudder passing through his very being, one roaming hungry spirit passing through another, terrible memories and times shared for a single instant, then vanishing like a fleeting nightmare. He saw the movement again, a flickering trace of swirling black, like a cloak, and then it was gone for good. The moment passed.

"Something the matter?" Gould asked, gripping Enoch Bale's arm as the Vampyr briefly staggered. There was concern in his glance, but something else as well: mockery, perhaps?

"I thought I saw someone," said the Vampyr, staring up at the gallery high above the colorful tiled floor.

"Probably a servant." Gould smiled.

"This was no servant," the Vampyr insisted.

"Then it was a guest," said Gould, an icy tone creeping into his voice. "The rooms upstairs are for their private use." Gould paused. "My friends are waiting."

The Vampyr and Gould entered the library. Gould carefully closed the door behind them. The room was large, the curving walls lined with books of suspiciously similar bindings, and like the entry hall it had an upper gallery reached by a winding iron staircase. The room was amply furnished with several sofas and leather club chairs with appropriate side tables and a large fireplace, the hearth dark and cold.

The centerpiece of the room was an immense round table, as black as night, a quarried slab of sparkling granite, polished to a brilliant gloss reflecting the shaded mantles of the gaslights overhead. There were twelve ornate chairs set around the circle, two larger ones with arms facing each other across the great expanse of darkly shining stone. In the center of the table, resting on a blood-red satin pillow, was a huntsman's arrow from another time, made from solid, buttery gold.

"The Assassin's symbol," said Gould, indicating the arrow and whispering to Enoch Bale as they stepped into the room. "And our method: we are hunters of wealth and our weapon is gold." He gave a conspiratorial wink. "Drew and Jimmy Fisk think it's railroads, but they're wrong. In the end it always comes down to the gold."

There were close to a dozen men about the room, talking in small groups or standing alone, some smoking cigars, some holding glasses, all dressed formally in black. Some, such as the crotchety-looking Daniel Drew, the biblical white-haired Thurlow Weed and the florid-faced Jim Fisk, the Vampyr recognized from his meeting earlier that day; the others Jay Gould introduced one after the other: the immensely fat and red-bearded William Tweed, deputy street commissioner for the city, George Barnard, the red-cheeked and red-eyed New York State Supreme Court judge, the mustachioed Fernando Wood, the previous mayor of New York before being summarily defeated by George Opdyke the Republican abolitionist who'd been responsible for Abraham Lincoln's presidential nomination, Wood's brother Benjamin, owner of the fiercely pro-slavery *New York Daily News*, Matthew J. Brennan, onetime head of the "Police Ring," risen from the terrible slums of the Five Points district of the Sixth Ward and now the city comptroller, the still hand-some Franklin Pierce, ex-president of the United

States, now abandoned and humiliated after a single disastrous term and little more than a desperate, albeit wealthy drunk, and last but not least, resplendent in his robes of office, was "Dagger John" Hughes, the once illiterate gardener's assistant from County Tyrone, risen by guile and the politics of betrayal to become the immensely powerful archbishop of New York.

Of the ten men, all had great power and most had great wealth. Of the ten, the most interesting to Enoch Bale was the archbishop; somehow it came as no surprise to him that his eminence was the only one of the group who was Damphyr, his cassock, bloody sash, silver crucifix and holy ring an unholy fraud. The Vampyr looked at the man curiously, wondering how he slaked the necessary thirsts and ravenous appetites of his kind. Glancing at the gleaming silver cross and the small figure impaled on it, the Vampyr reminded himself that the archbishop's professed religion was indeed founded on a bloody act; perhaps in some perverse way the man actually thought he was enacting some hideous version of their holy sacrament. It appeared from his expression that the archbishop had no inkling of the Vampyr's menace to him.

Gould spoke. "Gentlemen?"

Without further prompting the men in the room made their way to the table, each taking what was clearly his assigned seat. Gould sat in one of the larger, thronelike chairs and indicated that Enoch Bale should take the other. He did so. When everyone was in his place Gould rapped the cold black stone with his knuckles. "We are convened," he said. He paused for a long moment. From the other side of the mansion the faint sounds of continuing revelry could be heard. Finally Gould spoke again, directly to the Vampyr, facing him across the table's expanse.

"You come from a foreign land, Lord Bale, and cannot be expected to know about or even sympathize with our situation." He paused, a small smile appearing. "However," he continued, "there is no reason why that should stop you from capitalizing on our nation's present discord."

Fernando Wood, the recently deposed mayor, picked up the discussion. "Regardless of Mr. Lincoln's feelings about the plight of the nigger, this country survives on cotton. Our banks finance its growth, our insurance companies provide insurance for its transport, and that very transport is provided by New York's ships." The man paused and cleared his throat, his voice taking on the oratorical tone that he'd used so effectively in public office. "Cotton, Lord Bale, gives us sixty percent of our exports, and thirty-eight cents out of every dollar earned in this city comes from that single commodity. The war has slowed that somewhat, and production of war goods and materials has offset it for the moment, but when the war ends, cotton will once again be king. War is killing this city, Lord Bale; it is tearing this city apart. It must end, and it must end soon. There is already talk of the British giving aid to the rebels, and if that happens the Union will be finished and us along with it."

"His honor makes a dramatic plea," said Gould. "But dramatics aside, there is truth to what he says, and in that truth there is an opportunity for us all."

"All?" The Vampyr smiled. "Even someone from a foreign land, as you put it?"

"If he has gold enough," said Thurlow Weed bluntly, his voice clipped. "Do you have gold enough, Lord Bale?"

"Enough for what?" the Vampyr asked, just as bluntly.

"There is to be a draft on Saturday," said Gould. "The president intends to bleed New York for even more of its citizenry than he already has."

"And most of them from among my people, God rot the nigger-loving bastard," breathed the archbishop, his accent thick and dark with bitterness.

"My people too, your holiness," cautioned the fat man, Bill Tweed. "My informants tell me that most will be chosen from the Fifth, Sixth and Seventh wards."

"All Irish," said Matthew Brennan, the city comptroller and a close ally of Tweed's.

"All poor's more to the point," said Benjamin Wood, the ex-mayor's brother. "Not one of them able to afford the three-hundred-dollar substitute. Poor bloody Irish going off to fight the nigger's war while the nigger stays home and steals his job."

"I still fail to see the opportunity you mentioned," said Enoch Bale.

"The day for the draft was originally set to be Monday next," said Tweed, his pudgy hands folded across his enormous belly. "I have since managed to get that changed to Saturday morning."

"I'm not sure I see what difference it could make," said Enoch Bale curiously.

"A great deal," said Gould. "By making the draft on Saturday, the results will be printed in the evening papers."

"Front page," said Benjamin Wood, owner of the *Daily News*. "Guaranteed."

"Sunday will see the workers on their day of rest. A day spent brooding over the newspaper lists with all those fine Irish names and their sorry fate. Then drowning their sorrows in the city's saloons and gin joints, commiserating among themselves," said Gould. "With a little help from Comptroller Brennan and the archbishop, that grumbling can be turned into something else. There's not a soldier in the city left to give us any trouble; they've all been called away."

"Riot at the very least, perhaps outright rebellion," said Fernando Wood, a man who'd once expressed the idea that New York City should become a separate city-state and secede from the Union as the Confederate states had done, his pride still stinging from the thrashing he'd taken from the Republican Opdyke at the polls.

"Riot is all we need," said Gould, raising a placating hand. "Give us three or four days of chaos, and I'll guarantee us all a fortune."

"How so?" said the Vampyr.

"With the help of Mr. Drew's brokerage and seat on the exchange."

Drew spoke up, his words coming jerkily between puffs on his cigar. "Gold. We buy on margin over the next three days. As much as we can. Spread out the dealings so there's no appearance of a ring. Do it right, and between us we can corner the market. By Monday, if all goes well, there'll be a run on gold. Who knows how much the price could rise? The market price as of yesterday was twenty-two dollars per fine ounce." The heavyset man shrugged his shoulders. "Lincoln's people might find out eventually, but by then it will be too late." He smiled across the table at his friend Judge Barnard. "We have the law on our side, after all." He shrugged again. "We could double our money if things got bad enough."

"They'll be bad enough. I'll see to that," said Brennan, the onetime police court magistrate. "First we'll burn down the *New York Times* and Greeley's rag, then bust the heads of a few Metropolitans." He grinned wolfishly. "If Bill could provide us with enough free liquor in the saloons, things'll be all to the good. Nothing incites the mob better than a blazing fire and a wee dram."

"Consider it done," said Tweed. "Give the Big Six a chance to show their stuff." He puffed out his enormous chest. "Still the best fire brigade this city's ever seen, or likely to."

"You condone such actions, your eminence?" Enoch Bale asked.

The archbishop's thin lips twisted into a sneer.

"I'll suffer the flames of damnation to see my people served and the darkies put in their rightful place. The holy scriptures are quite clear as to what that place is, Lord Bale, or whatever your name is, they are indeed: they are the Children of Ham, the hewers of wood and drawers of water, that's what the niggers are, and certainly their souls aren't worth one good Irishman being drafted and dying for." The thin-faced man clutched at his silver crucifix and stared down the table, a belligerent glare on his angry face. "Does that suit you, your lordship, or do you suffer from the zeal of the abolitionist?"

"Any sufferings I might have are nobody's business but my own, Archbishop."

"And what of our business?" Gould asked. "Are you interested in our proposition?"

"Why wouldn't I be?" answered the Vampyr, careful to keep his tone bland. "As you say, I am no more than a visitor to your land, and I came here looking for opportunity, after all. This would appear to be one." Once again he felt the black, echoing shiver of the Other's presence. His throat filled with ash and he felt as though he was going to choke. He struggled against the feeling and kept his seat, forcing himself to remain absolutely still.

"The minimum ante into this game is a hundred thousand dollars in specie," said Thurlow Weed, his tone crisp and to the point. "Can you afford *that*, sir?"

"And more," the Vampyr responded. "I'd like some time to consider how much more."

"The deadline's tomorrow noon," said Gould. "A bank draft brought to Drew's brokerage will suffice."

"Tomorrow, before noon, then," said Enoch Bale. He could stand it no longer. He pushed back his chair from the table and stood. "But now I must bid you good night. It is late and I must be gone," he said abruptly. With that he turned and strode from the room without another word.

Gould frowned. "A strange man, to be sure," he said.

"How did you come upon him?"

"Booth found him at Barnum's Museum," replied Gould.

"A likely spot," said Franklin Pierce, the onetime president of the nation, speaking for the first time. "He's quite the specimen." The still-handsome man looked blearily around the table, his bloodshot eyes out of focus and his words faintly slurred. "Bit sinister, don't you think? Strange accent too, him?" He sighed heavily, his eyes half closing. He yawned. "I s'pose somebody's checked the man's bona fides, hmm? Lineage, Burke's Peerage, that sort of thing?"

"He was recommended by our young friend Adam," said Thurlow Weed. "His sources seem to be quite good, high and low. The lad's bound for better things, mark my words."

"Worth, was it?" Tweed said, stroking his heavy beard. "Well that's all right, then."

"I don't like the smell of this lord of yours, a foreigner," said the archbishop, his bony hand still gripping the silver crucifix hanging around his neck. "He stinks of the Devil's work."

"Don't worry," said Gould, staring thoughtfully across the table at the empty chair. "We'll know more about him by tomorrow. I've put young Lily on to him." He smiled darkly. "If she can't winkle out all his secrets, no one can."

CHAPTER 23

After retrieving his things from the footmen, the Vampyr stepped out onto the broad portico and stood for a moment, taking in the cleaner air in deep reviving breaths. He knew that the Other had been in the Assassin's Club that night, but he also knew that now was not the time to confront him. Behind him a figure stepped out of the shadows and approached him, coming forward into the pale light cast by the flickering gas lamps in the drive. It was a woman. She was beautiful, her skin pale and her auburn hair gathered up at the back of her long, slim neck. Around her neck was a string of perfectly matched pearls.

"I've sent one of the servants to fetch a hansom," she said. "Would you like to share it with me?" Her accent was languorous, almost a drawl. She wasn't native to New York.

"We haven't been introduced," murmured Enoch Bale. "It wouldn't be proper."

"But I already know who you are, my lord,"

she said. "Jay told me." She paused and smiled. "My name is Lily." She took another step toward him. "Lily Palmer."

"Madame," said the Vampyr, touching the brim of his topper.

"Miss, actually," the woman answered.

"You're a friend of Mr. Gould's, I take it, then?"

"Take it any way you like," the lady said, laughing lightly. "You still haven't answered my question about the cab."

"It would depend on your destination," said the Vampyr.

"I'm presently staying at the Saint Nicholas," she answered. "But my destination is still at question."

The Vampyr ignored the obvious suggestion. "I live on Gramercy Park," he replied. "It's only a matter of a few blocks and the night air is refreshing. It occurred to me that I could easily walk."

"How cavalier," said the woman who called herself Lily Palmer. "To leave a lady to the depredations of the night unattended. Is chivalry so dead in your part of the world?"

A hansom cab came rumbling down the drive, one of the colored footmen balanced on the step. The driver sat hunched in his seat, wrapped in a canvas coat, a dusty bowler crushed down on his head. As the cab drew up in front of the portico of the mansion, the footman nimbly dropped to the gravel and swung open the door of the hansom.

"Well?" Lily asked, staring at the Vampyr. "Shall we go?"

Enoch Bale gave her a brief, formal bow. "If you insist," he responded. He was fairly sure now of who and what she was, and he decided to play along, at least for the moment. Besides his curiosity, there was also the fact that it had been some time since he'd feasted on a young lady, and at the very least Lily appeared to be in excellent health.

She stepped up into the small carriage with the footman's help, and the Vampyr followed close behind. The footman shut the door and they moved off. The seat was narrow, and as they turned out onto Fifth Avenue and headed southward the woman swayed against him, one gloved hand reaching out to steady herself, gripping the Vampyr's arm through the cloth of his cloak.

"Strong," was all she said. He felt her thigh against his, felt her warmth, watched the soft heaving of her bosom in steady rhythm. He sensed the great flow pulsing just beneath the milky skin, and could just barely on the edge of his great senses hear the very beating of her heart. "Jay doesn't think you're a lord at all," she murmured. "Or if you are, you're one of those cousins of the czar you see so many of around the city these days."

"If that's the case, then why does he invite me to his club to meet his friends?" asked the Vampyr. He smiled. "Why does he arrange for me to meet a woman such as yourself, Miss Palmer?"

"Because he thinks you have money." She laughed. "You could be the son of a sailor and a fishwife, for all Jay Gould cares, just so long as you have the tin." She moved even closer to him, and he felt her hand on his thigh now, moving in small circles. He took his own hand and placed it over hers.

"There's no need for that, Lily," he said softly.

"You're not flattered by my attentions?" She paused, her lips curving into a smile, revealing her small white teeth. "Or you're not so inclined?"

"My inclinations are of a different sort altogether," he answered, looking the young woman in the eye. He saw the sudden look of disdain and smiled. "And not the kind you're thinking of."

"I can provide anything for any man," she said. "And if I can't, I know someone who can." She slipped her hand out from under his, then brought it to his cheek. "I know just the place."

"I thought you might," the Vampyr answered.

"Your skin is so cold," said Lily, frowning slightly, taking her hand from his cheek. "Your flesh is like ice."

The Vampyr cupped her own cheek in one gloved hand, the thumb under her jaw. He moved his palm a little, gently forcing her head back against the padded rear of the seat, examining the line of her long, slim neck. "There are ways to warm my flesh," he said quietly, his eyes fully on hers. "Ways you could not imagine in your most secret dreams." He saw the sudden fear and knew it was too early. He released her. There was more to know this night.

They trotted down Fifth Avenue to Eighth Street, then turned left. Lily had moved away from him a little, her thigh no longer pressing his, her hand no longer on his thigh. There was a nervousness about her now, an anticipation. She was frightened certainly, but there was something else there as well; an eagerness, a hunger perhaps?

The Vampyr whispered, "The Assyrian came down like the wolf on the fold, / And his cohorts were gleaming in purple and gold; / And the sheen of their spears was like stars on the sea, / When the blue wave rolls nightly on the Galilee."

Lily turned to him. "What did you say?"

"It's a poem," said Enoch Bale. "By Lord Byron. I met him one evening at the Villa Diodati, in Geneva. He was quite entertaining."

"Another lord, is he?" Lily replied archly. But she turned to look out the window again, the fear still bright in her eyes, unable to meet his look.

"There's another verse," said the Vampyr, and he quoted, "For the Angel of Death spread his wings on the blast, / And breathed in the face of the foe as he passed; / And the eyes of the sleepers waxed deadly and chill, / And their hearts but once heaved, and forever grew still."

The hansom turned right onto the Bowery, an impoverished version of Broadway to the west. Even with the first bleeding hints of dawn climbing weakly over Brooklyn and the river, there were still a few gin mills, dram shops and free-and-easies open on the gritty avenue. As well as the liquor emporiums there were warehouses and sweatshops aplenty, as well as dozens of pawnbrokers and small traders of every kind. The signs that the Vampyr could see were a babel of languages: German, Hebrew, Dutch, Italian, Greek and Russian.

At this early hour there was very little traffic on the avenue itself, but even now a few brewers' drays were drawn up outside one of the German beer gardens, draymen in leather aprons rolling huge casks down from the wagons on plank ramps to replenish the establishment's depleted stocks while the teams of massive Percherons waited patiently in their traces, stamping their feet heavily and leaving masses of droppings to steam in the early-morning air.

It seemed that half the buildings on the avenue offered some kind of amusement or entertainment, from musical halls to broken-down theaters, dance halls and shows of every kind imaginable. The stink in the air blowing in from the east was a mixture of coal gas, brewery hops and varnish. Suddenly, out of the semidarkness the giant-columned front of the Bowery Theater appeared like a Greek temple rising out of chaos then just as quickly vanished behind them.

The cab slewed to the left and they were plunged into the gray half-light that leaked down a narrow street lined on either side with rotting tenements that clawed into the air like brown and broken rotting teeth. The smell here was even worse than the chemical stink from the factories east of the Bowery. This was the odor of human filth and desperation. In the narrow spaces between buildings the Vampyr could make out crude galleries hung with laundry, rickety ladders and stairs, torn curtains over windows without glass.

"Not a pleasant place," he commented dryly.

"You have no idea, friend," said Lily without turning, her eyes keeping watch out the window.

"You might be surprised," said the Vampyr. For all the difference it made, it might have been one of the rookeries off St. Giles High Street in London, one of his favorite hunting grounds. Les Halles in Paris, the old Prenzlauer Berg in Berlin. They were all the same; poverty and ignorance knew no borders.

Enoch Bale smiled, gazing at the back of the woman's neck. The hair had fallen a little, wisps of it brushing the pale skin, translucent, each fragile bone in the elegant, delicate neck perfectly visible. He realized that he'd seen her before, blowing on the fat man's dice at the *crapaud* table. He also realized where she was from.

"*Tu es très belle,*" he said, speaking in French.

"*Merci, monsieur,*" she answered. She half turned absently, and he could see a faint smile of triumph on her face. It faded suddenly and she frowned. "How did you know I spoke French?"

"Your accent," he said. "You're from New Orleans. I'm acquainted with someone who lives there. He has an indigo plantation called Pointe du Lac."

"What's his name?" Lily asked. "I know most of the gentry there."

"You wouldn't know him," said the Vampyr. "He prefers to keep to himself."

The cab lurched again, and Enoch Bale saw that they had turned down one of the alleys between the looming tenements. The hansom pulled up in a rotting courtyard at the alley's end. There was filth and litter everywhere. Staircases with flimsy railings rose dizzyingly in all directions. Lines strung between windows sagged with ragged laundry, gray sheets flapping in the faint breeze. The only light came from the half-hidden square of purple sky high overhead.

"Here we are," said Lily. There was a creaking sound and the Vampyr turned just in time to see the woman dropping down through the open door on her side of the cab. She didn't bother to close it. The horse drawing the cab made a few small motions and the carriage rocked slightly on its heavy iron springs. There was no sound from the driver, hidden from view on his perch behind. Enoch Bale pulled open his own door and stepped down to the ground.

Almost on the instant, the driver's whip cracked and with a grinding lurch the hansom wheeled round in the narrow court, almost crushing the Vampyr against the wall of one of the tenements as it turned. The whip cracked again and out of the corner of his eye Enoch Bale saw the cab pause for an instant to pick up Lily, who threw herself through the still-open door before the hansom sped off the way it had come. The trap had been sprung. The Vampyr turned to see what Lily and her friends had prepared for him.

There were four of them, descending from the staircases all around him, slipping down from the rooftops where they had waited, watching for his arrival. These weren't Five Points bullyboys like Maddersly the prizefighter or the grotesque door minder Snatchem Leese; these were all Damphyr, hard men in long canvas dusters and heavy boots, dark cloth caps pulled low over bright, expectant eyes, their long incisors glistening wetly in the night.

The Vampyr stood alone, watching them descend the staircases. One carried a gleaming cavalry sabre, one the rag-wrapped and splintered end of a chair leg, while a third carried an army-issue boiling can with a wire bail for hanging over a campfire. There was a rich odor of turpentine and mothballs: the bucket was filled with camphene. The fourth creature carried a shotgun on a hanging strap with its barrels roughly hacked off a few inches short of the stock. The leader of the group. He reached the bottom of the steps before the others. He stepped forward, picking his way over the litter of broken bottles and other refuse that was strewn about the courtyard.

He sidestepped a barrel filled with scum-covered rainwater, then stopped, leaning one elbow on the broken and half-burned remains of a worn-out pushcart. A sign on the side of the cart said FAGIN FRESH FISH in faded pink. When the man leaning on the cart spoke, his voice was harsh and as dry as dust, with the faintest suggestion of a hissing lisp, like a snake.

"The master says there's only one way to kill you." He paused, then spit into the dirt and coughed. He spit again. "Cover you in camphene and then set you alight. Watch you burn until you're a cinder."

"Then take off what's left of your head and bring it to the master in a sack," said the man with the saber in his hand. He gave the blade a few swipes through the air, making soft, swishing sounds from his perch. "Anything less than that and you might rise again, or so the master says. If you really are one of the Nine, that is."

On the stairway next to him the man with the chair-leg torch reached into the pocket of his duster, then swept a match across the soot-covered brick of the wall beside him. He touched it to the soaked rags on the end of the torch and it flared to life, the flame yellow and smoking.

"Do it," said the man with the torch.

"Hold off," said the man with the shotgun. "Ain't every day we do this."

"The master said not to wait," cautioned the man with the torch.

"The master was right," answered the Vampyr.

He moved so quickly, there was no time to react. In a whisper of time and with no warning he stood before the man with the shotgun. The man raised the weapon but it was too late. The Vampyr gripped his wrist and broke it cleanly, bone splintering like a twig. The Vampyr struck at the horrified Damphyr like a snake, jaw moving and curved teeth dropping down and locking in a split second, then tearing into the face of the man and ripping first at his cheek and then at his mouth, chewing once, then spitting out the remains before giving his attention to the eyes. The man screamed blindly through his own gushing blood, and the shotgun dropped from his maimed hand. The Vampyr swatted away the man's weak struggles, then grabbed him with both hands beneath the jaw. He squeezed, the sharp, bony nails of his fingers digging deep into flesh and crushing bone, then twisted once, and hard, separating the skull from the spine with a wet snapping sound.

The man's bladder and bowels voided in a rush, and he fell to the ground. The Vampyr turned in time to catch the creature with the saber as the flashing blade came down. He slipped away to one side as the saber slid past his head, then ducked and brought his own rigidly held hand down in a blow that struck under the man's arm, momentarily paralyzing the shoulder. The Vampyr stepped forward, swung his cape up, blinding the man and confusing him, then lunged forward, tearing out the man's throat as smoothly as a butcher's blade.

The third man rushed ahead with his bucket of camphene, his eyes on the Vampyr and not his feet. He ran forward, screaming wildly, then stumbled on the broken wheel of the cart, almost dropping the container. By the time he'd regained his balance the Vampyr had retrieved the saber from the dying man's hands. With his arm low the Vampyr whirled, the blade extended, catching the running man just above the level of his belt.

He swept the saber across the man's belly, feeling the steel cut through cloth, skin, muscle and gut, twisted purple offal spilling down onto the already filthy ground. The man's furious screams ended as his mouth filled with blood and he sank to his knees. Almost idly the Vampyr swept the blade around a second time and the man's severed head tumbled backward into the dirt.

The last man, still holding the flaming torch, stood dumbfounded on the bottom step of the tottering stairway.

"Bring that to me," said the Vampyr, standing with the blood-soaked saber in his hand.

The man with the torch, eyes wide, stared at the carnage at the Vampyr's feet. He shook his head slowly and stumbled back up a step.

"Bring it to me or I will come and take it from you," said the Vampyr, extending his free hand. The man with the torch hesitated, then slowly stepped forward, shuffling across the courtyard, his eyes never leaving the bright, dripping blade in the Vampyr's hand. He stopped and held out the torch, his entire body shaking.

"Closer," said the Vampyr softly.

The man with the torch took another shuffling step.

"Closer."

He did as he was told. The Vampyr took the

torch, then leaned forward; his face, mouth glistening with fresh blood, was only a few inches away from that of the terrified creature. The Vampyr smelled muck, sweat and urine.

"You'd kill one of the Nine? You?" The Vampyr smiled a ghastly, glinting smile. "Tell your master that he'd best do better than this next time. Master, indeed!" He laughed. "Now, go!" He thrust the flaming torch into the frightened man's face. The Damphyr fled, running and stumbling down the alley, never looking back even once.

The Vampyr jammed the torch into the remains of the pushcart, then spent a few moments dragging the bodies of the three Damphyr into a pile beside the broken little wagon. He opened the boiling can of fuel and tipped the contents over the corpses. When they were thoroughly doused he searched in the shadows and found the severed head in the dirt. Holding it by the hair, he tossed it onto the sodden pile of dead men, then tossed in the torch. With a hellish sigh the camphene burst into life, a great fuming fire blossoming up into the purple predawn night. The Vampyr threw the saber and the shotgun into the flames and turned away as the first cries of "Fire!" began to ring out.

Lily Palmer awoke just before dawn in her single room on the sixth floor of the Saint Nicholas Hotel. Drifts of weak light leaked from divisions in the heavy velvet curtains across her window. Outside, barely heard, were the first sounds of commerce on Spring Street. Her heart was pounding and she felt short of breath, as though some great weight was pressing down on her chest. A nightmare. There had been a terrible nightmare and for an instant she felt a rush of relief. The day was here and she was safe. She'd done just as she was ordered, and now she'd have her reward.

She felt something sticky and wet in her hair, just below her ear. She tried to lift her hand to the spot, but for some reason she couldn't raise it from the bed. She turned to the left, lightheaded. She was confused. Surely the sheets covering her where white, not this terrible shining crimson? She blinked and saw movement. She stared, her eyes widening. Dear God in Heaven, it could not be. The young woman tried to scream, but nothing came except a rattling sigh. She knew then, with startling clarity and a strange sense of peace, exactly what her fate was to be.

"They failed," said the Vampyr, stepping from the shadows and looking down at her. She thought for a moment that she saw pity in those strange, terrible eyes, and then the slight light of dawn faded and there was only night. She lay dead below him on the sodden, bloody sheets.

"A waste," he murmured, then turned, his dark cloak sweeping around his ankles like a matador's cape, and then he too became one with the blank darkness.

CHAPTER 24

It was late afternoon by the time Carrie Norton
and Max Slattery reached the George Washington
Bridge and crossed the Hudson River into Manhattan. With Max behind the wheel, Carrie had
worked her cell phone almost constantly from the
moment they left Betsy Arnot's comfortable little
house on the pine-covered hill above the old cemetery. When she wasn't on the phone she was por-
ing over the transcript of Kate Warne's journal
given to her by the elderly researcher. At a pit
stop on the New Jersey Turnpike, Max had made
a few calls of his own; one to Diddy giving him
explicit instructions about the loft on Lispenard
Street, and several others to some well-placed
friends in the NYPD.

The storm that had broken upstate had followed
them back to the city, and the skyline of New
York was a stewing mass of brooding clouds and
flickering bolts of lightning. They came off the far

side of the bridge and took the off-ramp onto the Henry Hudson Parkway.

"I sure as hell hope you're right about this theory of yours," said the grizzled policeman as he drove south down the rain-drenched highway. "We will be in some serious doo-doo if you're not."

"In scientific terms it's not actually a theory," said Carrie. "It's more of a loose hypothesis based on some unsubstantiated information."

"In other words it's just so much bullshit," said Max with a sigh.

"That about sums it up."

"I'm starving," said Max.

"Why am I not surprised?" answered Carrie. "You only had a dozen of those Toll House cookies."

"That was then; this is now." He took his cell phone off the dashboard, flipped it open with one hand and hit one of the speed-dial buttons. "Diddy? Nancy Whiskey's. Twenty minutes."

Carrie sighed; she could feel her coronary arteries puckering up and shaking their capillaries in horror at the consequences of another bacon cheeseburger with fries and onion rings. Why did bad food taste so good and good food taste so . . . boring?

"Fat," said Max firmly. Carrie suddenly realized that she'd spoken out loud. "The human brain is programmed to love fatty foods because back in Stone Age times that's what got you through the winter. Fat. That's why vegetarianism is against the laws of nature. If we were meant to eat nothing but vegetables, we wouldn't have incisors and we'd have four stomachs like a cow."

"Speaking of incisors," began Carrie, "what do you really think about Betsy Arnot and her vampire theory? It's crazy, right?"

"I know some people believe they're vampires." Max shrugged. "I've actually met a few of them. There's even an organization called Real Vampires of New Jersey."

"No," said Carrie. "Tell me it isn't so."

"God's truth. Ever since Anne Rice wrote that book of hers, they've been everywhere."

"We're talking about something that happened a hundred and fifty years ago. There was no goth club scene back then."

"According to Dr. Morricone, the weird professor at Columbia, there was a serial killer loose in New York back in 1863."

"Named Adam Worth," said Carrie.

"Who Kate Warne, this Pinkerton lady, and her crazy friend with the weird name . . ."

"Echo Van Helsing."

"That's the one. She thought the serial killer was a vampire. Jeffrey Dahmer was a monster, Ed Gein was a monster, so was Ted Bundy and all the rest. It's semantics. Today's monster is yesterday's vampire. This guy back in the Civil War ripped people's throats out, so he's a vampire. If Jack the Ripper had ripped throats out instead of amputating women's private parts they would have called him a vampire too, I'll bet."

"So you don't believe any of it?"

"I believe that they believed, and I believe that someone's been re-creating the identical crimes in the present day."

"Why?"

"These guys need a motive? They're nut jobs. They do things because little green men with rabbit-ear antennas on their heads whisper in their ears. The Angel of Death is their buddy. In the Son of Sam case, Berkowitz thought he was getting orders from a demon-possessed Labrador retriever named Harvey."

"I wonder," said Carrie. "Maybe Adam Worth was a psycho, but the killings now seem too well planned and methodical, as though they had a reason, not to mention LinCorp's reaction to all of this."

"Love, lust, lucre and loathing," said Max.

"What's that?"

"Something I read in a book once. The four basic motives for murder: passion, sex, money and anger. I've been doing this for a long time, Trixie, and I know whereof I speak. The easiest murders to solve are the ones involving anger or sex. Wife picks up a five iron and clubs her husband to death because he's screwing around. Husband uses a five iron to club his wife because he wants to marry his mistress. Jealousy, screwing around, revenge, they all fit into that slot. The other big one is money."

"LinCorp?"

"That would be my bet. That's what Henry Todd Lincoln is all about, so it stands to reason.

Somebody's trying to make trouble for him. The murders and the body in the bog are the key, and five will get you ten that our man knows the reason why."

They turned off the West Side Highway at Canal Street and a few minutes later Max pulled the rental into a no-parking zone in front of one of the post office buildings. He clipped his laminated NYPD ON DUTY pass on the rearview mirror and they headed into Nancy Whiskey's on the corner.

As usual the bar was packed. This time the music on the PA was "Hell Ain't a Bad Place to Be."

"Lot of AC/DC," Max commented.

"Goes with the vampires," said Carrie. Max ordered a bacon cheeseburger with fries and onion rings along with a pitcher of Budweiser. Carrie settled for a BLT, no fries, and a Magners cider.

"Not hungry?" Max asked.

"Not suicidal," said Carrie. A few minutes later the food arrived and so did Diddy. He joined them at their table and ordered a Diet Coke to keep them company.

"Well?" Max asked, biting into his burger. Things dripped down onto his plate in a gooey mess.

"I did everything you asked," said the young cop, staring briefly at the mess on Slattery's plate. "Took a can of Krylon and sprayed over all the cameras, pulled out every microphone that I could find, pulled out the phone lines and unplugged all the computers. I went out and picked up a couple of HP laptops with WiFi hookups. You can either use your cell or ride the signal from the new Starbucks around the corner. I already checked and I'm getting a pretty good signal."

"How long ago was this?" Max asked.

"Hour, hour and a half."

"Caught with Your Pants Down" from the *Ballbreaker* album started wailing out of the speakers.

"Any minute now, then." Max grinned. He popped an onion ring into his mouth. His cell phone started thrumming its way across the table in vibrate mode. "Speak of the devil." He let it ring its way to the edge of the table, swallowed the onion ring, then scooped up the phone before it dropped onto the floor. He flipped it open. "Slattery." He listened for a moment, his smile growing. "You bet," he said finally, and closed the phone. He picked up another onion ring.

"Well?" Carrie said.

Max chomped down on the onion ring. "Officer Diddy here got their attention," he said, chewing. "We have an audience with Mr. Lincoln. 740 Park Avenue."

Diddy snapped his fingers, grinning. "We goin' uptown!"

CHAPTER 25

Seven forty Park Avenue was an eighteen-story limestone-sheathed cooperative apartment building at the corner of East Seventy-first Street in uptown Manhattan. It was designed by Rosario Candela, the renowned New York architect, and completed in 1930. Over the years its apartments, thirty-one, thirty-three or thirty-five of them, depending on who you asked, had been occupied by a continuous cavalcade of the wealthy, the powerful, the famous and the infamous.

For seventy-five years it had been New York's richest apartment building and one of the three or four most prestigious addresses in the world. Rockefellers had lived there, as had Vanderbilts, Chryslers, Schermerhorns, Bronfmans and Steinbergs. Jackie Kennedy grew up there, and Doris Duke sometimes entertained there.

The Explorers Club was a block or so away, the Frick even closer, and as the real estate brokers liked to say, it was close to some of the best churches and schools in New York, including Hunter College and Temple Emanu-El. Dolce & Gabbana as well as Versace and Giorgio Armani were just around the corner, and Sette Mezzo delivered if the right person asked.

Other than the Dakota, it was the only apartment building in New York to have its biography written. Officially there had never been a murder at 740 Park Avenue, although there had been several discreetly sanitized suicides and a number of robberies, almost inevitably inside jobs committed by disgruntled staff.

Henry Todd Lincoln, direct descendant of President Abraham Lincoln and his wife, Mary Todd Lincoln, self-described as the next mayor of New York, lived in 17C, one of the building's lavish two-story penthouses. By 740 Park standards, the apartment was quite modest, comprising only four thousand square feet, with nine rooms, not including two maid's rooms, a pantry, the kitchen and two large terraces. The apartment had astounding views west to Central Park and across the Hudson to New Jersey, north up Park Avenue and south to take in all of midtown.

After passing through the efficient hands and pointed questions of a doorman, a concierge and a plainclothes security officer in the lobby meant to make you think of a presidential Secret Service agent, Carrie, Max and Diddy were allowed into one of the building's ornate key-operated elevators and sent up to the seventeenth-floor penthouse.

The elevator arrived, the doors slithered open and they stepped out into a small vestibule done in marble checkerboard squares that in turn led to more marble and an enormous gallery stretching for thirty or forty feet, lit by chandeliers. The walls were hung with enormous mirrors in gilded frames, and the floor was covered with a pair of gigantic Persian carpets in rich deep pinks and greens depicting the classic tree-of-life pattern.

Standing directly in front of them was a very large man with a buzz cut and a face that looked as though it had been made of lightly tanned boot leather. He was wearing a dark suit and gigantic, highly polished black shoes, and he had a flesh-colored curly wire behind his right ear.

Max smiled. "I know you," he said. "Seibert, right? Brooklyn South, the Six-Six. Used to work Vice with Conklin."

The tanned boot leather didn't even twitch. "Follow me," the man said. He turned on one enormous heel and headed down the hall. He turned right into what was probably called the Library since there were a number of high, arch-topped bookcases recessed into the walls between the windows.

There were oil paintings in niches, each one with its own little light. Landscapes of places that never existed, portraits of horses that had never raced and dogs that had never hunted. The furniture looked mostly French and uncomfortable. The lamps on the side tables were original Tiffany, and a huge chandelier hung from the ceiling. A muted blaze burned in the marble-manteled hearth of the fireplace at the end of the room. The whole thing was straight out of the pages of *Architectural Digest*. There wasn't a thing in the apartment that divulged anything about the man who owned it.

There were two people in the room: Ryan Trusell, Henry Todd Lincoln's campaign manager, and Lincoln himself. Both were dressed in dark, chalk-striped suits and identical Harvard striped rep ties in dark red. Lincoln, tall, square shouldered and with his trademark thatch of JFK look-alike dark blond hair, stood with his arm on the mantel of the fireplace with a drink in his hand. Trusell was sitting on one of the plush couches with his knees drawn together writing something with a Montblanc fountain pen in a leather-covered portfolio.

"The three musketeers," said Trusell sourly as they stepped into the room. Lincoln gave an almost imperceptible nod and the heavyset bodyguard shimmered away.

"Detective Slattery and Miss Norton, I presume. The young gentleman in the horn-rims I am not so sure of."

"His name is Kling," said Max. "And he's a cop, just like I am. And it's Dr. Norton."

"My mistake, Doctor," said Lincoln, turning to Carrie. "No offense intended."

"None taken."

"Let's get down to it," said Trusell. "We understand you've destroyed some expensive LinCorp property."

"You understand correctly," said Max. "Illegal wiretap equipment, among other things."

"There's nothing illegal about tapping your own telephones," said Lincoln calmly.

"Surveillance cameras as well?"

"Security," said Lincoln. "As were the programs installed on the computers. All perfectly legal and aboveboard, I assure you. My three years at Harvard Law weren't entirely wasted."

"Nor mine," piped up Trusell.

"Frat buddies, huh? That's nice," said Slattery.

"Alpha Psi Upsilon, as a matter of fact," said Lincoln. "Since 1850."

"Before the Civil War, then," murmured Carrie.

"We're not going to get into this again, are we?" Trusell asked.

"The body we found at the Minetta site was that of a man in Civil War uniform. He'd been murdered," said Carrie. "There have been a number of recent murders that bear a remarkable resemblance to that of the murdered man at the Minetta site. Not only that, the present-day murders seem to have some direct relation to you, or at least your organization, by the fact that each of the modern victims was known to have ingested a gold-foil-wrapped coin—a replica of an 1863 double eagle—which your campaign manager had made for one of your fund-raisers."

"We've already been through all of this."

Max spoke up. "Not quite all. Tell them what you found out today, Officer Kling."

Diddy brought out his notebook and consulted

it. "William Henry Nichols, James Costello, Abe Franklin . . . Those names mean anything to either of you?" Diddy asked.

Lincoln shook his head. "Not to me. Ryan?"

"Never heard of them."

"How about August Stewart, Peter Heuston, Jeremiah Robinson, William Jones or Joseph Reed?"

"Never heard of them either," said Lincoln.

"What's this all about?" Trusell asked, irritated.

Diddy continued. "Joseph Reed was seven years old. He was beaten to death with cobblestones torn up from the street. William Jones, who'd been on his way home after buying a loaf of bread, was trussed up hands and feet, hung from a lamppost and literally roasted to death by a bonfire under him."

"This is all senseless," said Trusell. "What does this have to do with anything?"

"Joseph Reed, the little boy, and William Jones were murdered during the New York Draft Riots of 1863, along with all the others that were mentioned, and more. All of them were black."

"Your point being?" Lincoln asked.

"The point being that the murders committed in the last few months with your chocolate coins in their bodies were all black too. Not only that, the bodies were discovered in exactly the same places as the killings in 1863—exactly," said Slattery. "On July fourteenth, 1863, James Costello, a shoemaker, was murdered in his home at 97 West Thirty-third Street. On March fourteenth of this year a black man named Ben Eliot, a waiter at

Stout's Raw Bar, was found dead in the alley behind 97 West Thirty-third Street."

"A coincidence," scoffed Trusell. He slammed the portfolio on his lap closed and capped the fountain pen.

"Of the twelve recorded murders filed by the New York Metropolitan Police during the Draft Riots, nine so far have been perfectly duplicated since you threw your party with the replica gold coins," said Slattery. "Now you seem extremely interested in a hundred-and-fifty-year-old murder on one of your properties. I'd like to know why."

"Don't say anything," said Trusell urgently. "As your attorney I would advise you—"

"Shut up, Ryan," said Lincoln. He put his empty glass down on the mantel. "I'd be happy to answer the detective's question. Two words. Politics and money."

"Explain," said Max.

"Certainly," said Lincoln. "First, money. I agreed to the archaeological survey—paid for it—because I had to. It's the law and as you well know I'm a firm upholder of the law in this city. The fact that the site in question was a fetid, polluted slum a hundred and fifty years ago and could have no real historical significance to anyone but a few academics like Dr. Norton is irrelevant; the law is the law. At some point, however, the line must be drawn.

"This is, fortunately, not an old cemetery like the Negro Burying Ground. The fact that one man was killed there is not a factor when it comes to progress. My interest in Dr. Norton's . . . work is simply a matter of time.

"The longer I keep my people waiting to build that condominium, the more money it's going to cost me." He paused. "Then there is politics, specifically James Washington Stone, my so-called opponent in the mayoralty race. A man like Stone could easily take the situation at the Minetta site and turn it to his favor in exactly the same way as the same sort of people did in reference to the Negro Burying Ground."

"African Burial Ground," corrected Diddy mildly.

"The same sort of people?" Carrie asked.

"People with their own anarchistic agendas," answered Lincoln. "People who wish to interfere with the progress of this great city for their own shortsighted, short-term, and self-serving and self-aggrandizing reasons."

"I always thought it was to commemorate the deaths of a number of black men burned at the stake by the British for being traitors to the king of England," commented Diddy quietly. "I would have thought that would have made them American heroes."

"The same could be said of the potter's field in Washington Square Park," snapped Lincoln angrily. "I don't see anyone preserving that as a memorial."

"Maybe that's because nobody's trying to put up a building on it." Carrie smiled.

"Nevertheless," said Lincoln, "if Stone got hold of the information about your so-called bog body, or worse still, this information about the murders you're talking about, he could have a field day. That is the source of my interest in your activities."

"So under motive we put that down as self-serving, then?" said Max.

Lincoln eyed the detective coldly. "You must be close to retirement age, am I right, Detective?"

"I've done my twenty-five." Max smiled. "I could quit anytime now."

"With or without your pension?" Lincoln said.

"Is that a threat?"

"Take it any way you like," said Lincoln. "The chief is a good friend of mine."

"He's no friend of mine," responded Slattery. "I know too many secrets that could bury him and his career better than a mob whack job in New Jersey." Max turned to Carrie and Diddy. "Come on," he said. "I've had enough of this." He turned away from Lincoln and Trusell without another glance. A moment later the three were back in the elevator and on their way back down to the street.

"Did you believe anything he said?" Carrie asked.

"I think he's scared out of his wits," said Max. "And I want to know why."

CHAPTER 26

"We've stood watch in this dreary place for four days now," said Echo. "Maybe he's not coming." They were lodged in a foul-smelling room in a boardinghouse on Doyers Street opposite the headquarters of Dr. Chu Lo Sing, *Ah Kung* of the Low Gui Gow tong. It was late evening on Sunday and the sun was setting across the Hudson, the last pale rays of light washing over the ragged rooflines and smoking chimney pots of the city.

"He'll come," said Kate Warne. She was seated in a battered wooden chair and smoking a cheroot as she stared out the grimy window, barely covered by a pair of ragged curtains. Every few moments she used the stub of a pencil to jot down notes in an odd-looking deerskin-bound notebook.

"Maybe the doctor lied," suggested Echo, who was sitting glumly on the narrow iron bed that was the only other piece of furniture in the room.

"I doubt that very much," said Kate.

"Why?" Echo asked. "For all we know, he's in league with this Fu Sheng."

"Doubtful again," said Kate.

"Why?" Echo insisted.

Kate turned away from the window briefly. "Because this is New York and our Chinee friend across the way has to live here. Lying to a Pinkerton would be more trouble to him than it's worth. He likes to keep himself to himself. He knows I could bring the Metropolitans down on his head anytime I wanted. That's why he's cooperating." She turned and glanced out the window again, then bent to jot something down in her notebook.

"What is it that you're writing all the time?" Echo asked.

"Notes on passersby, just in case he comes in disguise. Some thinking I've been doing about your story; matching one fact with another to see what comes of it."

"It's not a story; it's the truth," answered the young woman vehemently. "Don't forget, I've seen him, met him in the flesh. I watched him with poor Lucy, holding her with his eyes. And then—and then she was dead."

"Of what exactly?" Kate asked.

"The doctors said anemia of some terrible foreign sort, but I know it was him!"

"How do you know?"

"The wounds in her throat when she was found in her bed. The fact that she had . . ." Echo fell silent.

"Had what?" Kate asked.

"Had lain with him, even though she was engaged to Arthur, Lord Godalming."

"You know this for a fact?" Kate asked, her pencil poised.

"Yes," said Echo, blushing furiously. "I do."

"How do you know?"

"Because Lucy told me she had done so. And because . . ."

"Because?" Kate prompted.

"Because I saw them!" Echo blurted out. She squeezed her hands together, fingers intertwined, eyes shut, tears coming from beneath her closed lids and trailing down her cheeks. "They were in the conservatory on the far lawn, among the plants. He had her pushed back against a table with her skirt up around her waist and his mouth was on her neck! I saw them through the glass and then he looked up and stared at me and I swear there was blood at his mouth. Oh, God! His eyes! His eyes! He saw me watching them and he didn't stop! He kept on and she was moaning and beating at him with her fists but he kept on and kept on watching me! Those terrible eyes!"

"Do you think perhaps that what you witnessed was nothing more than . . . passion?" Kate asked dryly.

Echo wiped her eyes and stared grimly across the small room. "I know what I saw, and I know what happened. A week later Lucy was dead. Three days after that my father was murdered with the same wounds on his neck as that young girl we saw in the dead house. The man we seek is an unholy demon, the Vampyr my father had been hunting for many years. He is the same, and he is here!"

Kate stared at Echo for a long moment, then slowly nodded as though coming to some decision. Outside the last light was fading. Night was coming. She turned back to the window and looked out again. Less than a minute later she straightened in her chair and leaned closer to the glass.

"The lamp!" she whispered. "It's in the window!"

"The signal!" Echo breathed. "The Chinese has come at last."

Echo reached the window just in time to see the door of the opium den open and a figure step out into the gathering gloom. Directly across from them the oil lamp was taken out of the window.

"Come on!" Kate said fiercely. "We'll have to make it fast!"

They raced out of the room, tumbling down the steep, dark stairway of the filthy, foul-smelling building to the front door. They stepped out into the street just in time to see the dark figure of the Chinaman, Fu Sheng, as he turned the corner at the far end of the street and disappeared from view.

Kate and Echo raced after him. As they went around the sharp angle of the street they saw their man again, recognizable by his long pigtail. He reached the corner of Pell Street and turned again.

Pell, like most streets and alleys in the district, was a tumbledown street of aging wooden tenements and sheds. Laundry drooped from clotheslines and ragged flags on long poles arched out from windows like the very ribs of death.

The cobbled street was slick with human waste, and the smells of a dozen different kinds of food spilled out of every window and doorway. A man dressed in rags, his feet bare and black, lay in a puddle by a doorway, curled up into himself, either dead or dead drunk. A huge rat appeared in the thin crack between two buildings and sniffed the air. The wet-furred creature trotted across the curled up man, then disappeared down a ragged hole in the stoop. The curled man never moved. There were no gaslights here, and the sun was fading with each passing moment. Echo felt the dry taste of fear in the back of her throat. This was no place for any man, let alone a woman, in disguise or otherwise. She looked about her; there were no cabs or carriages. She knew the great avenues lay only blocks away, but she might as well have been on the moon. This was a different world altogether.

Shouted voices could be heard, the accents mostly the round, incomprehensible drawl and drag of County Cork or the crack and trill of Mayo and Kilkenny. A barrow or two pushed by weary hawkers still rolled up the narrow street, and a few early drudges were on the stroll or standing on the corner smoking pipes and exchanging gossip.

The Chinaman's pace quickened as he turned up Mott Street and began moving north. An omnibus, half empty, trundled past, and without a wave the Chinaman darted into the street and climbed aboard.

"Damn!" Kate hissed, but then, blessedly, a hansom stopped at the corner of Bayard Street, disgorging two young swells in checked pants and top hats, both clearly drunk and up to no good. Kate gave a shrill whistle and caught the hansom before it could move off. She flipped a coin to the driver and they climbed aboard. She pushed open the flap in the roof. "Follow the streetcar!" she instructed. The cab moved off at a trot, the twin lamps at the rear of the horse-drawn omnibus acting as their guide. Kate and Echo stared out through the glass, watching the rear doorway of the bright yellow vehicle as it trundled heavily up Mott Street, the signs on the shops and small factories between the rows of tenements now in Hebrew, German and Italian. They crossed Canal Street, passing the derelict public bathhouse and laundry on the corner of Hester Street, and still there had been no attempt by the Chinaman to leave the bright yellow tramcar.

"Where is he going?" Echo breathed, staring ahead.

They crossed Grand and Broome with their she-beens and brothels, all alight and raucous, the streets full of drunks, spivs and revelers, all looking for some satisfaction, stupor or respite. Men in working clothes, dusty from the brickworks or streaked with oil and soot from the coal gasworks and the foundries, heaved themselves through the open doorways of the saloons, while aproned wives screamed threats down at the streetwalkers trying to tempt away their husbands' penny wages.

It was Sunday night. There'd been one day of rest and grace before the cycle repeated itself again, with less than no chance at all that the children of these men and women would ever see or know of anything either different or better. Most of the day had been spent in taverns, grumbling at Lincoln's latest slight to the workingman. From the rooftop of one of the tenements a Confederate flag was hanging limply in the still, fetid air, and a score of shop windows were soaped with the slogan DAMN THE DRAFT. The names had been printed in the Sunday papers and in a few hours there'd be hell to pay.

The omnibus finally reached Prince Street, and at the intersection it pulled to a stop. On the left were the walls of the old Roman Catholic Orphan Asylum, long since converted to a convent and a school for girls. Directly across from it and occupying the other corner was the imposing stone structure of Saint Patrick's Cathedral, the tall building and its accompanying cemetery occupying almost an entire block, all of which was in turn surrounded by a high brick wall.

"There!" Echo exclaimed, pointing. The Chinaman had dropped down from the rear step of the car almost before it stopped moving. He seemed to look in their direction, standing in the middle of the street for a moment, and then he ran. Kate rapped her knuckles on the roof and the driver's hatch opened.

"This will do," she said to the driver, and handed up another silver coin. The driver took it and tipped his battered bowler, and Kate and Echo left the cab in an instant, just in time to see the Chinaman slip through the side gate of the wall and into the churchyard.

"This isn't right," said Echo as they crossed to the convent on the corner, watching the Chinaman go through the gate. "Why would he come to a place like this?"

"Maybe he saw us following him," said Kate, pulling Echo into the shadows around the convent doorway. "Now he's trying to lead us astray."

"In a church?" Echo said.

"Maybe there's such a thing as a Roman Chinee." Kate shrugged. "Because he *is* going into the cathedral." They watched as the man with the long, distinctive pigtail stepped into the small, treed cemetery, then slipped into the main building through a narrow, arched doorway in the side of the building.

"Then we go in as well," said Echo, and she struck out across the street, following in the Chinaman's footsteps.

"Foolhardy child," muttered Kate under her breath, but she took off after Echo even though she was beginning to get a terrible feeling of foreboding about the whole thing. She patted her pocket as she zigzagged her way across the manure-strewn street. Her friend Barnabus was going up to Elmira on the next supply train, and it occurred to her that she might have him take the journal home for safekeeping.

She went through the gate and caught up with Echo just as the young woman was about to open the small doorway. She gripped the young woman by the elbow. "Perhaps a little caution is in order," the Pinkerton agent said quietly. "In my experience, rushing through doorways is never a good idea."

"But he's getting away!" Echo said, her hand on the door's heavy latch.

"He didn't come in here just to leave again," said Kate. "He came for a reason." She put a finger to her lips and gently took Echo's hand off the latch. She leaned forward, listening. She heard nothing. She turned and scanned the gloomy environs of the cemetery. Nothing but upright marble slabs, ghostly and pale in the dusk, huddled almost invisibly under the shadows of the young, arching oaks. Everything was as it should be: silent and empty, with no one lying in wait. She put her ear to the door once again and still heard nothing except Echo's ragged, angry breathing close beside her. Finally Kate nodded, gripped the latch and pressed down on the leaf-shaped thumb piece. She cautiously pulled the door open and they stepped inside.

Echo and Kate found themselves in a narrow stone corridor that formed an L-shaped passage. At the end they found a small room fitted with several tall, freestanding wardrobes, which proved to be empty upon examination, except for a small bouquet of flowers, abandoned and drying out on a wooden shelf below a narrow stained-glass window. Even in the fading light Echo could see the image in the colored glass: a young woman seated with a shepherd's crook in her right hand and a Bible on her lap.

"Saint Monica," she whispered. "We had a statue of her in our school in Amsterdam. She is the patron saint of weddings and married women. This is the bride's room."

"Whatever it is, it seems that our Chinee's not here waiting for his veil and train," said Kate. She sniffed the air. The man had left the pungent scent of the opium den on Doyers Street behind him like a trail for them to follow. "Smell that?" Kate asked. Echo nodded.

They let themselves out through an inner door and found themselves beside a row of confessionals, none occupied. Directly in front of them was the high altar, with a wonderfully carved and gold-leaf-encrusted reredos just behind, screening out the ambulatory and the lady chapel at the extreme end of the building. To their right there was the long nave of the church with its rows of wooden pews, flanked by a series of fan-vaulted columns on either side of the central aisle. The cathedral was silent and almost empty, the last mass said for the evening, the archbishop snug out of the rain in his residence at the edge of the cathedral grounds.

"Do you see him?" Echo whispered, keeping close to the rear wall of the confessionals. Kate leaned forward and looked.

"No."

There were no more than a dozen people in the towering building, all seemingly intent on prayer and none resembling the Chinaman. Most were older women and poor, their heads covered in scraps of rag in place of scarves. Kate and Echo could hear their softly mumbled prayers from where they stood.

The two women slowly made their way past the confessionals, Kate peering through the partially opened curtains over each to convince herself that they were empty. Beyond the confessionals was the massive Henry Erben organ with its great keyboard and pipes. On one side of the raised dais of the sanctuary was the bishop's throne and the more ornate pews for lesser clergy and the choir. They took a single step down into the nave, and against the wall Kate saw a carved stone screen, half hidden behind a bank of flickering votive candles and a tall wooden statue of the Holy Mother, gilt hands clasped in prayer, her robes a somewhat lurid and unlikely shade of blue.

Kate stepped around the slanted bank of candles and the garish statue and peered around the carved stone divider. Echo followed. In front of them, completely hidden by the narrow stone wall was a circular stone stairway that led down into the darkness. The scent of opium was here as it had been in the bride's room, hanging like an invisible mist. Above the descending staircase, carved into the stone, was a name and a phrase in Latin: HIC TOUSSAINT REQUIESCAT.

"Here rests Toussaint," said Echo. "Not very Irish."

"It's certainly odd," said Kate, with a wry smile. "The Irish seem to hate the Negro with a passion, but it was Pierre Toussaint, a Haitian man of means, who mostly paid for this place they all hold so dear."

"He's buried here?" Echo asked.

"They could hardly do otherwise, given the amount of money he spent on all this stone." Kate nodded, pointing into the forbidding darkness below the stairs. "He and his dead wife are down there in the crypt, along with our Chinee friend, I think." She turned away, plucked one of the heavy votive candles off its spike and came back to the stairway. "Come on," she said, and took the first step down into the hidden catacombs below.

CHAPTER 27

"He's right," said Carrie. Slattery and Diddy were sitting at the big examination table in the now debugged Lispenard Street loft eating takeout from the Province Chinese Canteen a block away on Walker Street. Carrie was eating tofu salad with soy vinaigrette with a side of bok choy, while Max and Diddy were happily working their way through aromatic overflowing and dripping short rib and kimchi sandwiches. It was early evening and the rain was still pouring down, rattling on the high windows that overlooked the narrow Tribeca street.

"Right about what?" Max asked, squeezing a packet of hot mustard onto the last half of his sandwich.

"Any kind of publicity about our bog body would just inflame James Stone and the Rollneck brethren," put in Diddy. "It could start a riot."

"So we can't go and interview Stone about

this?" Max asked. He put the bun together and took an angry bite. "That's not right."

"No, it isn't," said Carrie. "But frankly I have to go along with our slick friend on Park Avenue. If we interviewed him it would mean passing on information that would be prejudicial to Lincoln's interests, political as well as corporate." She sighed and speared a lonely-looking piece of tofu with her plastic fork. "In a sense he owns the crime scene. He could probably make a case that he owns the bog body."

"The body was a human being once," said Slattery. "You can't own a human being."

"You could in 1863," put in Diddy, raising a skeptical eyebrow. "My great-great-great-grandfather was owned by a man named Robicheaux at a plantation called Beaux Grande in Louisiana."

Max scowled. "This is a murder investigation," he said, wiping his mouth with a napkin. He reached out and grabbed a blob of *mantou* from the plastic container in the middle of the table and popped the gooey-sweet dessert bun into his mouth. "I'll be damned if I let him get away with this."

"We've got other directions we could go in," said Diddy. "Don't we?"

Max shrugged. "There's a direct link between the murder of Barnabus Coffin and the murder of all these people in the present day who ate the chocolate coins from Lincoln's thousand-dollar-a-plate fund-raiser."

"But there's no link between any of the dead people and Lincoln himself," Carrie said. "The fact that they're all black and that they were all found at exactly the same locations as the black people from the draft rights a century and a half ago could just be coincidence."

"You know it's no coincidence," said Slattery.

"Tell that to Lincoln's lawyer," Carrie scoffed. "And wait until he finds out about this vampire stuff." The urban archaeologist snorted. "I'd never work in this town again. I'd never work in Boston or Kansas City or anywhere else for that matter."

"Good BBQ in Kansas City," said Diddy.

"Shut up," said Max.

"Yes, sir." The young man grinned.

A sudden sound rang hollowly in the room. It was the strangest ring tone for a cell phone Carrie had ever heard.

"What the hell is that?" she asked.

"The Prince version of 'A Case of You,' the Joni Mitchell song where he leaves out the line 'O Canada.' Caused quite a row up north, I hear."

"They should count themselves lucky if that's all they have to worry about," said Max bitterly. Diddy got up, crossed to his desk and snapped open the phone. He listened for a moment, his eyes swiveling around to lock with Carrie's. The young man nodded, juggled the cell and jotted something down. He listened again for a moment, then closed the phone.

"Anything interesting?" Carrie asked.

"A message for you," said Diddy, a strange

note in his voice. "A man who said he had some important information about the sad death of Barnabas Coffin. He wants to meet."

"What kind of information would that be?" Max said skeptically.

"He says he was a witness to the murder," answered Diddy.

"Oh, right," said Max, laughing. "How old did this guy say he was?"

"He didn't," said Diddy. "But he said he knows all about the double eagle."

"Whoever he is, he's got good information," said Carrie, sitting up in her seat. "This is weird."

"It gets weirder," said Diddy, looking down at his notes. "He said to tell you that he knew a young lady named Echo Van Helsing and he was a friend of Kate Warne's. He knows about the journal."

"This is crazy," said Max Slattery. "How the hell could he know about that? We only just found out ourselves. Did he happen to mention the name of the man who killed Mr. Coffin?"

"He did, as a matter of fact," answered Diddy, his voice subdued. "A man named Adam Worth."

"I'll be damned," said Max. He reached out for another wad of *mantou* cake. "Where are we supposed to meet this guy?"

"The Temple of Dendur at the Metropolitan Museum. Five o'clock tomorrow afternoon. And there is no 'we.' He wants to talk to Carrie, alone."

"Not a chance," said Max. "This guy could be our killer."

"It's a public place," said Carrie. "You couldn't get much more public than that." She shrugged. "There's no two ways about it; we have to find out what he knows." She paused. "Did he tell you who he was? Did he mention his own name by any chance?"

Diddy nodded. "He said his name was Enoch Bale."

Ryan Trusell sat in his dark, wood-paneled apartment in the Dakota and brooded, a drink close at hand, one of his very politically incorrect Havanas smoldering in a cut-glass ashtray beside him. All the curtains were drawn and only one light in the room was on. He liked it that way. Even as a child he'd embraced the dark, perhaps because the shadows of darkness hid his sins, real or imagined.

The sins were real enough now. The greatest sin of all in the Trusell bible: the sin of failure. Lincoln was furious; the plan was coming apart the more that foolish woman and her fat cop friend investigated. The coins had been their own secret joke, thumbing their noses at a society that was so soft it didn't realize how weak it had become. The killings perpetrated by that lunatic Worth had been meant to provoke riots, to expose Stone's so-called Rollnecks for the thugs they were. As Lincoln had once said at an insiders-only party, "Lynching's gone out of style, so we'll let our black brothers hang themselves."

Not the sort of thing you'd say at a fund-raiser,

but it was what the money in this town really thought. Harlem wasn't a New York neighborhood; it was New York real estate. If you couldn't send the blacks back to Africa, the spics back to Puerto Rico or the rest of them back to Cuba or Mexico or wherever the hell else they were leaking into the country from, at least you could send them to New Jersey. Screw the melting pot, and screw your poor, your tired, your huddled masses longing to be free. The object is, has and would always be cold, hard cash. There was no growth potential in liberty. Not a pleasant truth, but a real one for the rich and the superrich in this country; that was Lincoln's credo, and in the past ten years he'd done everything to promote the idea. New York today, Albany tomorrow and then by God he'd show them how a country should be run! And Ryan Trusell would be along for the ride. Nothing too spectacular, no cabinet positions, nothing with a lot of work or exposure involved; something low-key and lucrative. Special counsel to the prez, that would do him just fine. He reached out for his glass of single malt.

"Not a chance," said a quiet voice from across the room. Trusell screamed like a little girl frightened by a snake. He dropped his glass. It shattered as it hit the floor. A uniformed New York City policeman stepped into the weak, sour light. "You screwed up, Ryan; you screwed up badly."

Trusell stared.

The man looked like a policeman. Sort of. He was wearing sergeant's stripes, but his right hand was missing and blood was dripping onto his carpets. Trusell gagged. He could see the clean-cut stump of bone sticking out of the bloody, ragged wound at his wrist. The man stepped fully into the light.

"You!" Trusell said in a whisper, recognizing the man at last. For the first time he noticed that the man had a gold coin in his good hand, passing it across his knuckles in a rolling motion like a conjurer.

"You were supposed to give me riots, Ryan, my lad," the one-handed horror muttered, his voice slurring as the jaw slipped down into its yawning position, the inside of his mouth a dark red maw. "You were supposed to give me the city, but instead you brought *him* back."

"No, really," stuttered Trusell. "We had an agreement, a deal!"

"Now I'll have to do it myself," muttered the horrible vision before him. The creature's eyes blazed. They were the color of old blood and quick death. "Come here, Ryan. Get your due."

"You promised . . ." Trusell moaned. "Eternal . . . power, life." He moaned again. He stood and then stepped forward unwillingly. The red mouth shifted and began to drip wetly, the tongue curling back out of the way like a coiling snake. The fangs glistened like polished ivory.

"I lied," said Adam Worth. Ryan Trusell screamed. Blood sprayed. The creature drank.

CHAPTER 28

Kate eased herself slowly down the steps, candle held high in one hand, her Colt Sheriff's revolver in the other. Echo followed, one step behind. The air coming up from below was damp and musty, filled with the smell of cold earth. Outside it began to rain, and both Kate and Echo could hear the sound of it hitting the slates of the cathedral roof high above them.

They went round four turns in the stone stairwell before they reached the bottom, exiting into a large vaulted chamber. The roof and walls were brick, whitewashed, and the floor was nothing but packed earth. The whitewash on the walls was peeling, showing great stains of rusty mold. At the far end of the chamber was an arched doorway.

Going through the doorway, they found themselves in a long corridor, barely wide enough for a single person to pass through. The ceiling here was also vaulted, the roof overhead lost to the faint light of the candle. It was a crypt, and Echo had expected to find niches with coffins or sarcophagi but there were none; the walls were flat, curving upward to the fanlike vault.

Finally the corridor came to an end and the two women found themselves in what appeared to be the central chamber of the underground vault. The room was circular, and from it four broad, dark passages led off in four directions, north, south, east and west. Around the walls of the round room there were large alcoves, each one filled with a large stone sarcophagus. Each one of the huge vaults had a name set into a stone rectangle in the wall. Kate read them, one by one, walking in a circle. "Seton, Heeney, Carrigan, Mooney, Lynch, Hargous, Leery, Dominic. Irish, each and every one." There was one empty alcove, but the name was already etched into the stone: Hughes. "Dagger John's already got his bed ready, I see." Kate grinned. Of all the niches it was the only one decorated with cherubs, twin obelisks and a pediment on which rested a marble orb carved with the archbishop's signature cruciform with a dagger point. Kate shivered slightly. "Damp place to spend eternity," she muttered.

"Where is Toussaint?" Echo asked.

"I suspect he's somewhere out of the way so all these godly Irish won't have to spend the time before Judgment Day with a man of color."

Kate turned and stood with Echo in the middle of the room. "Four directions," she said. She pointed left and right. "Those'll be the short passages, leading to the sides. The other two obvi-

ously stretch the whole length of the cathedral."
She shrugged. "You choose."

Echo turned on her heel, frowning. "Which passage would lead to the cemetery?" she asked.

Kate turned around again, trying to orient herself. She closed her eyes for a moment, thinking, then opened them. "That way," she said, pointing to the northern corridor. "Why?"

"Because if the crypt proceeds beyond the church, that will be the direction they'd build. Also, I saw a house at the far end of the graveyard. Probably the archbishop's residence. If he's anything like the churchmen in my country, he'll have a passage between there and the church to keep him dry on rainy nights like this."

"Smart girl." Kate smiled. "North it is."

They headed into the north passage, and both Kate and Echo saw immediately that there were rows of paraffin lamps on hooks close to the ceiling, the curving roof above them marred with soot. Using the candle Kate lit them one by one as they went along. Two women exploring down here alone was dangerous enough, but doing so trusting to the light of a single candle was simply foolish.

After fifty yards the corridor seemed to come to an abrupt end, the vaulting becoming ragged and the walls decrepit. There were scorch marks on the stone foundations as though there'd once been a fire. A roughly built low-ceilinged passage curved off to the right. Kate took the last paraffin lamp in the main corridor down from its hook and handed the candle back to Echo. She crouched down, shining the lamp on the earth floor. It was marred by fresh footprints.

"He came this way," murmured the Pinkerton agent. "You were right." In the silence of the crypt Echo distinctly heard the sound of Kate's thumb pulling back the hammer of the short-barreled Colt. "Come on." They stepped into the corridor and suddenly Echo knew that they were now beyond the confines of the cathedral and were traveling beneath the graveyard. Behind and around them, deep in the soil, were the bones of the dead.

Glancing upward, she could see that the low, flat ceiling over her head was dark with soot. The passageway, leading to either another chamber of the crypt or the archbishop's residence, was well-used.

After making their uneasy way forward for another hundred feet or so, they came to a branching of the passage. One corridor continued north, while the branch to the right, even narrower than the one they stood in, headed east.

"What do you think?" Kate whispered.

"This one must lead to the archbishop's residence," said Echo. "I think we should go to the right."

"Agreed," said Kate. "Very quietly, now."

They swung to the right, the crumbling brick walls of the tunnel brushing their shoulders, trails of cobwebs and even the pale venous roots of trees and vegetation in the ground breaking through the roof and brushing against their heads. The smell was different here as well; there was a dampness and a foul stink that could only come from the corrupted flesh in rotting coffins that were buried all around them. Within fifty feet Kate saw a faint light ahead. She turned and gestured to Echo for quiet. Echo nodded, her fingers dropping to her boot top and feeling for the silver-topped knife she'd taken from her father's possessions.

The narrow passageway turned abruptly to the right, clearly to avoid the flank of an enormous granite boulder, then straightened again for a few yards. Without warning the passage came to an end and Kate and Echo stumbled out into the light.

The chamber was small by the standards of the main crypt room beneath the church, but it was still impressive, domed in a single arch of un-whitewashed stone, lit all around with an array of paraffin lamps. Across the room was an exit, rough and framed in heavy timber. Beside the exit was a heavy metal chest and on top of that a leather satchel, some long object wrapped up in a cloak, a bowl, a flask and a tin cup. In the center of the chamber was a high, jet-black, polished granite sarcophagus ten feet long and four feet wide. On the side of the enormous stone object, carved in simple, upright letters, was the phrase they'd seen above the steps leading down into the crypt itself: HIC TOUSSAINT REQUIESCAT: Toussaint rests here.

On the polished top of the sarcophagus was a folded gray blanket, and on the blanket, laid out like the dead, was the half-naked body of a man.

He was tall, his hair long and black and spread out around his face. His eyes were closed and he was very pale. The skin of his torso was covered with a sheen of sweat that seemed almost luminescent. His chest and flat belly were perfectly hairless, muscles taut and powerful wherever they were visible. The shoulders looked incredibly strong, the arms sinewy, the hands powerful, laid calmly at his sides as though he was prepared to be sewn into his winding cloth. His hands were the hands of a pianist or a priest, the fingers lean and strong.

The body was that of a warrior, and like a warrior's body it was scarred. Scarred countless times, scarred incredibly and impossibly, long thin scars as though from a sword across his ribs, heavier scars writhing like worms up from his hips. Grooves torn across his chest as though from a glancing musket ball. There was a perfectly circular puckered scar at midchest that looked as though a bullet had blown directly into his heart. Half the wounds looked as though they could have been fatal, but all had healed. It was the body of a dead man, but the soft rise and fall of his chest showed that he still clearly lived.

"Dear Christ in Heaven," whispered Echo. "It's him! It's Draculiya, the man who murdered my father!"

The young woman rushed forward, dropping the candle. She stumbled as she reached down into her boot for the silver-handled knife and pulled it free. Screaming, she raised it high above her head, the black blade gleaming in the light from the paraffin lamps. Hidden by her gripping hand, deeply etched into the silver were the words COCHILLA MORTAJA, shroud piercer. The fiercely sharp volcanic glass blade had supposedly been part of the actual weapon that had dispatched the Aztec vampire god Xipe Totec, a creature that wore the flayed skin of a man and was also known as Yoalli Tlauana, the Night Drinker. According to her father, the obsidian had been a gift from the Aztec emperor Montezuma to the conquistador and conqueror Hernán Cortés. By her father's estimation, the blade was one of the few things that could actually kill a Vampyr, and from the appearance of Draculiya's partially clothed body, more than one had tried.

Her quest finally ended, Echo reached the sarcophagus and prepared to plunge the needle-sharp black blade into the creature's heart. Still screaming incoherently, tears of rage streaming down her cheeks, she gripped the knife in both hands and raised it above her head.

The Vampyr's eyes opened and stared up at her without fear. Without any fear at all, only curiosity. Horribly, clutched by some terrible vertigo that made her sway where she stood, Echo felt herself almost falling into the jade green pupils, the irises blazing like the corona of some distant and eclipsing sun. From the far side of the room, at the wood-framed exit, came the sound of a voice. Fu Sheng, the Chinaman.

"Hold," he called out clearly, a revolver in his

hand. He stood in the narrow exit, bowler hat fixed squarely on his head, long queue down his back, his arm unwavering as it pointed the pistol. If he was any kind of a shot, Kate thought, he could blow out her brains before she had a chance to raise her own weapon, or worse, kill the young Van Helsing girl.

An instant passed. Somehow, still falling into the deep green pools of the Vampyr's eyes, Echo managed to break free of their hypnotic grasp, and with a deep, terrible sigh she brought the blade down in a killing blow meant to pin the creature's still-beating heart to the top of Pierre Toussaint's granite tomb.

Snake quick, the Vampyr's arm came up and his hand grasped her wrist in an incredibly powerful grip, wrapping around her arm like a stone manacle. The point of the obsidian blade hovered no more than half an inch above the dead white skin of his terribly scarred chest.

"I did not kill your father," said the Vampyr. "And the one who did now holds your brother, Matthew, hostage."

CHAPTER 29

It was still raining the next day as Carrie climbed out of the taxi at the corner of Fifth Avenue and Eighty-second Street. She paid the driver, climbed out of the cab, popped her ARCHAEOLOGISTS: THE COWGIRLS OF SCIENCE telescoping umbrella and crossed at the lights. She climbed the wide set of steps up to the neogothic facade of the block-long Metropolitan Museum of Art and went through the doors into the immense vaulted lobby.

Her wet sneakers squeaked as she crossed the marble floor and checked her umbrella. It was late and the museum was already emptying out. Carrie flashed her pass at the cashier, crossed the immense echoing hall to the main corridor and turned to the right. She went through the whole medieval wing without a glance at the stupendous array of paintings and artifacts, finally emerging into the glass-walled, glass-ceilinged Sackler Wing at the far northern end of the museum.

There was an array of stunning Egyptian sculpture on her right but the real point of interest in the glittering, ultramodern hall was the Temple of Dendur, a gift to the United States from Egypt for their help in rescuing artifacts during the construction of the Aswan Dam and the eventual flooding of the Nubian Plain.

The temple as it stood in the museum was in two parts, a high rectangular gateway that was once surrounded by a mud brick wall, and the entrance to the temple itself, a long, truncated rectangle fronted by two huge pillars. At one time the temple had been built into the side of a hill overlooking the Nile, the river now represented by a long reflecting pool in front of the granite stage that covered half of the Sackler Wing's football-field-sized floor. There were lights set into the glass ceiling, but at this time of day the temple was lit with natural light flooding in through the enormous slanted window that filled the entire north wall of the building. Outside, even in the pouring rain, a group of kids were playing touch football on the grass field outside the wall while a stream of cars plugged the length of the Eighty-fifth Street extension across Central Park.

The sound of the rain on the huge window was a pleasant thumping drone that was somehow comforting inside the big, austere room with its ancient temple. Suddenly Kate found herself thinking of the sound of the rain on the roof of the old lady's house above the old cemetery, and not for the first time in the past twenty-four hours she wondered whether she'd been foolish for coming to the Met alone. She had argued her point about the temple being a public place to Slattery, but the truth of it was that a quick scan showed there were no more than half a dozen people in a room the size of the main concourse at Grand Central, and most of them seemed to be wandering toward the exit.

"Crap," she said softly. She wasn't a cop, she didn't have a gun and what use would a gun be anyway if she was actually meeting a vampire. Even if that wasn't likely, the person she was meeting *believed* he was a vampire and that was even worse. "Crap," she muttered again.

"Hardly that," said a tall man who'd suddenly appeared beside her. "The Egyptians might have given your country something a little more interesting, like the temple of Horus of Miam at Aniba or the Temple of Amun at Wadi es-Sebuam, but one shouldn't complain."

Carrie turned, her heart beating like a triphammer in her chest. The man standing beside her at the reflecting pool was at least six foot three and was dressed from head to toe in perfectly tailored black. Hugo Boss or Armani.

"Brooks Brothers," the man said, apparently reading her mind. "I've shopped there since my first visit to New York." He had an accent she couldn't quite place, something soft and foreign, barely there at all. She stared at him.

His skin was pale, his nose long and aquiline, his cheeks a little hollow, his chin square. His hair was long, falling to his shoulders and as black as ink. His eyes, the lids a pale taupe, were an extraordinary shade of green.

"It's you," whispered Carrie. "It's you, isn't it?"

"That would depend on who I'm supposed to be," he said calmly.

"If you've shopped at Brooks Brothers since your first visit to New York, when would that first visit have taken place?"

"Late spring, 1863," the man responded. "I was actually heading for Montreal but there was a little problem off Cape Race and I wound up here instead."

"You don't look a hundred and forty-five years old," said Carrie. For a man who thought he was a vampire, he didn't look crazy at all.

"I age well," said the man, his smile gentle. "People tell me it's in the blood."

"You really expect me to believe that?" Carrie said. The man's stare was incredibly powerful. She looked away for a moment. Horribly, it seemed that they were now alone in the enormous temple complex. She looked in the other direction. The football players were gone and so was most of the traffic she'd seen passing; it was down to a trickle. It seemed darker too. She looked down at her watch. It was after seven. She been here for more than two hours and she didn't remember anything. It was impossible, but it was fact.

"Now do you believe it?" said the man in black.

"I'll scream," said Carrie. She took a step back.

"No one would hear if you did," said the man.

"And there's no reason for you to do so anyway. I mean you no harm, believe me."

"This is crazy! The museum's closed!"

"I have an arrangement with the guards," he said. "I come and go as I please."

"This can't be happening," said Carrie, the pounding of her heart making her breath come in short little gasps. It was hysteria, mass hypnosis, some kind of poison gas. It was David Copperfield making the Statue of Liberty disappear. It couldn't be true.

"It is," said the man. "Watch." He reached out and let his fingers gently brush her hand. Suddenly they were standing on the granite slab beyond the pool, the temple close enough to reach out and touch. They'd traveled across the entire huge room in the blink of an eye.

"How . . . ?"

"Time is elastic," said the man softly. "It can be folded and stretched, walked through like a picture gallery, seen through a glass. Elastic but unchangeable. A force, like gravity." He reached out again, took her palm between his thumb and forefinger, gently pressing it into the warm stone of the temple's slightly sloping side. "Feel," he said. "This place stood by the Nile for two millennia. Look out. There is the museum wall, but once it was a broad river under a burning sun. A man stood here with a dressing adze and smoothed the stone, and another came after him with a stone-etching chisel and carved this row of papyrus stalks, and a thousand years later one of Napoleon's men carved his initials and the date A.S. JUILLET 14 IEME, 1798. Two hundred years after that the temple sits in a glass box in Central Park while the rain pours overhead. In its first two thousand years I doubt these stones knew rain more than once or twice, and now they regularly witness snow. Imagine it."

"Who was A.S.?" Carrie asked. "You sound as though you knew him."

"I knew him. I know him still. In those days he called himself Adamo Selva. He was, among other things, Napoleon's astrologer."

"You know your history—that's for sure," said Carrie, her heart slowing as she began to believe the man beside her, dressed all in black.

"I *am* history," he answered. "One of Nine, almost the last of my kind."

"So I'm supposed to believe that you're Bram Stoker's Dracula?"

"Draculiya," he corrected. "And Bram Stoker never knew me, nor I him, though I saw the play once on Broadway in 1924 with Lugosi playing me. He was far more frightening than I was."

"You know how insane this sounds?"

"Of course," the dark man answered. "It's the twenty-first century; no one believes in vampires anymore." He touched her hand again, a single finger stroking the ball of her thumb, the sensation feather light, and suddenly the temple was gone entirely. Her eyes opened and she found herself surrounded by rich black leather in the rear seat of a limousine, the dark man at her side. She turned and looked out the window. There was nothing to see but darkness. No lights. They weren't in Manhattan any longer. Ahead of her was a rosewood bar and beyond that the opaque black glass barrier dividing the driver's compartment from the rear.

"Where are you taking me?" said Carrie. Oddly she felt not even a hint of fear, almost as though she'd been drugged. What was happening to her could not be happening to her, but it was and somehow that was all right. The dark man turned to her, the green eyes cool.

"Your friends followed you to the museum. They were shadowing you, no doubt to ensure no harm came to you. I decided we were better off without them."

"Max? Diddy?" Carrie asked sleepily. The dark man's voice flowed over her like soothing water.

"That's right."

"You didn't say where we were going."

"Home," said Draculiya. "We're going home."

"Where's that?" Carrie murmured sleepily.

"Dracula's castle—where else?"

CHAPTER 30

As dawn broke, a restless city roused itself from a drunken, angry stupor, and like horrible, furious human bees they began to swarm in the first bleak light of morning. The rain had stopped, mist lay as thick as fog on the ground and screaming bloody murder came to New York City.

Railroad yards, machine shops, shipyards and foundries were all quiet. The sun began to rise over the ragged rooftops of Five Points and the other poor wards of the giant metropolis; the fog began to shred and tear and the people marched. Hundreds, thousands, tens of thousands armed with the righteous indignation of a mob. Gathering in swirls were men, women and children armed with torches, clubs, sticks, knives and broken bottles, fueled by gin and the boiling anger of an entire race maligned since Cromwell crossed the Irish Sea and made his slaughter at the Black Castle of the Byrnes.

The signs said NO DRAFT and KILL THE NIGGERS,

but in their savage hearts the mob knew that neither thing was at the root of their fury. Wealth and privilege were the enemies, the black man was the scapegoat and their greatest weapon was their stubborn, angry stupidity, for a mob is only as smart as its dullest wit, and if ever there was a mob of sodden dullards, this was it.

There had been fifty thousand casualties at Gettysburg two weeks before, and these people were not about to go peacefully into that kind of hell for the sake of Abe Lincoln's proclamation of the nigger's emancipation while the Irish had yet to see their own. The next draft draw was set for ten thirty in the morning at the provost marshall's office at Third Avenue and Forty-sixth Street, and the mob, first a trickle, then a flood, was drawn to it like flies to fresh-killed meat.

A dozen Metropolitans were there to guard the office, but by eleven a call went out across the police telegraph for fifty more. Violence began to spread, fires began to burn and people began to die. William Seward, the governor, forewarned by his friends at the Assassin's Club, was conveniently vacationing in New Jersey.

The mob split into a dozen branches, some concentrating on the plunder of stores such as Brooks Brothers and Tiffany's, others rioting in front of the pro-Lincoln offices of Horace Greeley's *New York Tribune*. Still others sought out the homes of policemen and known Republicans, while a separate throng moved up Fifth Avenue, looting, pillaging and destroying property as they went.

By noon whole sections of Broadway were in flames, tram cars overturned by main force, women with huge flensing knives slaughtering the horses and butchering them into likely cuts before they fled back to their verminous warrens, clutching the dripping roasts and haunches in bloodsodden aprons.

One furious harridan, stinking of rum, was arrested by a lone constable, an Irishman named Ryan Howard, late of the Coombe in Dublin. Screeching at him, she turned and in one stroke of her butcher's blade she slit his throat from ear to ear. The crowd around her cheered, then tore the dead man's body into pieces. A cry went up throughout the mob—"*Kill the niggers!*"—and they did.

By late afternoon the surges from the lower wards turned on the Colored Orphan Asylum at Fifth Avenue and Forty-third Street, burning it to the ground although by then the children had been evacuated. At five o'clock, the city wreathed in clouds of smoke from dozens of fires, a black coachman named Abe Franklin met the mob at the corner of Twenty-seventh Street and Seventh Avenue while trying to escort his elderly mother to the safety of a friend's home.

Running into the house, he and his mother were chased by a group of thugs who crushed his skull with a brick, then dragged his body outside, stringing him up from a lamppost with a length of rope, then beating his unconscious form with clubs and fists. Interrupted briefly by a patrol of soldiers, they returned to the dangling body, hacking at it with knives and finally slashing out his eyes and slicing off his genitalia, carrying the severed flesh away on the tines of a pitchfork like a prize.

At seven that evening, the fires on Broadway now out of control, a roving host of almost five thousand rioters found their way into the streets of Greenwich Village, seeking out plunder in the warehouses along the waterfront, burning everything in their way and giving chase to fleeing residents of the area like baying hounds after a hare.

By nine o'clock, the police telegraph lines cut in most sections of the city and the troops quartered in City Hall Park spread out across the island so thinly as to barely make any headway against the seething hordes, they turned their attention back toward Broadway.

A young father, William Jones, desperate to feed his children, had purchased a loaf of bread and was returning to his tenement home of Clarkson Street when a small band of rioters trapped him, half of them women who worked together at a laundry on Elizabeth Street. They set upon him instantly, beating him with makeshift weapons made from clubs of wood studded with roofing nails as well as claw hammers they'd looted from a hardware store on Leonard Street.

Bleeding from a dozen wounds, the man was stripped of his clothes and strung up head down from a lamppost in the same fashion as the unfortunate Abe Franklin. When he showed no signs of life they piled up broken crates beneath his dangling body, doused them with kerosene and lit a fire underneath him, roasting him alive, listening to his horrible screams of agony while they danced around the lamppost, singing.

At ten, with full darkness fallen on a city lit like daylight by the towering flames of a hundred blazing fires, the writhing mob that roamed the streets of Greenwich Village sought out new worlds to conquer. Crossing Sixth Avenue, the smell of bloody, battered flesh hot in their nostrils, they turned into the narrow reaches of Minetta Lane.

Echo Van Helsing and Kate Warne stayed in the catacomb beneath the cathedral cemetery through the night and listened, sometimes unbelieving, to the Vampyr's strange tale, all the while under the watchful eye of the Chinaman, Fu Sheng. The Vampyr told them of the approaching sickness that would soon overwhelm him, told them of the Nine and the ancient Order of the Dragon, the near mythic *Drachenorden*; the secret alliance of the Vampyr kind, dedicated to protecting the rights of the weak, mortal and unfortunate preyed upon by their half-breed cousins the unholy Damphyr, the blood lusters, the killers-for-joy who had roamed the earth almost since time began.

He also told them of the Tenth, the Other and the Fallen, who was the Damphyr's leader and was the creature who'd really murdered Echo's father, the renowned metaphysician and naturalist Abraham Van Helsing. Known variously through the ages as Memnoch, Gaheris, the mysterious Gwalchmai ap Gwyar, or Adamo Selva the Astrologer, the Other had craved the bloody mortal power of the Damphyr and chafed at the strict discipline and sacrifice practiced by his fellow Vampyrn.

He told them of his ancient home, of Budapest and Prague and of the dark secrets of Berlin. He told them of the strange, elusive, eellike Acqua Damphyr in Venice and the ghostly Damphyr Blanche beneath the streets of Paris. He told them of London and his escape, of the wreck of the *Anglo-Saxon*, the death of one Enoch Bale and the rebirth of another. He told them everything and they listened, transfixed.

Through the ages, the Nine became eight, then seven and now six. The Other, calling himself Adam Worth in this war-torn world, had battled with the Vampyr Draculiya more than once, never defeating him, never being defeated, always withdrawing to fight again in some other place and era. The time had come to do battle once again.

The Vampyr told them of Gould's plot to raise the price of gold by bringing riot and fire to the city, aided by Adam Worth's regiments of Damphyr, spread throughout the city's poorest districts, their job to fan the flames of violence and hatred, taking their own grotesque pleasures unseen within the greater horror.

At dawn Fu Sheng slipped away through the secret exit from the crypt, returning an hour later to report that the riot had begun. He went out again at noon and did not return for several hours. When he did return, his shirt and his dark suit coat were drenched with blood, though not his own.

"The rioters are everywhere, my lord. The city is in flames. I had to fight my way back here. The telegraph has been cut and the roads out of the city are blocked. The police are having little effect. The army, what there is of it, is fighting in the streets. It is chaos."

Kate, slumped against the wall of the dingy chamber, shook herself, like someone waking from a dream. Echo's eyes were still firmly fixed on the figure of Enoch Bale as he stood, fully dressed now, leaning on the huge sarcophagus of the long-dead Haitian, Toussaint.

"We must . . ." Kate began. She shook her head again, then spoke a second time. "We must get help."

"What help could there possibly be?" Echo said, her voice barely above a whisper. "We are beyond God now. We are in a world of darkness." She sobbed once, a small ragged cry. "Matthew!" she moaned. "What have I done?"

"We'll find your brother and deliver him from my old enemy," said Draculiya. "I make that vow." He turned to Kate. "What were you thinking, Mrs. Warne?"

"That this is madness, but that something must be done, and quickly. If New York is lost to the mob, then the war is lost."

"I agree, but what can you do?"

"My friend Barnabus is working as a longshoreman on the Hudson piers until his new ship is ready. If I can get to him he can take me across to the Jersey shore. There's a colonel attached to the provost general's command at Gettysburg. His name is Alan Sharp."

"And what can he do?"

"Send men. The Seventh New York was stationed here. A forced march could bring them to the city by Wednesday night, the following morning at the latest."

"Would they come?"

"If Lincoln knew about Gould's plot? Yes, I think so."

"You can reach the president?" the Vampyr asked a little skeptically.

"I did him a favor once. Honest Abe owes me."

"Which pier?"

"Twenty-four, at the foot of Vesey by the Barclay Street Ferry."

"Fu Sheng!" commanded the Vampyr. "Accompany Mrs. Warne to the foot of Vesey Street. See that she finds her friend, and see that no harm comes to her."

"Yes, my lord." The Chinaman nodded with a small bow.

"I can make it on my own, thank you very much," said Kate stiffly.

"Fu Sheng will accompany you," said the Vampyr in his odd, insistent voice. There was no room for argument. Kate still had her small pistol in her lap, and she raised it experimentally. Her limbs were heavy, almost as though she'd smoked opium from the den on Doyers Street. She knew that with his strange hypnotic powers the Vampyr could have taken the gun from her at any time he wished, but he hadn't. She looked at the Chinaman in his blood-stiff clothes. Better to have him as an ally than an enemy.

"Agreed," she said finally. "But not without Echo."

The Vampyr seemed to shimmer across the room, his feet barely touching the earthen floor of the crypt. In an instant he was looming over her, his long jet hair hanging around his face like a cowl. He reached out his hand to Echo and she rose to meet him, her eyes never leaving his.

The Vampyr spoke quietly to Kate. "Miss Van Helsing will stay in my care. She has an appointment on Minetta Lane, and so do I." The dark figure's voice seemed to deepen and fill the room, his eyes burning into Kate's very heart. "Now, go."

And she did just that.

CHAPTER 31

Late in the Civil War a surgeon attached to the Ninety-fifth New York Infantry, a man named Major Robert S. Sparks, invented a concoction for pain relief composed of a combination of chloroform, capsicum, Indian hemp, alcohol, tincture of cannabis and opium. Needless to say, it worked. Major Sparks, who played fanciful Schumann *papillons* on the piano between amputations and who became known as "Painless Bob," died from an accidental overdose of his own medicine, but not before selling the recipe to an apothecary of German extraction who lived in New York.

The apothecary, whose name was Gustav Wolff, took out the capsicum, replaced it with peppermint and bottled the sweet-tasting mixture under the name "Chloromemdium." According to the advertising for the product, it cured cholera, diarrhea, insomnia, toothache, cancer and any sort of headache. It was also available in a "Ladies" formula for the relief of the pain of "accouchement."

The drug, approved by none other than Pope Leo XIII, with a medal to prove it, sold like hotcakes, first in New York and then all over North America, Great Britain and even Europe. Gustav changed his name to George, dropped one *F* from Wolff and began building a castle on Eriskay Island on the St. Lawrence River border of New York State, an area that had become a favorite place for the scions of the patent medicine industry to build opulent summer residences, probably because of the proximity to the Canadian border, which was convenient for the surreptitious removal of untaxed income skimmed from already questionable profits.

In George Wolf's case, the river border was less than two hundred yards away from his private island. He worked on the castle for years, the plans changing and expanding as he went along. There were battlements, towers, dungeons, a grotto and a great hall hung with dozens of hunting trophies that he'd bought wholesale from a bankrupt taxidermist in Rhode Island, supposedly re-creating the hunting lodges of his homeland, although the closest his cobbler father had ever come to a wild boar was the making of a pair of hunting boots for a Prussian cavalry officer in Hanover. Wolf, now a multimillionaire, called the castle and the island Wolfschanze, or "Wolf's Lair" a name that remained until World War II and its unfortunate and embarrassing connection with Hitler's headquarters near Rastenburg, Poland. At that point the name was prudently changed to Castle Island.

George Wolf completed his stone and oak-beamed fantasy in 1903, with his flagship medicine, Chloromemdium at the height of its popularity. Within a few years of the summer residence's completion, George Wolf's beloved wife, Louise, died, and with her died the snake-oil salesman's interest in his castle. He never occupied the place, nor did he sell it. By 1910 more and more coroner's reports were referring to bodies found in rooms full of empty bottles of George's elixir, and in 1914 George Wolf went belly-up. By 1918, a broken, tired and heartbroken old man, George Wolf became a statistic in the great Spanish flu pandemic and faded quickly from memory, having left no children behind to carry on his name.

The castle languished, left to occasional vandals and the harsh winters of that part of the country. The Thousand Islands Bridge Authority purchased the island from the state of New York for a dollar, intending to lease it to the Coast Guard as a base for catching the rum runners prospering in the area, but the Coast Guard never took the place over, let alone maintained it, and the decay worsened.

In the 1930s title passed to the Catholic Church, which originally intended to use it as a summer retreat for the archbishop, but when that proved to be an unpopular decision they changed their plan first to a summer camp for Catholic orphans, then a home for unwed mothers and finally briefly passed the declining property over to a Catholic military academy.

The church had little use for a military school on an island in the middle of the St. Lawrence with all the attendant problems, so the property was sold in the late forties to an evangelical association, but after losing their tax-exempt status the group in turn sold Castle Island again. Between 1956 and 1972 it was owned in turn by an artists collective, a reclusive millionaire, a Korean love cult eventually indicted for tax fraud and a British newspaper baron who never even bothered to visit.

For thirty-five years after that the castle languished, empty again until it was purchased by a German venture capitalist with the coincidentally prescient name of Vlad Jorstadt, a man who collected private islands and bartered them as a hobby. The last time Castle Island was up for sale was through Sotheby's Properties at twenty-two million dollars. There were no takers.

Carrie slept and did not dream. To her it seemed that no time at all had passed. She heard the sound of tires on gravel and opened her eyes. The man who called himself Enoch Bale turned to her and smiled.

"You slept well."

"Where are we?" Carrie asked. She still felt sluggish and vague. All she really wanted was to go into that dreamless sleep again and wait until this bad dream ended. The man who sat beside her was a specter from some terrible fever, a demon lover of monstrous power who could hold her rigid with a glance and turn any kind of fortitude to water in her veins.

"Come and see," he said. He opened the door of the limousine, then turned and offered her his hand. She took it and stepped out of the car. It was dark, so she knew it was still night. The rain had stopped, but dark, dangerous clouds scudded overhead and in the far distance she could see the flicker of lightning.

They were at the end of a gravel road. To the left was a large, dark building and a long dock leading out into inky water. A mist had risen on the water, pale but heavy enough to be called a fog. There wasn't a breath of wind. There were no lights on in the building that must have been a yacht club once upon a time, but Carrie could faintly hear music. Big band music.

"Benny Goodman," said Enoch Bale. " 'Stomping at the Savoy.' He always plays it when he comes up here to perform for the gentry."

"Plays?" Carrie was sure he'd used the present tense and that didn't make any sense at all.

"I told you, time is elastic." He smiled. "The blink of a dinosaur's eye."

"Why are we here?" she asked.

"We have an appointment."

"Where?"

"There," he said and pointed. For a moment she thought he'd changed into some kind of cloak that brushed against his ankles and shrouded his up-raised arm. His hand pointed to the fog-covered water, and, blinking, Carrie found herself halfway down the dock. Her companion was standing in an old-fashioned inboard runabout, a mahogany Chris-Craft Cadet from the late twenties. The power-ful engine rumbled and once again the Vampyr offered Carrie his hand. The fog was steadily be-coming thicker. She turned and looked back over her shoulder. The old building had disappeared but now she could see lights shining through the thickening mist. The music had changed as well.

"That's 'Moonlight Serenade,' " whispered Car-rie, staring back through the twisting fog.

"Glenn Miller," the Vampyr replied. "They all play at Scobie House." He paused. "In their time."

Carrie felt dizzy for a moment, and it seemed that the only way to maintain her balance on the old wood dock was to keep her gaze firmly fixed on those luminous green eyes. Reality began to shred around her as though the very fabric of the world was falling away. Over the water, quite near now, she heard the sound of volleys of musket fire, the blast of cannon and the des-perate screams of dying men. Or was it only thunder?

"Come," the Vampyr urged, "we mustn't be late."

Carrie nodded absently, took the extended hand and stepped down into the boat. She sat down on the seat beside her companion. Behind her the music was very clear, rich and full of melody.

Somewhere a woman laughed, the sound full of life. The Vampyr pushed the throttle of the Chris-Craft forward and they headed slowly out into the fog.

CHAPTER 32

Minetta Street was madness, a bedlam of screaming horror, a single curving block of Hell itself
that ran from the intersection of Sixth Avenue and
Bleeker Street in the south to Minetta Lane in the
north. Flaming barricades blocked both ends, the
tumbledown barriers of tables, chairs and broken-
down carts and barrows guarded by an assort-
ment of whores, thieves, murderers and worse,
most of them black and few of them armed with
anything more lethal than a blacksmith's hammer
or a rough-made cudgel.

The narrow cobbled street, deep gutters thick
with night soil overflowing from the backyard cis-
terns, had once been a place for tradesmen and
families of moderate wealth, but those days had
vanished long ago; what was left was a collection
of plain, three-story brick buildings and tottering
five- and six-floor tenements, their foundations
rotting in the muck that was once Minetta Creek
and that was now a sludge- and rat-filled sewer

that led invisibly to the Hudson River, spewing out the city's filth beneath Pier 47 at the foot of Clarkson Street.

It was hardly a place where anyone would expect to find any sort of reasonable plunder, but on that Monday night in July it was in the mob's way. Three snaking arms of the marauding horde, burning, terrorizing and murdering their way from west to east, came together from Bleecker, Sixth Avenue and Carmine Street, where the roasted corpse of poor Abe Franklin hung suspended from a lamppost.

With a single furious moan of hatred, the mob converged in the intersection, then fell upon the barricades, tearing away the improvised bulwarks and fighting hand to hand with the defenders. The pitched battle lasted less than five minutes. Those able to run ran for their lives. Those who couldn't were trampled underfoot. It was a rout and a massacre.

A hundred died, some beaten so badly their brain matter spread out on the cobbles in large, slimy patches. A baby, torn from its mother's arms, snatched away by an aproned laundress up from the wretched hell of Five Points, was swung around by one arm like a child's doll until the arm was literally torn from its tiny body. The laundress's drunken companion then spiked the dying infant on a pitchfork and marched about with it like a proud soldier trooping the colors.

A surge of men and women broke windows, smashed doors and scuttled through the rabbit warren of the tenement rooms, stealing what they wanted and destroying everything else in their path. But like any plague, it passed. The mob swept over like a swarm of locusts, then turned north again, heading for Washington Square, the little street strangely silent, small fires burning here and there, the cobbles covered in blood and broken glass.

The pitchfork, the gray sagging flesh of the infant dangling, stood up against a wall beside the eviscerated body of its mother, disemboweled with a filleting knife, coils of her entrails trailing into the filthy gutter, her blank eyes staring up without expression at the corpse of her child.

The street wasn't entirely empty, though; shadowy figures flitted from building to building, whispers could be heard, calling in wailing chirps and rattling warbles. Something was there. Something less than human. In the dark, smoky sky above Minetta Street, nighthawks swooped and dove, feeding on the clouds of moths attracted to the rioters' fires.

Leaving the crypt beneath the graveyard of Saint Patrick's Cathedral, Kate Warne followed the Chinaman down a fetid, earthen-walled tunnel lit only by the man's guttering linen-wrapped torch soaked in paraffin. She knew that every step she took was one step farther away from the young Van Helsing girl and the strange scarred creature whom she'd seen lying on the Haitian's grave.

Removed from the sound of his hypnotic voice

and those startling, seething eyes, she'd felt his hold on her diminish and with it her belief in his unholy tales of a life everlasting, fed by the blood of the innocent, humankind turned into nothing more than herds of soulless milking cows, or even for the simple pleasure of the slaughter.

Eventually the tunnel ended beneath a brick-lined arch and they turned into a much larger passageway. It stank, but not like a sewer, and Kate realized that she was following the course of one of the old rivers that ran beneath the streets of the city and were being charted by Allan Pinkerton's particular friend, Brigadier General Egbert Ludovicus Viele of the Corps of Engineers.

Following Fu Sheng, she continued along the narrow walkway above the sluggish stream and wondered once again whether she'd been wrong to leave Echo behind. But then again, what choice did she really have? If Gould managed to corner gold, it was as good as giving New York to the Confederacy. The city was fundamental to the Union, and if it seceded under financial pressure or simply declared itself an open city, then all would be lost; the president would have no choice but to occupy the city, bleeding masses of infantry from the Army of the Potomac to garrison it. The president had to be warned, and above all the rioting in the streets above her had to be stopped.

After what seemed hours, the Chinaman stopped and Kate saw a series of iron rungs set into the brick like a ladder. Fu Sheng pointed upward and waited. She would be forced to go ahead of him; the Chinaman was leaving nothing to chance. Kate climbed.

The iron ladder led to a trapdoor, which Kate pushed upward. She boosted herself up, followed by Fu Sheng. For a moment she thought they must have walked around in circles underground because there could be no doubt that they were in a crypt; lead vaults let into narrow niches in the walls of a gloomy underground chamber.

"Where are we?"

The Chinaman made no response, but simply pointed to a stone staircase at the far end of the crypt. She went to it and climbed, eventually coming up behind a carved wooden pulpit. The pulpit was crowned with a wooden, white-painted coronet and six white wooden feathers. The church was neither grand nor ornate. Two rows of white Corinthian columns marched down the nave, and the altar stood under a simple, slightly flattened arch. Light was offered by a row of hissing gaslight chandeliers that stood in a long row between the columns above the central aisle that ran between the simple pews.

Kate immediately knew where they were: Saint Paul's Chapel on Vesey Street, no more than a few blocks from their destination. Whatever else this Draculiya was, he kept his word. The church was empty and the doors were barred against the rioting and looting outside. Saint Paul's, despite its name, was a church for Episcopals, not Romans, and wealthy Episcopals at that.

Fu Sheng led her off to one side, then unbarred

the small door that led outside to the small cemetery. The air was full of smoke as thick as fog, and the Chinaman handed her a bandanna, indicating that she should tie it over the lower half of her face. She turned and stared at the glow of flickering light that outlined the steeple of the church. Broadway was on fire, and the air was full of white-hot cinders, dancing like fireflies across the night sky. They headed out onto Vesey Street.

The market street had been hard-hit earlier in the day, fruit stalls and barrows overturned, awnings ripped to shreds and windows smashed. A toy store had been vandalized, and broken dolls and push toys, brightly colored in reds, yellows and blues, lay on the sidewalks. A fishmonger had been raided and for the better part of a block the street was awash in oyster shells and rotting fish. The upper stories, mostly small manufacturing concerns or coffeehouses, seemed to have fared a little better, but Kate and her guide were the only ones willing to take a stroll along the vandalized and plundered thoroughfare.

They reached Washington Street and the docks, but the ferry slip was abandoned and there was not a soul to be seen. Far off across the river she could see the faint lights around the canal basin at Paulus Hook. She heard a brief whistle and what sounded like the cocking of a pistol.

A man stepped out of the shadows around a warehouse close to the pier. "Don't move, either one of you thieving bastards! And put up your murdering hands.'' The man was black, of medium height with powerful arms and slightly bowed legs. He had a handsome, open face and deep brown eyes. He was wearing a brass-buttoned pea jacket and off-white canvas trousers, flared at the cuff: what passed for a seaman's uniform in the United States Navy. He also had a pistol in his hand.

Kate pulled off the bandanna covering her face and grinned. ''Guarding an empty pier, Barnabus Coffin?''

''Last ferry's gone. Anybody ain't on it is likely dead by now.'' The man laughed and lowered the hammer on his heavy Colt Navy, letting it hang freely from its braided lanyard. ''Kate Warne, as I live and breathe! What in the name of all that's holy are you doing here? And playing at being a man again.''

''Looking for you, as a matter of fact,'' she answered. ''But first I should introduce you to the man who brought me here. A friend, I think.''

''What friend?'' said the sailor.

Kate turned. There was no sign of Fu Sheng. The Chinaman had vanished.

CHAPTER 33

Barnabus Coffin found a fisherman's skiff tied up at the foot of the wooden steps leading down from the pier. He seated himself between the thwarts, fitted the long slim oars into their tholes and waited for Kate to seat herself in the stern before he pulled out into the river. He rowed easily, with a sailor's stroke, and they left the burning city behind them.

"They came out of nowhere," said her friend as he rowed. "There were hundreds, maybe thousands, some of them with their children, most of them women. At first the ferryman said he didn't take niggers on his boat, but my friend convinced him that taking them to safety was the right thing to do." He bent his chin down toward the big Colt revolver stuck through his belt. "I told him I'd shoot his drays if he didn't take them."

The ferry in question was an old-fashioned barge powered by a team of horses walking a treadmill that turned a paddle wheel. "I don't think he much liked me." Barnabus grinned. "His name was O'Toole." He laughed, still rowing hard. "I threw him over the side on the return trip so he wouldn't give any more trouble."

Kate watched over her friend's shoulder. From the looks of it, Barnabus was heading for the Pennsylvania Railroad depot on the Jersey side. She looked into the dark, oily water of the North River, the local name for this part of the Hudson. There was debris floating and bodies too, most black but a few white as well, and more than one or two in army uniform, all moving sluggishly downstream on the tide. She turned and looked back over her shoulder.

The city was in flames from Maiden Lane to Washington Square and beyond. Broadway was the worst off by far, and Kate could see the flames like fiery pillars halfway across the river. She could hear the faint ringing of the fire reel bells, but she knew nothing would truly quench the flames of the rioters' fury except musket balls and a bayonet's point. She found herself thinking of young Echo Van Helsing and the monster she'd left her with who now didn't seem such a monster after all. But if not him, who had killed that savaged streetwalker they'd seen on the slab in the dead house at Bellevue and all the others like her?

Kate put the dark thoughts out of her mind for the time being. The city was on fire and there was only one way to stop it being razed to the ground. She felt her journal in her pocket and had a sudden thought. She took it out along with her pencil and scribbled a quick message. She tore the page from the journal, folded it once and handed both the journal and the message to Barnabus. He took both, pausing briefly in his labors.

"What do I do with these?" he asked.

"What's the quickest way to Gettysburg?"

"By rail?" Barnabus asked.

"Yes."

The sailor thought for a moment, frowning. "North to Elmira, then the Gettysburg and Hancock or the B and O, doesn't make much difference either way."

"Then, do it," said Kate. "Give the journal to our friend Johnny Jones the grave digger. Take the message to a colonel named Alan Sharp at the provost's office in Gettysburg."

"What about you?"

"I've got to send a message to the president; then I'm going back to the city."

"You're crazy, Kate; you can't go back there!"

"I have to."

"Where will I find you when I'm done?"

"Look for me on Minetta Street," she answered. "Now, row!"

The Vampyr and Echo thundered across the city on a wagon whose reputed owner was only too glad to sell it for a pair of double eagles, which meant it was probably stolen in the first place and the horse thief was merely turning a quick profit before scuttling off to see what else he could loot in such an opportune environment. The Vampyr had brought nothing with him except the long item wrapped up in his cloak, and he'd made no further mention of their destination other than the name: Minetta Street.

It was no great distance to travel from the cathedral. In ordinary times it could have been accomplished by traveling west a few blocks to Broadway, then north to Great Jones Street and west again to the place where Sixth Avenue came to an end just above Carmine Street. But these were no ordinary times; Broadway was closed off by almost every fire brigade company in the city, and flaming debris from a dozen gigantic blazes blocked their path.

The Vampyr turned the wagon down Crosby Street instead, guiding the cart horse through the litter on the cobblestones. Crosby was well known for its saloons and brothels catering to blacks, but tonight all was dark, the windows shuttered. They turned again on Broome, finally crossing Broadway well below the worst of the fires, then headed north, threading a careful passage through the streets of the Fifth Ward and farther, into the Eighth.

Everywhere there was evidence of riot; it was as though the streets had been a battlefield. There was litter and broken glass everywhere, gas lamps, their mantles smashed, spouted huge naked flames like rows of immense torches. Carts and wagons were overturned, horses had been slaughtered and farm animals, sheep and pigs mostly, roamed in roving, aimless herds, the pigs snuffling their snouts into the bloated corpses of dead horses and human bodies.

At last they reached the shattered barricades where the occupants had made a foolish attempt to stem the riot's tide. Someone had put some straw-filled mattresses and a manure wagon to the torch and they still smoldered, sending up a few small spikes of fire here and there as the hot summer breeze from the river fanned the flames. Now the street was abandoned.

Echo, still half in a trance, stared down the dark, narrow, sinister length of the curving street. Just at the curve she thought she saw movement, a shadowy, long cloak spread like the giant wings of a bat. On the cobbles other things moved. Small things with shining eyes.

"There's something there," she whispered.

"I know," said the Vampyr. He reached behind the seat and pulled out his cloth-wrapped package. He unwrapped it and Echo's eyes went wide. As the cloak was pulled away, it revealed a massive two-handed sword almost five feet in length, the pommel set with a bezel enclosing a dark stone speckled with red like tiny droplets of blood. The hilt was wrapped with heavy gold wire and the crosspiece was made of silver. The steel blade was sharpened on both edges and the runnel down the blade's length was broad and ugly. The steel was strangely patterned down its length, like watered silk. Except for the stone in the pommel and the gold wire, the sword had no decoration.

"Damascus steel. Sharp enough to cut the Devil's tongue in two and made by Voelundr, or so I was told. I took it from a heretic Cathar knight in 1209," said the Vampyr. "He had called himself Adam-Roger de Carcasonne back then. He told me he regretted losing the weapon. I'm here to give it back to him." The Vampyr dropped down from the wagon and held his hand out for Echo.

"Is there a purpose to my presence?" asked the young woman.

"Of course," the Vampyr answered, handing her down to the ground. "I need your good heart and the black-glass dagger of your father's if I am to sleep peacefully when the sickness takes me. If you do not come I will almost certainly fail, and any chance we have of saving your brother will vanish."

She stared up at the pale figure standing beside her. He held the massive sword almost casually in his hand, the blade half pointing down the shadowed, twisting alley. "All right," she said at last. "For Matthew," she whispered.

And they stepped around the smoldering barricade and entered the narrow, cobbled passage.

The building was a rat's nest of rooms, most of them windowless. The halls were barely wide enough to let two people pass. The rooms were further subdivided and rented out so that sometimes a hundred people lived in a building designed for twenty.

They came down the narrow hallways and through the doorways like wraiths in ragged blue, their eyes bright red and half glowing in the darkness. Their terrible gaping mouths hung open on impossibly hinged jaws, shining fangs like splintered, freshly polished piano keys, tongues like bloated, coiled worms writhing within bloody mouths.

They screeched and screamed as they crowded toward Echo Van Helsing. She cringed in terror at their approach, huddling back against the passage wall while in front of her the great sword swung and lunged and hacked as Enoch Bale cut a swath through the raging host of Damphyr who stood between him and his objective. He decapitated some and others he simply cut through the middle, hacking at heads and arms and legs, splitting skulls down through chins, blood gushing upward and everywhere, splashing the walls in long splashes, filling the corridor with a foul odor as the creatures' bowels released. A fallen torch sputtered against the floor; then flames began to lick at the layers of dry wallpaper. Soon the corridor behind them was on fire and the wretched tenement began to burn.

"Come!" the Vampyr ordered, and Echo followed as the Vampyr cut a murderous path through the wretched creatures, slipping and sliding on their offal. She clutched her father's dagger in her hand. Her face was spattered with the Damphyrs' blood, half blinding her, the stench of their torn flesh choking her and making her vomit. Even through all of that she realized that they were all wearing uniforms or parts of them, some blue, some gray, all red now, their draining blood making them all allies.

"*Caedite eos!* Kill them all!" cried the Vampyr, echoing the famous crusaders' call against the heretics. He finally reached the end of the hallway and found the cellar door. He kicked it open with one booted foot and turned to Echo. "He's here!"

He plunged downward into the darkness.

Echo Van Helsing screamed. Deep in the half-flooded cellars of the slumping, dangerously tilted structure above their heads she'd found her brother Matthew, bound to a pair of old beams lashed together in an X, his head hanging upside down. He was naked and appeared to be unconscious. He was very pale. The only visible wounds were two punctures at the neck, crusted with congealing blood, and another set high on his right thigh, just above the femoral artery.

"Draculiya," said a pleasant voice. A man stepped out of the shadows beside the terrible crucifixion. "Always the knight, always ready to help a damsel in distress." The man who spoke was young, no older than twenty-one or so, and dressed in a worn and bloodstained Union army uniform. There were sergeant's stripes on both arms, and a cavalry sabre hung from his wide leather belt. He reached and stroked the white flesh of Matthew Van Helsing's torn thigh. "I was never much of a one for damsels myself."

"Matthew!" Echo moaned. She rushed forward, but the Vampyr's upraised arm kept her in check.

"There's nothing you can do for him now," he said. "Adamo has used him to feed on."

"And very tasty he was, dear Count. Very tasty indeed. A virgin, in more ways than one." The creature looked at Echo and winked broadly. "But no longer, in more ways than one." He laughed at his joke and Echo struggled against the Vampyr's grip.

"It's time we ended this," the Vampyr said, lifting the sword.

"You know that's not going to happen," said the other creature. His jaws worked and his own wolfish fangs appeared, glistening and wet. "We can live and die a thousand times and it will not end. That is our horror and our joy, Draculiya, to go on forever, to see it through to whatever choking ending is the fate of the world."

With a scream of rage Echo fought her way free of the Vampyr's restraint and lunged forward, the black obsidian blade plunging toward the other creature's heart.

Stumbling through the filthy wreckage of the basement, she came at the smiling, slack-jawed creature who awaited her so patiently, one hand resting carelessly on the terrible device that held her brother, the other hand resting just as carelessly on the butt of the pistol stuck through his broad leather belt. Calmly he drew the weapon, lifted it and pulled back the hammer, aiming the long barrel between her heaving breasts.

"Such a pity," he said quietly. "Such a waste."

Beside him, Matthew moaned terribly. The creature's finger tightened on the trigger.

"No," said a voice out of the darkness. "You shall not have her."

The Vampyr's blade came sweeping down out of the deep shadows in the horrible low-ceilinged chamber, not at the creature's neck, but at his wrist, slicing through flesh and bone as though they were nothing. The fingers of the severed hand twisted in spasm, and the pistol fired up into the rafters. The hand fell into the mud at Echo's feet, briefly spurting black blood before it shriveled into a corrupted liquefying jelly that drained into the earth. Screeching in pain, his good hand gripping the horror of his amputated wrist, the creature twisted away and vanished backward into the deeper shadows at the back of the rotting basement chamber. From above Echo's head there was a terrible crash and the sound of flames. The Vampyr stepped forward.

"Hurry," he said to Echo. "We must hurry now. Your brother."

Echo nodded and they turned their attention to the ravaged, emaciated form spread-eagled on the horrible device. They cut him down and, moaning terribly, he fell into the Vampyr's arms. Enoch Bale carried him like a child, Matthew's face pressed into his shoulder. Ahead of them the roof above their heads was beginning to smolder and smoke, wisps of choking fumes twisting down like fog from the burning building above them, creaking ominously now, with seconds left before it collapsed.

"Follow me," said the Vampyr calmly. He strode ahead toward the small, below-street-level door that led into the well beside the steps. He smashed his booted foot through the rotted, dry-as-tinder wood, Echo close behind him, and they were outside at last. Coughing with the sudden clouds of smoke that began to billow around her, Echo stumbled up the stone carved steps and reached the cobbled street.

"Miss Van Helsing!" a voice cried. Echo peered through the smoke. There was a carriage a few feet away, a single horse plunging and stamping on the cobbles as the fiery building behind Echo began to collapse in on itself. Flames rose, spurting from the windows. Greasy black smoke billowed everywhere. Echo peered through the cinder-laden smoke and saw Kate Warne trying to soothe the terrified beast as the Vampyr laid poor Matthew across the carriage's padded seat. A waft of smoke blinded her, and when she looked again the Vampyr had vanished. Sobbing, she threw herself toward the waiting carriage and safety at last.

CHAPTER 34

The old Chris-Craft didn't look old at all as it cruised slowly through the heavy fog, the man who called himself Enoch Bale seated at the polished wooden wheel. He piloted the boat carefully, listening for echoes. Every few minutes an island would appear out of the thick mist like a dark ship, tall pines like naked masts stripped of their sails, standing like ghosts in a dead-calm sea. Some of the islands had names and Enoch Bale told them to Carrie, his voice calm and formally polite: Atlantis, Twilight, the Rock, Toothpick Manzanita and Eagle Wing.

There was a long period after that where the water was empty and Carrie felt as though she'd been carried to the end of the world, but finally she saw the spires and battlements of a castle rising through the edge of the fog, and off to one side, the glow of a small blinking channel light.

As they came closer, the island resolved itself out of the foggy curtain. It was no more than a hundred yards long, bare rock at one end dropping steeply down to the still water, the other end crowned with old blasted pines, ravaged by winds and storms, bent and almost bare with age, but living still. In the center of the island, high on a bare stony bluff, was the castle.

It was something out of Stevenson or Poe and certainly not of the world Carrie knew. It was enormous, a high square of quarried stone with spired bailey towers at each corner. At the front of the castle was an outer barbican complete with drawbridge, the crenellated curtain walls notched for archers on the fire-step parapets, the windows nothing more than narrow slits. There was a small, square wooden dock and a zigzagging set of stone steps that led up to the castle gate.

The fog twisted around the castle in ragged skeins, but even from the water it was clear that the place was in a terrible state of disrepair. The conical roof of one of the bailey towers was a shattered ruin, the leading of the roof gone, stone tiles shattered and broken, the huge oak beams exposed like a rotting skeleton. Large sections of the barbican had crumbled and the iron portcullis stood half raised, its rusted bars like broken teeth. Someone had used a can of white paint and scrawled IVY RIDGE '89 in three-foot-high letters on the barbican tower. It was a bleak place. Old. Forgotten. Worn.

Enoch Bale the Vampyr throttled back the engine, then switched it off. They glided the last few hundred feet in silence. When they bumped into the rope fenders, the Vampyr stepped out, grabbed the forward line and tied them off. Once again he extended his hand to Carrie and once again she took it.

"You live here?" Carrie asked.

"When it suits me," he answered, then smiled. "Perhaps it reminds me of home."

Carrie realized that she was still holding the Vampyr's hand and dropped it. She wrapped her arms around herself. The air was oddly warm for such a fog, but she'd felt a sudden chill run up her spine and she shivered. She looked up at the castle. For a second she thought that the front tower had repaired itself and that lights were shining from the slit windows in the curtain wall. She heard laughter and the babbling hum of conversation. A woman dressed in a medieval gown with a tall conical headpiece appeared beneath the portcullis, a man in a knight's jupon standing beside her. Both of them had champagne glasses in their hands. They faded in the fog, and then were gone. The castle was in ruins once again. She blinked and felt the grating vertigo snatching at her again. She swallowed bile behind gritted teeth.

"George Wolf used to give costume parties in the castle's heyday," said the Vampyr, watching her. "They were very popular with the summer gentry. Billy Murray sang at one of them." She heard a high, crooning voice coming faintly from somewhere high up the bluff, echoing inside the castle walls:

I'm a Yankee Doodle Dandy,
Yankee Doodle do or die.
A real live nephew of my uncle Sam,
Born on the Fourth of July.
I've got a Yankee Doodle sweetheart,
She's my Yankee Doodle joy.
Yankee doodle came to London,
Just to ride the ponies.
Say, I am a Yankee Doodle Boy.

The song faded slowly, like smoke. Carrie shivered again and gathered her arms more tightly around her. "I'm going to die here, aren't I?" she said, her future suddenly as clear as glass.

The Vampyr answered with a wistful smile. "Death, like life," he said, "is only a state of mind." He reached out and touched her cheek softly, then took her by the hand. "Come," he said, and she went with him to the stone steps and began the climb up to the ruined castle.

Carrie and the Vampyr, Enoch Bale, climbed up the long stone stairway that led up from the floating dock at the water's edge, eventually reaching the short path that led up to the barbican. They paused there for a moment, and through the wisps of clinging fog Carrie saw that the rusted portcullis was flanked on either side by two great stone dragons, tails twisted, each with three enormous leering heads, eyes bulging, curved fangs holding back great stone tongues.

"The one on the left is Zmey Gorynych, supposedly killed by my ancestors; the other is his brother, Tugarin, who escaped. To kill them you must cut off all three heads or they will grow back again."

"This is all crazy," whispered Carrie, staring at the great granite beasts.

"I can't dispute that," said the Vampyr. He strode beneath the rusted, half-open portcullis and Carrie followed.

Once through the dark portal, Carrie found herself in the castle courtyard. She could see the sliver of a crescent moon through the scudding clouds overhead. The courtyard was empty except for a single tree, a huge oak, half as high as the castle walls surrounding it. The tree was dead, struck by lightning long ago, its great trunk split into three clawing spikes like the heads of the dragons guarding the gate. Below the ruins of the tree there were the remains of an old well, its circular wall crumbled.

From where she stood, Carrie could see just how much the castle had decayed. Sections of wall had tumbled down, piles of stone spreading out to reveal the ruined interior of rooms. Stone stairways led nowhere, the far bailey towers were open to the elements and most of the flagstones in the courtyard were cracked or broken, weeds and grass growing up through the spaces in between. There was no music here, no singing and no costumed guests. All of that had clearly been her imagination. This was dry dust, one past trying to emulate a more distant one, all of it for nothing, all of it gone the way of all things.

She turned to the so-called Vampyr, ready to tell him she'd had enough and that whatever drug he'd given her was wearing off.

"This is all bullsh—"

"They're very near," the Vampyr said. "We must be careful, now." They stood in what had once been the castle's great hall. Faint moonlight slipped in through the narrow, deep-set windows. No fire burned in the massive hearth; there were only ashes. A thick coating of dust shrouded all the furniture, cobwebs stretching from the huge hanging iron chandeliers in ragged strands that stretched down to the table far below. The stuffed severed heads of a score of animals stared blankly across the room at one another, their glass eyes glazed by time. Wolf's gruesome hunting lodge menagerie.

The Vampyr reached beneath the great stone mantel of the fireplace. He drew out a massive gleaming sword, the same sword he'd carried into the tenement only a few moments before. With the sword there was a smaller weapon, a dagger with its blade encased in a shining silver scabbard. "Is all this a dream?" Carrie asked.

"No," answered the Vampyr. He handed her the dagger. "It's real enough."

"Why have you given me this?" she asked, sliding the blade partway from its sheath. The hilt was heavily carved and silver; the blade was shining black. Obsidian. Volcanic glass created in some

ancient fire, its edges so sharp that scalpels made
from it were used in modern cardiac surgery.

"No Vampyr can kill another. The death blow
must come from someone with a human heart."

"You expect me to—"

"They're here," said the Vampyr, and suddenly
they were everywhere.

They had come in through the windows and
down the chimney of the great hearth in the hall
like a horde of insects or like bats and ravens with
black beating wings. Somehow they had been
beaten back, and Carrie and the Vampyr managed
to climb up the stone stairs to the roofless upper
bailey, then out onto the fire step. Looking over
the castle wall, Carrie had seen that the ground
below was a moving, slithering wave of them,
slipping out of the water, their ancient uniforms
dripping, faces gaunt, eyes bright, bones showing
through torn cloth, black blood oozing from time-
less wounds.

"Sweet Jesus!" Carrie said softly. "What are
they?"

"The unbelieving dead. Damphyr, come to help
their master," the Vampyr answered.

Carrie stared. "Not you?"

"No," said the Vampyr, shaking his head. He
pointed along the parapet. Overhead there was a
sudden streak of lightning, and thunder crashed.
"Him." She turned and stared at the terrible appa-
rition that stood before them. "Adamo," the
Vampyr said. "You've come at last."

"Welcome."

The lightning cracked enormously once again, filling the air with sudden ozone and raising the hairs on Carrie's neck. Below them the already shriven oak burst into flames as lightning struck it for the second time in almost a hundred years. The old branches began to blaze like wooden bones.

"Draculiya," said a voice. "You've brought my old sword again." He glanced at Carrie. "And another damsel."

He wore an expensive tailcoat and a top hat. He had a ginger beard and carried a silver-headed ebony stick, every inch the London gentleman of the late nineteenth century. His face was fuller, the weak chin covered by the beard. He looked for all the world like someone out of a BBC version of *Sherlock Holmes*.

"Adam Worth," said Carrie, suddenly making the connection.

"The very same," said the man with a horrible smile. The jaw unhinged, and he leered at her with a gaping, bloody-mouthed grin. He turned to Enoch Bale, who stood with the sword upraised. "She looks familiar to me."

"Well she might," said the Vampyr. He took a step forward. Worth stepped back, taking him very near the edge of the fire step.

"A long way down for some," he said.

"It's over, Adamo."

"That old song." The mouth dripped. "My old sword."

"No more of your horrors. You've done enough harm."

"Don't be silly," the drooling horror said. "I've only just begun." The laugh grew into a screaming crow of triumph. "This is my hour!"

"This is your end."

When it came, it came without warning and without fanfare, ten thousand years of dead, dreamless life erased in a single slashing instant.

The creature turned away from both of them and trod one more step, taking him to the very edge of the parapet. Twenty feet down was the ruined end of a stone stairway. Carrie watched as he crouched, gathering himself for the leap. He straightened, arms held out before him, but he was a single heartbeat late. With two steps the Vampyr reached him and so did Carrie. The huge sword swept around, lopping off the creature's head in a single spurting stroke as Carrie plunged the obsidian dagger between the other Vampyr's shoulders.

The screaming demon head of Adam Worth spun out into the abyss and the body plunged downward, impaling itself on the broken fiery limb of the burning oak tree like a butcher bird's prey upon a thorn. The head struck the cobblestones in the courtyard, the skull splitting open with a rotten, bursting sound. Something black spilled out like sand or ash and then whirled away and vanished.

The Vampyr stared down into the courtyard, watching as the flaming tree consumed the terrible burden of Worth's decapitated corpse. A foul stench rose in a noxious cloud and was swept away on the breeze. After a moment the Vampyr turned away, went to the parapet and took the sword by the pommel. Swinging it around his head in a huge arc, he let it go, flinging into the air in a long, high curve. It straightened as it fell, slicing through the thinning fog, striking the dark water without a ripple and disappearing. He turned back to Carrie.

"Is it done?" she asked.

"Perhaps," said the Vampyr. He inclined his chin and for the first time Carrie saw that she was still clutching the obsidian dagger, the black blade thick with something foul-smelling and glutinous. She lifted the blade slightly in her hand.

The Vampire smiled at her, wistfully again. "There are worse things," he said quietly.

"Worse than dying?"

"Worse than living forever. Alone. Worse than the terrible sleep that slows my life to a standstill yet speeds me to dreamless eternity."

She held the blade toward his chest. She knew that she could kill him now, this creature from the same past as the thing burning to ashes in the flaming tree, but something held her hand at bay. "You could stop me. You know that. You could do it easily."

"I would not," he answered simply.

"What happened in the tenement?"

"Worth had crucified young Matthew, fed on him. Adamo managed to escape. We saved Matthew, at least for a time. Though eventually Echo had to . . . end his life for the sake of whatever remained of his poor soul."

"How did Barnabus Coffin die?"

"He came to Minetta Street, searching for Kate. Adamo must have been hiding in the sewer there until he was sure we were gone for good. He would have been hungry by then. He would have needed to feed."

"The murders now?"

"Adamo returned. He liked nothing better than provoking his Damphyr minions. He corrupted the man Trusell, offered him eternal life, offered Lincoln the power he craved. I came back to stop him."

"And your fate? You haven't spoken about what happened to you."

"I found Fu Sheng. The sleeping death came over me as it always does eventually. Fu Sheng kept it at bay with his medicines until a place was found for me to rest. The very crypt we had stayed in at the old cathedral, as a matter of fact. When I woke again, I left New York, I thought forever."

"Echo?" Carrie asked. "She lost her father, her brother, even you."

"After Matthew died she left New York and went with Kate back to Chicago for a time, but the memories they shared were too painful for her. After leaving Kate Warne, Echo never spoke of what happened again. She married and settled in a little place called Hazel Dell, Illinois."

"My great-great-grandfather came from Hazel

Dell, Illinois." Suddenly she saw. "Are you trying to tell me . . . ?"

"That you are Echo Van Helsing's direct descendant? Yes."

Carrie stepped forward, the dagger raised. She moved until she was standing no more than a foot away, the black blade almost on the Vampyr's heart. Her own heart thundered and she could feel the heavy pulse beating in her throat. She thought of the boy Matthew on his horrible cross, remembered the clotted blood and the punctures in his neck. Thought of Echo, alone.

"Is it always like that?" she asked, taking a half step closer. So close she could almost hear the ponderous, powerful beating of the pale creature's heart and knew that he could hear her own.

"No," he said. "It can be very gentle. Peaceful, in fact."

She saw him on a raft in the cold waters off Cape Race, a dying Irish boy in his arms. She turned aside and walked to the edge of the parapet. She threw the dagger as hard as she could and didn't even wait to see it fall. She turned back to the Vampyr. Raised her head, bared her neck without any hesitation.

"Show me," she said.

"There can be no turning back."

"I want to know. Past, present and future."

"As you wish," he said. He put his hand behind her neck and brought her gently forward, the set of his jaw changing fractionally, the long, steel-hard fangs descending.

"Make me see!" Carrie whispered, and closed her eyes.

Later they rested on the crumbling stones of the abandoned castle and watched the pink early light of dawn come up in the east.

"I want to know it all," said Carrie, sharing the eternity of time and sadness that now joined them. "I want to know everything."

"Listen, then," said the Vampyr. "Listen while I tell you a story."

AFTERWORD

"Just a moment, ladies and gentlemen, just a word before you go! We hope the memories of Dracula won't give you bad dreams, so just a word of reassurance. When you go home tonight, and the lights have been turned out and you are afraid to look behind the curtains and you dread to see a face at the window, why, just pull yourself together and remember that after all

THERE ARE SUCH THINGS!"

—Hamilton Deane in the onstage role
of Abraham Van Helsing, 1924